THE TRUTH *about* HAPPILY EVER AFTER

THE TRUTH *about* HAPPILY EVER AFTER

karole cozzo

Swoon READS

Swoon Reads • New York

A SWOON READS BOOK

An Imprint of Feiwel and Friends
and Macmillan Publishing Group, LLC

Our books may be purchased in bulk for promotional, educational,
or business use. Please contact your local bookseller or the Macmillan
Corporate and Premium Sales Department at (800) 221-7945 ext. 5442 or
by e-mail at MacmillanSpecialMarkets@macmillan.com.

Library of Congress Cataloging-in-Publication Data is available.

ISBN 978-1-250-12797-6 (hardcover) /
ISBN 978-1-250-12798-3 (ebook)

Book design by Eileen Savage

First Edition—2017

10 9 8 7 6 5 4 3 2 1

swoonreads.com

To Laine and Aug, the heroes of more of
my real-life stories than I could possibly count

PART I

the end

chapter 1

I SLEEP WITH ALL MY BEDROOM WINDOWS open as habit, so I'm roused from my sleep by the repetitive shrieking of a great blue heron that must be nesting near the man-made lake in the center of the apartment complex. *Where are my soft-spoken finches and friendly bluebirds?* I wonder with a dreamy smile. Not in Tallahassee, apparently.

The heron is loud and insistent, refusing to be ignored. I need to get out of bed, anyway—a long, busy day awaits. I picture Jake's face—that bemused close-lipped smile, those gentle blue eyes—and memories of last summer flood my mind and my heart. I throw back my covers in a burst of anticipation. A long, busy, *fabulous* day awaits.

My feet hit the ground and I pause, as it crosses my mind that no matter how I arrange my schedule, there's no way to squeeze in my daily workout. I run through the computations automatically—how many workouts I've completed this week to date, how long each one was, approximately how many calories were burned, and if the number's enough to make up for the special dinner I have planned. I squeeze my eyes shut, trying to power down the invisible calculator. I'll fixate on it if I let myself, and I have too many other things to accomplish today.

I need energy. Protein. Protein is a must.

Eating a carton of Greek yogurt at my kitchen counter, I wait for the frying pan to heat so I can whip up an egg white omelet with spinach and tomato. The loaf of fresh-baked bread calls to me from the bread box, but I turn my back and ignore it. *No bread.* Look-overs are in two hours.

Then, carrying my plate and mug to the table when the omelet's finished, I eat facing the window, drinking my coffee through a straw. It's a practice Jake ridicules mercilessly, and I get it, but I don't think *he* fully gets my commitment to my job. When you make your living off your smile, when your smile might be the highlight of a little girl's vacation, you take good care of your smile. You buy whitening strips in bulk at Costco, you favor lipstick with blue-based undertones for maximum pearliness, and sometimes you drink your damn coffee through a straw. Playing princess isn't nearly as easy as I'm sure some people like to believe. It's a dream job, but it's still a job. There's work involved.

I linger over breakfast, enjoying the feel of the sun's rays on my skin as they make their first appearance over the horizon and through the window, listening to the familiar sounds of a community coming to life around me. I like the company of the neighbors I don't know. It wasn't my plan to live alone, but when hunting those coveted three-month sublets, you take what you can get. Me, I prefer the company of others, and a single costs more than I'd like to spend on rent. I tried to talk Jake into being roomies, but right away I'd sensed his hesitation. So I'd laughed the idea off, dropped the subject at once.

It doesn't matter that his name's not on the lease agreement. He'll be spending enough time here, anyway. Just like last year.

I shower after breakfast, then walk through the apartment in my robe, guy-proofing it the best I can. I put the tampons back under the sink. Hide the little notebook beside the scale that I use as a log. Unload the snacks I picked up at the twenty-four-hour convenient mart late last night after work. I wrinkle my nose at the bag of Funyuns I deigned to purchase. They're probably the most disgusting excuse for food on the planet. But he loves them. And I love him.

Then I end up back in my room, grimacing at its decor. It's a girl's room, and there's not much that can be done about that. A wooden plaque over my vanity reads, SHE LEAVES A LITTLE SPARKLE WHEREVER SHE GOES in iridescent paint. The walls are covered in turquoise and gray ZTA memorabilia, much of it bearing the sorority's symbol, the crown. Next to my door is the poster of Audrey Hepburn that I look at before leaving every single day. I BELIEVE IN PINK. I BELIEVE LAUGHTER IS THE BEST CALORIE BURNER. I BELIEVE IN KISSING, KISSING A LOT. I BELIEVE IN BEING STRONG WHEN EVERYTHING SEEMS TO BE GOING WRONG. I BELIEVE THAT HAPPY GIRLS ARE THE PRETTIEST GIRLS. I BELIEVE THAT TOMORROW IS ANOTHER DAY AND I BELIEVE IN MIRACLES. I've had that poster since forever. It's ripped and curling up at the sides. But it reminds me to smile, and it makes me smile.

Taking one final, futile sweep of my room, I gasp in horror when I notice It still sitting atop my bookshelf. My wedding binder.

For the record? I know the binder concept is antiquated (Hello? Pinterest.). I have a Pinterest account I use almost daily, teeming boards titled "Outfit Ideas," "Cinderella," "Princess

Love," "Zeta Life," and "Fashion Nexts." But there is something about my wedding binder . . . and I want it to be tangible. I like to hold it in my hands. It's pink and sparkly and even involves some floral lace.

I have no idea how Jake would feel about its existence, which actually predates him, but I sense he wouldn't feel particularly thrilled about it.

A pang of loss and longing pierces my chest. Last summer, a future together had seemed so certain. A ring from Jake . . . someday . . . hadn't seemed so out of the question. Now . . .

I shake my head, stuffing the binder, along with my negative thoughts, under a pile of romance novels. *"A pessimist sees the difficulty in every opportunity,"* I coach myself. *"An optimist sees the opportunity in every difficulty."*

This summer is about growth. Reconnecting. Not trying to get back to where we were, but getting someplace even better. We'll figure out the road map as we go.

I nod decidedly, hang my robe inside my closet, and peruse its offerings. It's time to get dressed. My summer wardrobe consists of gauzy white pieces with gold accents—scarves and belts and shiny thong sandals. But for look-overs, black, with its slimming properties, is the only color that makes sense. I root around until I find a clean pair of cropped black yoga pants and a matching workout tank.

I lean forward toward the full-length mirror, assessing myself, biting my lip. *You have nothing to worry about.* My log assures me this, daily, in black and white. The numbers on the scale are unchanging. I work out religiously, and I haven't put on weight. My last period was two weeks ago, so no blemishes are on the horizon, either.

As confident as I can be, I grab my tote bag with the glass slipper decal and head toward the door. I notice Kallie and Luke's wedding invitation on the counter from when I opened the mail yesterday, and I fight the urge to squeal. I love me a good wedding, and this one's just around the corner. Better yet, it's an *Enchanted Dominion* wedding, the marriage of two people who met while in character, at the park. Kallie's living the dream.

So many fabulous events to look forward to this summer . . . the wedding . . . the Character Ball in August . . . I've been waiting for summer forever!

When I step out, Rose, one of my neighbors, is locking up down the hall. I do a quick double take, making sure it's not her twin sister before greeting her, but the girl's dress—short and black, with a pleated skirt and wild fuchsia rose pattern, confirms my initial assumption. It must be Rose.

"Hey, lady," she calls over her shoulder. "Off to the gym, per ush?"

"I wish. Look-overs."

She lets out a low growl, which basically sums up how we all feel about look-overs. "That practice should be outlawed. But at least you know you have nothing to worry about."

I smile in appreciation of her reassurance.

"Are you working today?"

Rose is a fellow park princess. She's Rose Red. And she more or less loves the coincidence of it all. I love that she loves the coincidence of it all.

"Yeah." She grimaces. "Over at the Enchanted Beyond, though. Chrissi's off, my sister's at ED, and the new roommate's at training."

"New roommate?"

"Yeah." Rose nods, gesturing over her shoulder with her thumb. "Katie's out."

"What happened? She was only here for, like, three weeks."

"Naked Rapunzel is what happened."

I almost drop my keys. "What?"

"Yeah, so Katie wasn't the brightest bulb," Rose tells me, leaning against her door and folding her arms. "She let her boyfriend take pictures of her wearing nothing but the wig. Strategically placed, of course. Then she cheated on him. Real smart move. The pictures were up on social media in less than an hour after he found out."

"'Don't post unsavory princess images on social media,'" I recite. "'Don't post *any* princess images on social media.' That's basically rule number one!"

"Yup. So she's out, and Harper's in."

"Harper?" I cock my head. "Do we know her?"

A lot of us have worked at the park for a while, and there are few strangers in the cast.

"No, she's a newbie," Rose tells me. "Last-minute casting call or something. A shortage of Beauties. I know nothing about her. Except that she's flying in from somewhere up north today."

"Well, it can't be any worse?" I say, trying to be encouraging. "Than Naked Rapunzel?"

"Truuue story." Rose grimaces. "I think everyone's gonna be around later if you want to stop over. You could meet the latest member of the Princess Posse."

I smile at the term. "I would love to, but . . ." My smile grows even bigger. "Jake's getting in tonight, too."

She raises an eyebrow. "The illustrious Jake finally shows his face!"

The two of them just missed each other last year. Jake left in August, and Rose and her sister, Camila, arrived in September.

"I'm so damn excited!" I admit.

"No worries, then," Rose replies, pushing off the door. "Have fun with your lover."

I push my tote up on my shoulder. "Thanks. I will."

We exit the building in opposite directions, and I make my way toward the nearest shuttle station that will take me to the main park. I greet everyone along the way—the groundskeepers in identical brown uniforms who keep our fabricated downtown area pristine, fellow cast members whose faces I recognize even if I don't know their names. The shuttle approaches just as I arrive, and I skip aboard and claim a seat near the front.

It's a quick, ten-minute ride to the Enchanted Dominion, which is why so many cast members live in the Lakeside apartments. With so many young people on the scene, looking for hook-ups with convenience, it's pretty much just like being at college.

I've barely finished humming the Enchanted Enterprises theme song when the glimmering spires and turrets of the Diamond Palace come into view over the palm trees. Here is the thing—It. Never. Gets. Old. I have seen the Palace, the central feature of the park, come into view over these same trees countless times, dating back to when I was four years old. And every single time, the sight steals my breath just a bit. Every single time, I have to bite back my urge to squee. I really believe this place is infused with magic.

There are some who wait their whole lives to take in this iconic sight, some who get to do so only once in a lifetime. The thought of these people makes me sad. I can't imagine not getting to lay eyes on the Palace almost every day. *That's* how much I love this park. *That's* how much I love my job. I feel like the luckiest girl on earth, and it makes the hard work all worth it.

It's why I make the two-hour trip from the southern part of the state a few times a month during the school year, just to pick up random shifts. And it's one of the reasons I can endure look-overs. My stomach flutters nervously. Not that they ever get easier. It's almost like they're waiting for you to fall off your game, become complacent the longer you've been on the throne.

I enter the park through the employee gate and take a detour from the park's main corridor to the hidden employee path, following its twists and turns by memory. I'm almost to the human resources office, still lost in my look-over worries. I'm pulled back to reality when I hear the rapid approach of running feet from behind me, and then . . . someone sort of *leaps* onto my back and almost tackles me with the force of their hug.

My body crumbles under the weight of my attacker, but they've freed me before I actually fall over. "What the . . ."

I whirl around and find a grinning Miller Austin behind me. Any sense of irritation dissipates at once.

Miller's arms are spread wide. "What up, Princess?" he asks, before pulling me into a huge hug.

Miller is exactly my height—five foot seven—and he's got this stocky build about him. He's incredibly active and physical, but hugging Miller is still like hugging a teddy bear. I take a step back and smile at him. "Miller! I didn't think you were back this summer! Aren't you . . ."

"Graduated? Yes, as a matter of fact I am. For two weeks and counting, a fact I'm committed to ignoring as long as possible. Real world, whaaat?"

I giggle. It's good to see Miller again. We didn't hit it off at first, but . . . we got there. We're friends now. It's practically impossible *not* to be friends with Miller.

"So you're honestly working the park again?"

"Yeah, I wasn't kidding." He rubs his short, scruffy beard with the palm of his hand. "I *do* have an agenda, a practical reason for being down here this summer. Otherwise, I'm delaying adulthood as long as I can get away with it. There's no shame in my game."

"Well, cheers to that. Best place on earth for it."

I mean, we basically work in a glamorous, oversize playground for children.

He studies me for a minute, then asks, "How's life been, Lys?"

"Life is good."

It's an automatic answer. Life is always good, isn't it?

"Jake's getting in tonight," I tell him. "He's back for the summer, too."

Miller pauses for a beat, then grins again. "Aww. Prince Charming's back in town. Good stuff."

I snort at the idea. Jake would never actually play a prince. He's an emergency responder in the park.

I nod toward Miller. "So are you moving up in the world this summer or what? You've paid your dues. They have to be willing to let you out of fur by now."

He shrugs. "Maybe if I'd asked them to. But I'm staying in fur by choice. That's my pedigree."

That's right. I'd forgotten that Miller was technically a part of the University of Delaware's cheerleading squad, embodying the school's mascot, the six-foot-tall fightin' blue hen.

"I'm not tall enough to play prince, anyway."

"I think you make the cut."

Miller laughs. "You're too nice, Alyssa. I know where I belong." He pats his roundish belly. "Me and my incredibly impressive physique."

I roll my eyes in response. "You're probably onto something. I'm off to suffer look-overs." I clutch my sides, feeling somewhat queasy.

Miller quickly assesses me, blond hair to flip-flops. Then he averts his eyes before saying, "Come on, now. You know you'll nail it. I can't believe they even have the nerve to call you in."

"Sweet of you, Miller." I smile, then shrug. "But whatever. It's policy. Fair is fair." I take a quick glance at my watch. "And I need to be there, like, now. But we should hang out sometime. Where are you staying this summer?"

"Lakeside."

"Groovy. Me too."

"I'm sharing a sublet with Yael. You know her?"

"Umm . . . vaguely?"

An image comes to mind, a hipster type with bright maroon hair and nerd glasses. She's a fur character, too.

"Yeah, we're buddies," Miller says. "We kept up on e-mail during the year, so when I started asking around, she ended up having a spot in her place."

"Cool." I look at his friendly face, smile again, and bump my fist against his. "It's supernice to have you back. Have someone to put me in my place, ya know?"

"That's what I'm here for, Princess." He turns to go but calls to me before leaving, "And say 'hey' to Jake for me, okay?"

"Will do."

There's a bounce in my step as I walk the rest of the way to

HR. I freakin' love the sense of community among cast members. I love being back with my people. The Enchanted Enterprises theme park complex is huge, comprised of three different parks and employing thousands upon thousands of workers. And still it feels like being home, surrounded by family. Running into Miller before look-overs . . . it was a welcome distraction and a nice little boost.

I push the door open, happy to see Diana is working today. She's one of my favorites in the HR department, and she's, well, female at least. It's always a little creepier when a man's doing the looking over.

"Let's get you on your way as quickly as possible, shall we?" she says as a means of greeting. She briefly glances up from her iPad. "No sweat for you, right?" I smile, refusing to let any self-doubt show, and she steps closer to confide in me. "Thank you for making my job easy. I had to send Alana home today. She could barely zip her gown. Twelve pounds in ten days, how does that even *happen*, as hot as it's been? We all should be sweating the pounds off."

Diana looks at me, but I don't have an answer for her.

She shrugs. "Who knows? Maybe a bad breakup she wouldn't cop to, or something." She grabs my shoulders and turns me to the side. "Let me get a shot of your silhouette first."

I turn dutifully, closing my eyes and reminding myself I've suffered much greater humiliations. The ladies on the Panhellenic Council at Coral State College would swear on their pearls that Zeta actives *never* forced pledges to strip down to their skivvies to circle in permanent marker areas on their bodies in need of liposuction.

That doesn't mean it never happened.

At least look-overs have a *purpose*, separate and apart from utter degradation. With so many different girls playing princess, someone has to keep an eye on character consistency and integrity. Park-goers pay a lot of money for us to get it right, to make dreams come true.

Once Diana is done inspecting my body from every angle and recording my weight after it flashes on the screen of the electric scale, she steps forward to inspect my face. She studies my complexion, commands me to smile so she can see my teeth. Then her shoulders collapse in relief and she gives me a hug. "You look great, Sweet Pea. You're my all-star, Alyssa. Keep up the good work." She laughs. "If this was an orchestra, you'd be my first chair Cinderella."

I exhale a quick sigh of relief and smile back at her.

I'm proud of myself.

And I don't have to do this again for almost two weeks. Thank you, sweet Jesus. I hightail it out of there.

I'm still in my street clothes, so instead of navigating the underground tunnel system that ensures no two Cinderellas are spotted at the same time, I walk through the park to one of the hidden changing areas, where I'll get into costume, hair, and makeup for the morning and afternoon parade routes. I feel my black clothing absorbing the already-scorching heat of the sun as I walk, and I'm not entirely eager to change into my heavy, formal silk gown. But I'll do it, and I'll do it with conviction.

Just before I walk inside the changing area, I pause. I close my eyes, inhale a deep breath through my nose, and center myself. I envision the Alyssa part of me dropping into the soles of my feet, fading away. It's time to become Cinderella.

It's a long, arduous process, but when I'm done, I *am*

Cinderella, and I know I'm doing her proud. Riding in the golden coach as the finale to the parade route, my vehicle pulled by real white stallions, is an honor.

I do the parade route, a long loop around the entire park, twice with only a short break in between. It is only May, but it is crazy hot. My hair is limp and damp, itching my scalp and neck beneath the hairpiece. The armpits of my dress are soaked, chafing painfully every time I stand to wave to the masses. By the afternoon route, hunger pains are assaulting my stomach and making me weak in the knees.

But the crowds break out in applause when we come into view to end the show, people leap to their feet to take better pictures, and some little girls even burst into happy tears. I wave and smile like my life depends on it; I make eye contact with as many of those little girls as possible. I love every single minute of it.

By the time I'm done, the late afternoon sun is reflecting against the mirrored panels of the Diamond Palace, bursting into a million rainbow facets. Another beautiful day in the park.

Tonight is sure to be even more beautiful than today, and I can't wait for the sun to set.

chapter 2

I'M *SO* NOT A COOK. MY MOM'S NOT A cook—for the better part of my life, dinner consisted of takeout from trendy Italian or Asian fusion restaurants as she attempted to shuttle my sisters and me to our various activities while my dad worked long hours—so no one had ever taught me.

But I can YouTube with the best of them, and I'd done a trial preparation after watching a professional make the recipe online. I'd shared the meal with Rose, Camila, and Chrissi, and they'd seemed to enjoy it.

Now, the chicken breasts are pounded to an even thickness and battered to perfection, the contents of a jar of gourmet roasted tomato sauce are simmering on the stove top, and a bowl of Parmesan cheese I'd grated myself sits beside it. The crème brûlée is chilling in the fridge, just waiting to be caramelized. I'm ready.

I glance at the clock, confirming that I'm still right on schedule. It's go-time for dinner in T-minus thirty minutes. I've checked

Jake's flight status, and I know it's still on time. I can guesstimate how long it will take Jake to collect his bags, get a cab, and travel to the complex. He promised he'd come directly here.

Since this afternoon was such a scorcher, I take my second shower of the day, then dress in a gauzy white calf-length peasant skirt and a subtly cropped white tank top. I let my hair dry naturally and fasten my diamond tiara studs—an end-of-summer present from Jake—onto my earlobes. Then, for sentiment's sake, I slide my feet into the jeweled flip-flops I'd been wearing the day we first met, at the beginning of last summer.

I WAS MORE excited than a kid going to bed on Christmas Eve the night before my new hire orientation at the Dominion. But that next day, I'd gotten stuck on campus later than expected thanks to the World's Longest Anthropology Lecture. There was a ridiculous amount of traffic for midafternoon on a Tuesday, the trip taking me nearly three hours instead of two, and I got there way later than intended. I pushed through the gates and took to running at full speed through the park toward the main HR office, where I'd had my final interview-slash-audition.

Sprinting in flip-flops simply doesn't work. As I made my way down a side corridor, I felt the rubber sole of my shoe catch on an uneven stone a second too late to do anything about it. The next thing I knew, I was splayed out on the walkway, problematic shoe no longer on my foot.

I sat up and twisted around, trying to get my bearings, and all of a sudden . . . there he was.

"Hey, are you okay?"

Backlit by the setting sun, Jake was tall and gorgeous. A serious, scholarly looking kind of gorgeous, with disheveled light brown hair, soft blue eyes, and these cute horn-rimmed glasses. He dropped to his knees at my side and immediately flipped open the lid of a large plastic case he carried.

Glancing at it, I noticed the red first aid emblem on its side.

"I'm okay," I finally managed to answer. Then, in confusion, "Where did you come from, Mystery Medical Man?" It made him smile.

I hadn't even heard anyone walking behind me.

"I had to double back to the medical center." He patted the first aid kit. "Forgot I needed to bring this bad boy with me to orientation." Then he glanced down at my knees—one was scuffed and white, the other was torn open and bleeding. He gestured toward the kit. "Is it okay if I . . . ?"

"Sure." I nodded. "Thanks."

He expertly tugged on a pair of blue latex gloves, and I found myself smiling as he examined my superficial wound with as much concern as I imagined he'd examine a broken bone.

"This is nice of you. I'm Alyssa."

"Nice to meet you, Alyssa," he answered, quickly tearing a piece of gauze from the roll. "I'm Jake."

"You're heading to orientation? Me too."

Jake glanced over at me as he continued to work. "Another new hire?"

I nodded with so much emphatic excitement my entire body shook like a wriggly retriever pup and Jake had to bite his lip to keep from laughing. "I'm so excited. Guess I was literally trying to run faster than my legs could carry me."

"I'll have you back on your way in no time." He smiled.

"I gather you're going to be on the first-response team?"

"Yep. I've worked as an EMT since I was seventeen."

"You a local boy, Jake?"

I'd perused every single website I could find about the ins and outs of working at the park, so I knew a lot of the medical staff hails from the area. I guess it's less appealing than being character actors, who come from all over the country.

"Not a bit." He shook his head. "I go to school in Philly. Drexel. Ended up down here this summer on a lark, because my aunt does PR for the park and promised me it would be fun. Said I needed to mix things up a bit, live a little, before I seriously consider med school."

"I think I have to agree with her." I winced in anticipation as Jake hovered over my bad knee, spray bottle of antiseptic in hand. But seconds later, I relaxed. "That didn't hurt a bit."

He smiled at my comment, that cute little close-lipped smile, the corners of his eyes crinkling. "These things don't sting anymore. You must not have skinned your knees in a few years." He blew a breath of cool air across the knee, aiding the spray in drying, and then placed a bandage over the wound.

The gesture gave me goose bumps. "Thanks. Again," I told him.

He didn't answer me. Instead, he reached over to retrieve my lost flip-flop. Jake positioned himself at my feet and slid the shoe back into place. Then, gently, he took one hand and helped me to stand. He smiled down at me. "You're all fixed up, Cinderella," he said quietly.

He took my breath away just like that. *How did he know?* I

couldn't get over the perfect irony of my *first* official day as an Enchanted Princess—I mean, the Palace was even in the backdrop—and I was convinced at once that Jake had shown up, right then, to be my personal Prince Charming. I mean, if the shoe fits . . .

We'd walked side by side to orientation, conversation coming easily, and sat next to each other, arms brushing, as seasoned employees gave a very genuine spiel about becoming "the heart of Enchanted Enterprises" and the importance of embodying the Enchanted spirit each and every day in the park. Then we'd separated, as I joined the group of character actors and he joined the medical staff. I'd felt his eyes on me throughout the session, though, and I could almost feel his warm skin still touching mine.

Jake had waited for me after, even though I noticed his group wrapping up fifteen minutes before mine did. When I approached him, he looked down toward the ground, hands clasped behind his back.

"Just wanted to check in on you. I mean, your knee. Make sure it feels okay, that you have full mobility."

I bit back my smile. What a terrible attempt at flirting. The cut was *maybe* an inch across, at most.

"I'm okay," I assured him, smiling coyly up at him. "I'm sure you provided top-notch care."

He was quiet for a minute. "You seemed like you were having a blast tonight." Jake flashed me a quick smile. "Lovin' every minute of it. Like you're really what this place is all about. Seems like it's more than just a job to you."

"It is."

Jake looked into my eyes. "You don't see dedication like that too often. It's nice."

Ten minutes later, he'd worked up the courage to ask for my number. We were inseparable the rest of the summer.

SO THESE STUPID shoes . . . the painful stubbed toe, the scar on my knee . . . it was all worth it. And of course I'm going to wear them tonight.

I fasten my watch around my wrist. If my timing is on point, Jake will be here in approximately fifteen minutes. Time to cook some chicken.

As I walk toward the kitchen, a rumble of thunder in the distance catches my attention and I look out the window. The sky has darkened since I went into my bedroom, and I frown at what has become of such a perfect day. Summer storms come out of nowhere in Florida. I'm glad his flight has already touched down.

I boil the water for the pasta and sauté the chicken, smooth a red-and-white-checkered tablecloth over my small kitchen table, and light the candles atop it. The chicken turns golden. The pasta is a perfect al dente. I put the entrée into the oven to keep warm and sit down to wait, smile already on my face.

Fifteen minutes passes.

Fifteen minutes is nothing, I remind myself. Fifteen minutes is a long taxi line, a patch of traffic on the freeway. Did I expect my estimation to be perfectly precise?

At thirty minutes, I call his cell phone. It rings through to voice mail. I start to worry that the chicken is going to dry out and that the pasta will clump together, even though I poured on a bit of olive oil. I mentally debate putting everything in the fridge and reheating it when he gets here.

Forty-five minutes. I start to worry about food poisoning and with a heavy sigh, go ahead and put everything in the fridge. I sit back down and stare worriedly out the window, stomach growling. The sky is nearly black; a downpour is imminent.

I dial his number again. This time I leave a voice mail.

"Hey, baby, it's me. Just checking in and making sure you're okay. Hopefully you're on your way here. It looks like it's going to storm. Call me if you can."

An hour after I expected Jake to be on my doorstep, I open the bottle of wine I pestered one of the older princesses on staff to purchase with this evening in mind. It's red, to go with the meal, and since I'm still alone in the apartment, I drink it through a straw.

It goes right to my head, and does nothing to calm my stomach, which is a mess of nerves, or quell the pounding of my heart against my chest. What if something happened? What if something is for-real wrong? How long will it take before I'm forced to consider that?

I stare sadly into his bowl of wilted salad. Where is he? He promised he'd come *right* here. . . .

For the next half hour, I'm paralyzed with indecision and helplessness. And I'm starving. If it hits two hours, I *will* eat, I tell myself.

Then, about an hour and fifty minutes after it was supposed to, my doorbell finally rings.

I literally hurl myself in the direction of the door and fling it open, smile about to split my cheeks, and find . . . a drowned rat.

I mean, I think it's actually Jake, but it's kind of hard to tell. His hair is soaking wet, still dripping onto his face, matted against his forehead. A few strands are covering his glasses, which are muddled with raindrops and half fogged over. His button-down is more wet than dry, and his khaki shorts are the color of mud.

"Oh my God, Jake! What happened to you?"

The taxi surely dropped him off right outside the door. How did he end up like this?

Without waiting for an answer, I pull him inside, dart to the bathroom to grab a towel, and press it into his hands.

Then I pause, looking up at him. He's here. Jake is really *here*. In person.

"Oh wait . . . first . . . ," I say. I push onto my tiptoes so I can brush my lips against his.

Jake pulls back.

Just for a millisecond, and he corrects the behavior right away, leaning down to kiss me back, but . . . it's noticeable.

When our lips actually meet, I can feel his smiling against mine, but there is something artificial about it. I did some acting in high school, and I feel like we're onstage before an invisible audience.

But, considering his appearance, there is clearly a story, and who knows how dramatic it is, so maybe I should let him tell it first before jumping to conclusions about his behavior.

"I was getting so worried! I knew your flight was on time, but then almost two hours passed, and I couldn't get ahold of you . . ."

"I'm sorry, Alyssa." When his eyes meet mine, his are pained, and I can tell his apology is real. I think I finally see Jake again. "It was crazy, honestly. There was this cab, and this . . . *criminal* cabbie, and a hit-and-run. The cabbie took off, and it was this old guy on a bike he'd hit, and we had to make sure he was okay, and wait to report the story to the police and wait for the ambulance, and . . ."

"We?"

Jake freezes, his expression a mask, but then shakes it off. "Yeah, I mean, I shared a cab with someone headed in this direction . . . but anyway, the guy was okay, but at first it was fairly dramatic because he wasn't making sense. I didn't have any kind of kit with me, so I tried to run to the nearest pharmacy, and anyway . . ." He pauses to take a breath. "I didn't even hear my cell in all that chaos. I'm sorry." He quickly presses his lips against mine again.

I relax a bit. Of course Jake was just helping someone. This is a story that makes sense.

"It's all right," I tell him. "I'm just glad you're okay. Okay and here."

I squeeze his hand and press myself against his torso, not caring in the least that it's still very damp.

Jake doesn't relax into the hug. "It smells great in here," he says instead. Then, eyeing my wineglass, he grins and asks, "You boozing alone, though?"

"Well, I was about to give up on you." I glance toward the refrigerator, where my likely ruined dinner is hanging out. "I, umm, . . . wanted to surprise you with dinner."

"Thanks, Lys."

I frown. "I hope everything will still taste decent? I made your favorite, chicken Parm. A ton of it."

He smiles, but it looks strained. "That's awesome."

"Go ahead, sit down." I wave him over to the table. "Have a drink, relax, and I'll get everything warmed back up."

"Let me grab some dry clothes first."

While he changes, I pour him a glass of wine, and then he sits down and drinks it. Quickly.

I boil the water, again, to cook a new batch of noodles. "Did you hear how your finals went?"

"I passed organic chem. Organic chem is over! Forever."

I raise my glass in his direction. "Cheers to that. Congratulations."

Jake is on a premed track, and organic chem is a rite of passage. He wants to go to med school after graduating next year, and he hopes to specialize in child psychiatry.

He's quiet for a minute, twisting the stem of the wineglass between his fingers. "And in other good news . . . I got the CHOP internship for the fall."

I set the slatted spoon down and stare at the stove top. Because he's such an all-star scholar, Jake is ahead of schedule in terms of credits and has been looking for an internship for the fall. *Which* internship has been a source of contention. He was considering something in South Carolina, which would have been awesome and allowed for weekend visits. But his first choice is a rotation at Children's Hospital of Philadelphia. Meaning when summer ends, he's gone again.

"That's . . . good."

It's all I can manage.

I hear him sigh. "I know you were hoping for it to work out differently, but this is such a great opportunity, Alyssa."

I know it is. He's explained to me the role of child life specialist before. It's pretty much the noblest thing I can think of, being the person to coach children and parents through life-threatening surgeries, supporting their mental health during some of the most difficult times of their lives.

It's so wrong of me to begrudge him this success. His wanting to do it . . . it's one of the reasons I love him.

So I lift my face bravely and find a real smile. "I'm proud of you," I say honestly. "You'll do great."

"Thank you," he answers stiffly.

I dish up dinner, take two, and as I carry our plates over, I catch him staring pensively out the window. "You okay?"

"Yeah." Jake rubs at the back of his neck. "It's fine. I'm fine."

I sit down across from him, smoothing my skirt. Something is nagging at me. I've been waiting for this night for so long, and something about it . . . I don't know. I haven't seen Jake since Valentine's Day, when I'd insisted he fly down, and I feel all confused as to why it's not living up to the expectation.

I have this problem a lot, though. Where reality doesn't live up to the anticipation of something I've envisioned in my head.

Jake cuts his food and nods toward me. "How'd your finals go? Were they questions like, 'pleats—yay or no way?'"

I tilt my head and reach across the table to poke his hand with my fork. "Very funny. LOL."

Jake just *loves* to joke about my fashion merchandising major.

"There were actually a lot of business courses this semester. My finals were mostly math, Professor Genius."

His eyes sparkle. "Professor Genius?"

"Yeah, that's what I'm going to call you. If you keep mocking me."

"I'm not mocking you. Someone's got to pick out people's clothes. Lord knows it's a skill I don't have. I look much more together when I'm in your company."

Jake winks, and I'm smiling for real, and I think I'm finally relaxed and enjoying my food . . . until I look across the table a moment later and realize it doesn't seem like he's enjoying his. I watch him, and he's pushing it around his plate more than anything else, taking tiny bites of chicken and ignoring the noodles altogether.

"I'm sorry," I say. "It probably tasted better before. I just wasn't sure if I should keep it hot or . . ."

"No, no, no!" he assures me quickly. "It's excellent, I swear. It's just . . . well . . ." Jake hangs his head. "Everything ended up taking so long, trying to get here, and I hadn't eaten lunch. After everything got sorted out with the accident, I . . . I ended up stopping and grabbing some pizza on my way here."

I set my fork down.

Don't cry. You will not cry.

But the damn YouTube videos, the grocery list, the money I'd spent on ingredients and supplies, the thought and the effort . . . how worried I'd been . . . and Jake had grabbed *pizza.*

It's not his fault. He didn't know.

Of course he didn't know. Because nothing is in sync *anymore.*

My throat convulses, and I feel the pressure in my chest, and . . . oh *no.*

Tears are *not* part of our perfect first evening together.

"Be right back," I whisper. I stand abruptly and turn my face so he can't see my glistening eyes. "Just running to the bathroom."

I'm quick, but I'm not quick enough, and before I can duck inside the small powder room, I feel Jake's hand closing around my wrist, stopping me in my tracks.

He turns me around, his eyes scanning mine. "Whoa. Hey. *Hey.* What's wrong?"

I shake my head, still trying to keep him from seeing my face, but I feel them, a couple of tears, spill onto my cheeks.

Jake takes my face in both hands and forces me to look at him. "I'm sorry, baby," he apologizes quietly. "Really, I'm sorry. I didn't know you were cooking."

"It was supposed to be a surprise." My words are choked as I fight to keep more tears from falling. "I just . . . I worked so hard, and I have dessert ready, too . . . crème brûlée, and I bought that stupid little torch, ya know? And now it's all ruined, and I just feel like . . ."

I feel sad.

I feel sad, and I'm pretty sure it's not just about dinner, but dinner is something I can wrap my head around being sad about.

"I know you worked hard, and I really appreciate it, okay?" He taps my chin. "Look at me."

I raise my watery eyes to his gentle baby blues. "It was so good of you. You are so good, and"—his eyes sweep over me—"you look gorgeous, Alyssa, and I'm . . . I'm happy to see you. I am, you know that, right?"

My head falls.

Suddenly I'm blurting out the truth. I only have the nerve to speak to the carpet, not Jake, as I say what's on my mind. "I'm just not entirely sure you one hundred percent want to be here."

In Florida. With me. Any of it.

When I make myself look back up, uncertainty is flickering in his eyes. I hate it. It's not what I want to see there.

"Look. I know these past few months, we've had a rough patch." Jake squeezes my hands. "But if I didn't care to figure this out with you, if I wasn't interested in fixing that, I wouldn't be here, okay?"

I don't answer him. I don't want to acknowledge that this is *hard* now. I just want it to be fixed. Now.

Last summer had been effortless.

"Come here," he whispers.

He tugs on my arm and draws my body against his for a real hug. It's one I really need.

"Don't be sad." He squeezes my sides. "Where's that torch? Let's go set some sugar on fire, okay?"

I start laugh-crying against his chest. "Okay."

"I always have room for my favorite dessert." Jake kisses my temple.

He hugs me one more time, turning to lead me back toward the kitchen, and I decide maybe the night can still be salvaged. After all, dessert is the best part of any meal, and everything is better with a little sugar sprinkled on top.

chapter 3

ON MONDAY AFTERNOON, I LEAVE THE PARK after a full day comprised of multiple appearances at the Princess Brunch and meet-and-greets at the Diamond Palace. I walk out with Chrissi, who's often at my side during meet-and-greets, embodying my fairy godmother. Enchanted Enterprises opted for a younger, more spritelike godmother in their movie rendering of the classic tale, and Chrissi more than fits the bill.

I'm not even sure if Chrissi's five foot; she's petite and somewhat unkempt, with this wild dark blond hair that is perpetually twisted up in a messy bun. She dances through life with the grace and stamina of a ballerina on speed, constantly surrounded by this fluttering energy field that sometimes causes me to stare at her back to see if actual pixie wings are sprouting there.

We talk as we walk—well, *Chrissi* talks, the way she often does without taking a breath. "And I mean, it's laughably ridiculous that the second Memorial Day rolls around and the princess summer squad is in town, Kellen's already organized a party to harass the newbies, but on the other hand, it's a beautiful night and who doesn't love a good courtyard party, so I told Rose—"

She stops suddenly, midsentence, and stares at me. "Pause. What is that face?"

"What face?"

"*That face.*" Chrissi points at me. "This week . . . knowing the big countdown was almost over . . . you've been smiling so hard it was like you were going through auditions all over again, excited as you've been." She shakes her head. "So today I expected, I dunno"—she's still carrying her magic wand and waves it in the air as she makes her point—"mussed hair. Dreamy smiles. Swollen lips. But you seem down."

I realize I've automatically plastered a wide smile on my face in response to her mentioning its absence, something I do as a reflex. The Enchanted Princesses are *never* to be caught without a smile. So it's easy to protest. "What do you mean?" I touch an index finger to my lips. "Still smiling here."

But Chrissi keeps looking at me, and even though my mouth is cooperating, a worried little sigh escapes through my nose.

It makes her stop in her tracks. "Seriously. What's wrong?"

I pause, then slowly lower myself onto a nearby bench, making sure I choose my words carefully. No need to make any of this seem like a bigger deal than it is. After all, Jake himself had reassured me.

Hadn't he?

I shake my head to clear it, hair brushing back and forth over my shoulders. "It was tough, us being apart so long. Conversations just didn't flow the way they used to. Inside jokes weren't quite as funny anymore since we never had a chance to make new ones. I guess I just thought the second we were back together, everything would gel right away. Just . . . naturally."

"Just naturally?" Chrissi plops down next to me. "You surprise me, Alyssa."

"What's that mean?"

"You're an Enchanted girl at heart. And relationships are like anything else." With a giggle and a grin, she produces a tiny canister of glittery pixie dust from her bag, uncorks the top, and blows some in my direction. It coats my shoulders, and she nods with satisfaction. "You need a touch of magic to make them work. To make them really come to life."

My eyes widen and I throw my hands up. "I brought the magic! Trust me!" I spend the next several minutes detailing my perfectly planned romantic meal, my efforts all the way from dredging the raw chicken to setting the sugar crystals on fire.

And when I'm done, Chrissi's staring at me skeptically.

"What? It was amazing!" I assure her.

She cocks her head. "The concept that the way to a guy's heart is through his stomach is super outdated." Her eyebrows disappear beneath her bangs, and her tongue appears in the corner of her mouth. "There's another type of magic they appreciate much, much more."

I giggle. "Chrissi!"

She puts her hand on my knee. "No, I'm serious here." She shrugs. "Us girls, we have this tendency to want all the emotional stuff to feel perfectly aligned in order for the physical to be good, right? But guys, they're backward that way, most of them anyway, and sometimes, surprisingly, getting physical together can make the other stuff click. Help all involved parties relax a little bit and just have some fun together. Reconnect. Ya know?"

I stare at the lazy crowds passing us by, considering. I'm not sure I do.

"So maybe you should do something to really knock his socks off."

Hmm. Jake and I had had, like, four opportunities to be in the same place at the same time since last August. I had thought mere proximity would be sock-knockin' worthy. Yet . . . he hadn't even stayed over that first night. He said he was beat from the trip and needed to get settled in his apartment before he started working, but . . . maybe I could have stepped up my game a bit.

I chew on my lip as I glance at Chrissi from the corner of my eye. "You really think?"

"Yeah. I do. At the very least, a little effort on the sexy and seductive front can't hurt." A second later, her eyes widen and she sits up straight. "I know! We should go into downtown tonight. Go over to Bare with Flare."

"I just can't take that store seriously." I laugh. "I mean, that sign . . ."

"No, it's cool now," she assures me. "I heard they're carrying that new Enchanted Beneath It All line."

I sit up. "Really?" *Now* my interest is piqued. I'd seen some online samples of the new princess-inspired lingerie line, and they were supercute.

"Yup." Chrissi stands, pulls me up, and we resume our course toward the exit. "So let's go home and shower. Then we'll meet back at our place and go shopping. I'll tell the girls."

A moment later, she looks at me again. "And screw Kellen's party," she adds quietly. "We can just hang out and have some girl time if you'd rather."

I smile gratefully back at her. "That's sweet of you. But I told Jake I'd grab a late dinner with him when he's done tonight."

She actually winks at me. "And after our trip, you'll be the most appetizing thing on the menu."

I fall over giggling, jabbing her with my elbow. "You're ridiculous." Then I throw my arm around her and plant a kiss on her cheek. Because I do feel much better after talking to her, like my head is clear and like I actually have a plan to make things better. "Thanks for trying to help."

She's waving her wand in the air again. "No need to thank me. What kind of fairy godmother would I be if I *didn't* help you bring a little magic?"

I PICK UP Chrissi and Rose at their apartment. Rose and I have to remind Chrissi she needs shoes, because she starts walking out the door without them, but eventually we're on our way.

I talk fashion with Rose as we clomp down the outside stairwell, pointing toward the green-and-black, palm-patterned dress she's paired with shiny red sandals. "Your dress is supercute. ModCloth again?" She has a bit of an addiction. I think mostly because she's obsessed with the catchy names they assign their items.

She nods. Then grins. "It's called a girl's best *frond*."

"Cute," I say again.

Rose runs her finger along the fabric of my dress. "This is really nice. Has to be Lilly, right?"

I nod in response. I don't bother to say it's from two years ago and that I snagged it off eBay for twenty bucks and had to bleach it twice to get rid of a makeup stain around the neckline.

The three of us talk park politics, share bits of gossip, and update one another on returning cast members as we walk, and ten minutes later we've made it to the downtown shopping and restaurant section of the complex. I see the sign for Bare with Flare, a cheesy neon creation that portrays a teddy bear wearing lingerie and doing some type of PG-13 striptease, at the end of the block. It does little to convince me that we're on the right track here.

However, the second we step inside, my eyes are immediately drawn to the front right corner of the store, where they've highlighted the new arrivals from the Enchanted Beneath It All collection. With a squeal, I make a beeline toward the familiar color combinations and the signature elements of the Enchanted Princesses.

There are undies comprised entirely of tiny satin red roses, silky aquamarine camisoles bearing the Little Mermaid's scales, and, be still my heart, a Cinderella bridal line that's all white, each item accented with countless tiny crystal hearts. There are sets in Rapunzel's signature emerald green and gold, sets in Beauty's signature royal blue and crimson. The pieces are individually, and collectively, delicate and beautiful, each bearing a tiny, hidden golden silhouette of the princess they're representative of.

Beside me, Chrissi flips impatiently through a rack, dislodging several hangers. "Surprise, surprise. No fairy gear. That's not right! Fairies are supersexy!"

Rose, who's inspecting a deep red low-cut chemise from the Rose Red collection, clucks in sympathy. "Poor Chrissi."

I'm too busy filling my arms with every last Cinderella signature item to comment.

Chrissi turns to me, and then frowns. "Um, no."

"No?" I hold up a pair of white silk panties, the back of which is practically see-through thanks to a large mesh heart cutout. "These are so hot!"

She snatches them away and shakes the hanger. The tiny undies shimmy in the air. "These are white! And gold! And Cinderella! Everything you own is white and gold and Cinderella."

I cross my loaded-down arms over my chest. "Not entirely true."

"*So* entirely true," Rose chimes in.

Chrissi reaches past Rose and grabs something from the red and black section and turns around to present her pick, a red lace bustier and coordinating boy shorts. A subtle rose pattern borders the top of the bustier and the bottom hem of the shorts. "I betcha next week's paycheck that Jake has never seen you in red lace. This will make him sit up and pay attention. *This* is magic."

I have to admit it's a hot little combo, and in the spirit of doing something new and different, I agree to try it on. I'm kind of surprised when I turn around and look in the mirror, because I'm so unused to wearing bright colors. I look . . . okay, I look pretty sexy, but I can't say that I look like myself.

I meet my own gaze in the mirror. *Why should* not *looking like myself have to be part of the plan?*

I turn around and redress before giving it any further consideration.

When I emerge from the dressing room, Chrissi raises her eyebrows and I begrudgingly admit, "It might be a good pick."

"Knew it." She nods in satisfaction, grasping a chocolate-colored teddy bear wearing a, you guessed it, teddy.

"What is that?"

"It's the Bare with Flare bear." She grins. "I'm totally buying it."

I shake my head. "Where's Rose?"

"She's still trying on." Then she actually shoves me toward the register. "You go and pay before you change your mind."

When we leave the store fifteen minutes later, Rose glances at her watch. "What time is Jake done tonight?"

"He's working till eight. Then he has to take the shuttle back and shower."

Chrissi links her arm through mine. "So you're gonna come back and watch *The Bachelorette* premiere with us, right? I know you can't resist the notion of love at first sight."

I chew on my lip. "I don't know. If I watch the premiere, then I'll watch next week, and the week after that, and then before I know it I'll be trying to arrange my work schedule around being home on Mondays at eight o'clock."

"That's what DVR is for."

"Come hang out," Rose says. "I'm not even heading down to the party till at least ten."

So I extend my arm and tell them, "All right. Twist my arm. Go ahead, twist it."

The two make a big show out of actually twisting my arm until it feels like taffy, and we're a giggly bunch as we make our way back through town and back to our building.

As we walk down the hall, it occurs to me that I still haven't met Naked Rapunzel's replacement, and I ask about her. "Hey, do you think your new roommate's going to be home?"

"She has to be back from training sooner or later," Chrissi says, "but we all know those are long days."

"She's working out all right, though?"

"Oh yes." Chrissi nods. "Harper's a dee-light. I really adore her." She's quiet for a minute. "She has some family stuff going on, but she's a sweetheart."

Chrissi doesn't elaborate. She's good at keeping secrets like that.

Camila is at home, however, and I greet her when we step inside. "Hey, Camila."

"Hi," she says distractedly, glancing down at her laptop. She has on her glasses, her hair is pulled back in a low ponytail, and I notice she's wearing a T-shirt that reads, HOME IS WHERE THE WIFI CONNECTS AUTOMATICALLY.

Seriously. It's hard to believe she and Rose are twins. It's hard to believe they're sisters. It's hard to believe they're related in any way.

Here's what Rose and Camila have in common. They are both stunningly beautiful—Vietnamese American, with long, silky black hair, delicate features, and slender figures.

Here's what else they have in common: nothing. Rose wants to be a makeup artist for television and theater and attends cosmetology school. Camila finished college in two and a half years and has an assistantship for grad school at MIT awaiting her. She's spending a year in between Yale and MIT playing princess somewhat against her will, at her sister's insistence that she have an adventure before she turns into "the most stereotypical smart Asian girl *ever*." Rose's words.

At this point, Camila has been here for nine months but still seems immune to the Enchanted magic. She continues to act like playing princess is some form of cruel and unusual punishment. Needless to say . . . I don't really *get* Camila.

But still I try. "Did you get your summer schedule yet?"

Schedules shift a bit around Memorial Day, when the daily crowds grow even huger during the summer season.

"Yes," she answers tersely. "But, shocker of shockers, Rose is insisting on taking all the Rose Red shifts. I have protested vehemently that we are *identical twins* and it would be appropriate to switch things up from time to time. I don't know why I always have to be the meek, pea-brained sister of the two."

Rose throws her hands up. "Camila, work with me here. I *am* Rose. You are White. It makes sense, and it's easier to stay in character than to keep switching back and forth. Messes up my vibe. And Snow White's not pea brained! She's just . . . thoughtful and less . . . fiery."

"She's boring and inane."

"You think every princess is boring and inane."

"Fair enough." Camila shrugs. "I think I might have rather spent these last few months—thank you, *God*—as a fur character."

Rose groans for a solid twenty seconds, and I jump in to change the subject.

"You should have come shopping with us, Camila. It was fun."

Her mouth twists up wryly in response. "Lingerie shopping isn't my idea of a group event."

To be honest, I'm not sure what *is* Camila's idea of a group event. She's a textbook introvert.

"I think that's something you do in private," she says, making the mistake of continuing.

Rose can't help herself and pokes her sister in the side. "Guess what? I know what you look like naked. I don't know . . . I think it's that whole *identical twin* thing."

Camila inches away from her sister and straightens her T-shirt, and Rose rolls her eyes in my direction at her stiffness before heading to their room to put her purchases away.

While Chrissi grabs some snacks and turns to the channel for

The Bachelorette, I text Jake to let him know he should head to the girls' apartment rather than mine. Then we settle in on the couches, and within ten minutes of meeting the new bachelorette and this round of crazy-as-ever contestants, I know I'm in for the season.

I'm totally engrossed in the latest contestant introducing himself to this season's star of the show, because I swear I recognize him as an older sorority sister's ex, and I don't even hear the door to the apartment open.

Then Chrissi squeals. "Oh yay, you're back! Now we can introduce you to Alyssa." Chrissi grabs my arm so that I turn around, and my eyes follow hers to the doorway. "This is Harper!" she exclaims, looking at me. "Isn't she a perfect Beauty?"

Harper stands in the doorway, looking exhausted and sweaty, still clutching her huge purple-and-gold princess training manual.

I quickly assess the new girl. I know my Enchanted Princesses, from the shapes of their faces to their hairlines to their hidden birthmarks. Harper's complexion isn't spot on and her hair's too straight for her to be considered a *perfect* Beauty, but she's pretty enough and definitely has this . . . bookish air to her. And when she smiles over at me in greeting, I have to admit her smile is dazzling. She'll do well in the park.

I get up and walk over to shake her hand. I wish it was a commercial break, but princesses remember their manners. "Hi, Harper. I'm Alyssa. Welcome to the Princess Posse."

She shifts her binder to her left arm. "Thanks. It's nice to meet you."

"We're rivals, did you know that?" I fold my arms and wink at her.

Her face wrinkles in confusion. "What? I don't . . ."

"Enchanted Dominion factoid: pictures with Cinderella and Beauty are the most highly sought." I shrug. "Some girls actually compare their numbers at the end of the day." I put my hand to my chest. "Not me, though. So silly."

Her shoulders relax. "I had no idea. I can't imagine doing something like that." Harper looks me over. "You're a perfect Cinderella. You're seriously stunning."

I like the new girl.

"You're sweet, Harper."

Chrissi rearranges herself on the couch and points to a bowl of sour watermelons on the coffee table. "Harper, get yourself some candy, pronto. You've survived your first week in princess training, girlie!" Then she rolls her eyes toward me and Rose. "We all know what a painful process that is, all those quizzes and rehearsals and fittings. And that's *after* she had this totally dramatic trip down here! Alyssa, you would not believe this story; her trip down was insane! And there was this guy—"

"Chrissi!" Harper interrupts her new roommate with a hiss. "We are *not* talking about him, okay? I've decided to pretend the whole *trip* never happened. Officially deleted from memory, as quickly as he disappeared."

I helpfully change the subject. "Well, congrats on making it through the first week. It's the most grueling; trust me. Except for the requisite stint in fur." I head back to the couch, leaning down to pick up a piece of candy. "Are you an actress, Harper? Or studying acting, at least?"

Harper's face becomes guarded. "Umm, no." She doesn't come over to the couches, and fiddles with the long chain around her neck instead. "I was actually prelaw. I just . . . I just . . . needed to do something different. This summer . . ." She inhales a deep breath. ". . . I just needed to get away."

An endless moment of awkward silence follows.

Harper stares down at the ground, and when she eventually raises her head, I think there's a trace of tears in her eyes.

But she smiles until they recede, in true princess style, and says, "Let's talk about something else." Now she does make her way over to us and extends her hand. "And where's that candy? Give me, like, ten handfuls."

The clouds break, and Harper perches on the arm of the couch, joining us to watch the next segment of the show before announcing she's in desperate need of a shower after a hot day in one of the park's employee auditoriums.

Fifteen minutes later, the door opens again, and this time I most certainly do notice.

"Jaaaake!" Chrissi screams when he comes walking in, gently knocking on the door at the same time. She spreads her arms wide in greeting. "Welcome back!"

I smile up at my boyfriend, studying him. He looks happy and relaxed, wearing a tight gray T-shirt, loose jeans, and gray New Balances. I can tell his hair is damp and he's just showered. I hop up and walk over to give him a hug. Plus he smells yummy.

I kiss him and ask, "How was your day?"

He raises his eyebrows uncertainly. "How was my day? There was a considerable amount of vomit involved in my day. Comes with the territory when you're stationed at the base of Marauders' Mountain."

I wrap my arm around his middle and turn toward Rose and Camila. "Hey, girls. So this is Jake. Jake, this is Rose and Camila. Camila wears glasses; that's the easiest way to keep it straight."

He does a double take. "Oh wow! Yeah, you're twins."

It is easy to miss it.

"Good to finally meet you, Jake," Rose says. She narrows her eyes and squints up at him. "Hey, your favorite color doesn't happen to be red, by any chance?"

He looks thoroughly confused. "Uh, not really. Why?"

Her face is innocently blank. "Oh, I just have a feeling it's going to be."

She and Chrissi collapse into each other in a fit of immature giggles, and I just shake my head at Jake. "Just ignore them. Talk to Camila instead. She actually knows how to act her age."

Camila looks sort of irritated about the proposal, having to talk to a guy. Having to *talk*.

Once Rose gets herself together, she makes more of an effort to be appropriate. She clears her throat. "Are you staying here at Lakeside, too?"

"Yeah, a few complexes over. Next to the grocery store." Jake turns his face and plants a quick kiss atop my head.

I smile against his torso. Between the shopping trip, the girl time, and his PDA, I'm definitely feeling much better about things.

Suddenly I hear Harper's voice from down the hallway. "Chrissi, I hope you don't mind I used your conditioner. They didn't have my brand at the store and I haven't—"

We don't have a chance to warn her that there's a boy on the scene and she appears before us, wet hair dripping over her face and back, wearing nothing but a short purple towel that barely covers all the parts it needs to. She stops at once when Jake comes into view, a surprised little gasp escaping her throat, and she struggles to wrap the towel even more securely around her torso.

My body is still pressed against Jake's, so I feel his stiffen at once. At first his expression is that of a deer caught in headlights, and then his eyes dart wildly, as if looking for an escape.

It's an uncomfortable run-in, for sure, but certainly he's seen girls wearing much less. Any given day at the complex pool, as a matter of fact. We should just be adults, offer a quick introduction, and allow Harper to get some clothing ASAP.

"Sorry for the lack of notice about the guy," I apologize, wincing. "This is my boyfriend, Jake."

The look of shock on Harper's face changes to something else, something I can't quite read. Even though you'd think she'd be darting out of there as fast as she could, she seems frozen in place, and it takes her a minute to find her voice. She swallows hard. Smooths her wet hair. Lifts her chin and once more tucks the end of her towel inside the other end. "Alyssa's boyfriend. Jake. Okay." Harper smiles widely, but it's not the natural one that I thought was so pretty earlier. She manages a quick, stiff wave. "So nice to meet you, Jake."

He hadn't relaxed a smidgen. It takes him a minute to remember social norms, but eventually he does respond. "Hey." He glances down. "Nice to meet you, Harper."

Moving robotically, Harper twists toward the others. "Get dressed. Right. I should do that." She backpedals into the room she shares with Chrissi, eyes still on Jake, and then we hear the door slam.

I look up at him. "Do you know her or something? You both . . . look like you saw a ghost."

He's staring after her closed door. "Yeah, I did sort of do a double take. She looks like someone I went to high school with.

Thought it was her for a minute." He takes a deep breath, then finally looks back at me, expression still distant, but his smile in place. "So. Dinner? I'm starving."

"Sure, just let me get my stuff." I walk back to the couch to pick up my shopping bag, still trying to shake the unsettling feeling that lingers in the room even after Harper has departed. What *was* that?

Jake lifts his hand in greeting to the girls. "Chrissi, good to see you again. Rose, Camila, really nice to meet you finally."

As soon as I return to his side, he has his hand on the small of my back, turning me, pushing me toward the door with slightly more force than is needed.

And once we're in the hallway, even though he claimed to be starving just a moment ago, he takes my hand and gestures in the direction of my apartment instead. "You know what, hon? Actually I don't know if I feel like going out to eat tonight. Maybe I'll just scrounge something up or order something. I think I'd just rather stay in and . . . hang out."

His words warm me and dispel the odd feeling from inside the apartment. Now this feels like last year, when we had the best times doing absolutely nothing at my apartment, just hanging out.

"Sure. Sounds better to me, too," I answer at once.

"Yeah. Let's just . . . stay in."

The rest of our night is about as perfect as I could imagine. He merely rolls his eyes and smiles when I find *The Princess Diaries* on television and doesn't protest when I leave it on. He makes us popcorn. He holds me in his arms. He accepts my invitation to stay over.

And as it turns out, I don't even need to open my shopping bag to get him to say yes.

I'm all smiles as I crawl into bed beside him in a loose T-shirt instead. This is more like it. Seems like my Prince Charming is back in the building.

chapter 4

THE FITNESS CENTER IN THE MIDDLE OF Lakeside's downtown area is a four-story, gleaming, angular monstrosity that doesn't quite fit amid the narrow boutiques, coffee shops, and chain restaurants surrounding it. It takes up nearly an entire block, and I'm guessing it's considered an eyesore by the few non–health conscious residents of the complex. But the fitness center was built to meet a demand, a fervent, fanatical type of demand, as the complex slowly but steadily came to house such a large number of Enchanted Enterprises cast members.

I make my way inside, jog-climb the three flights of stairs to the main fitness studio, and survey the scene as I stuff my tote bag in the last empty cubby in the wall. If there was a phrase to describe the fitness studio, I'm pretty sure it would be "you can tell just by looking." Cast members self-segregate themselves in the various areas of the gym.

Those who portray villains, males and females alike, camp out around the free weights or wait impatiently for GRIT classes to start. They maintain fierce expressions even when working out, interested in bulk, muscles, and strength.

The show performers, who do elaborate stilt work, tumbling, and complicated fusion dances, are here for flexibility and endurance. Their muscles are lean, their bodies wiry, as they pound the belts of the treadmills or contort themselves in advanced yoga classes.

The princes? Linger by machines postworkout, logging stats into their Apple watches and posting them to Instagram.

And then there are us princesses. Typically we have a monopoly on the elliptical or step machines. A lot of the princesses favor the barre classes that focus on posture, balance, and toning one's core.

I'm totally comfortable at the fitness center; it pretty much parallels the rec center at Coral State. It's just here I work out next to fellow princesses instead of sorority sisters. The show performers replace the scholarship athletes. And narcissistic guys? They're the same everywhere you go. I'm so glad Jake's not a gym rat!

I scan the cluster of elliptical machines, making a beeline for the last one in the row when I see that a girl is stepping off and wiping it down with a cloth. I'm an elliptical girl. On the elliptical, I can listen to Taylor Swift, Meghan Trainor, old-school Britney Spears, zone out, and almost pretend I'm dancing instead of exercising. I don't actually *like* to work out, and I really hate running. I work out because I have to. I do so out of habit, because I'm terrified if I don't do it ritually I'll stop altogether. Really, the only thing that makes me happy about going to the gym is crossing it off my mental to-do list when I leave.

Climbing on, I put my water bottle in the cup holder and

stuff my earbuds into my ears. I select my favorite bubblegum pop playlist and get moving. It makes my head hurt when I try to read or watch TV at the gym, so I distract myself by people watching instead. Well, princess watching, to be more specific. I'm in the second row of machines, so I find myself staring at the backs of my fellow cast members.

I stare at Tara's legs as they rotate furiously in my line of vision. *That's what I wish my legs looked like, those stick-skinny legs I'll never have no matter how many calories I burn. I know Jake tells me no guys really like legs that skinny. But I do.*

Gracie is working out two machines down from her. *She really does have the perfect boob-to-waist ratio.* I'd heard some of the girls say as much in a show rehearsal last week. *You'd think they're fake, but they're not. They're just naturally perfect.*

Alexis, who plays Rose Red on some of Rose's off days, walks past. She's tiny and looks like an Olympic gymnast. *It's an unnatural advantage, I swear, being that tiny and lithe. Does she even* need *to work out? She looks perfect as she is, and I bet she never gains weight, no matter what she eats.* I pump my legs faster.

I pretty much spend the entire first part of my workout assessing my coworkers, comparing myself without meaning to. It's impossible not to. We're in Florida, it's hot and sticky most of the time and even worse here in the gym, and the princesses work out in colorful sports bras and yoga pants that fit tighter than a second layer of skin. Despite the humidity, most of us work out in full makeup, even though we're all well aware how bad it is for one's pores. We're forced to acknowledge the perfection of others; we're forced to face reminders of how easy it would be to fall off our game if we *didn't* come every day. There are so many other girls who are just as pretty.

But this is a job. And it's all part of the job. If you care, anyway.

I turn my head, noticing that the girl working out beside me is staring down at her machine's screen in concentration, lips moving as she performs some type of mental computation.

I'm sure I know every last formula that she may be applying. I know exactly how many calories you have to burn to rid your body of an extra pound. I know how many calories are in most beers and mixed drinks, a chart I was required to memorize while pledging, and exactly how many extra minutes of cardio are required for each extra drink. An image of the BMI chart has been committed to memory.

I'm sure not a math whiz, and thinking about it, I have absolutely no idea when I started running the numbers. I guess it dates back to high school cheerleading days, when girls first started throwing these terms around and measuring their self-satisfaction in comparison to other girls rather than themselves. Then in the sorority, with its rules about not being seen eating fast food in public and scheduled gym outings, it's just more of the same. All the girls I have always associated with routinely run the numbers, too. It's part of our culture, part of our lexicon.

I don't really know girls whose minds *don't* work this way anymore.

With my music pumping and a gym full of distractions, time passes quickly, and the next thing I know, my workout is already half over. Internally, I relax, which I can't really do until my daily workout is out of the way. It's why I prefer to get it over with early; otherwise I'll just keep thinking about it.

Good for you, I tell myself, drinking some water. *Way to get it done. It's all downhill from here.*

When I put my empty bottle back into place, I see Harper making her way toward a treadmill. I haven't seen her in four days, since I met her at the apartment, and I try to catch her attention to say hi. Even though I think she can see me from her angle, I guess she doesn't, because she just keeps walking purposefully toward the treadmill with her head down. Her earbuds are in, so maybe she's already lost in her own little world.

I stare at her as she climbs aboard the treadmill. There's not a single other princess in the row of treadmills, but her choice doesn't surprise me. There's something about her that keeps her from fitting in with the group in a perfectly natural way. I watch her, curious, trying to figure it out.

It turns out that Harper's a runner. Like, a legit runner, hitting the treadmill with such intensity and speed she's likely already elevated her heart rate from the fat-burn to cardio range. She's got a runner's butt, too—full, round, and capable looking. My butt has never looked like that.

Harper's all business as she runs. Her face is serious, and she appears to be reading something on her phone, the way she keeps swiping its screen, something I could never manage. She's wearing a loose T-shirt and running shorts, the exception to my "you can tell just by looking" rule. I really wonder how she ended up down here.

Because she basically sprints the whole time, she finishes before I do, chugs her water, and adjusts the speed of her machine for her cooldown. My elliptical switches into cooldown mode soon after, and I decide I'll wait till she's done, make a point of saying hi.

I don't know the seemingly sad story that brought her here, but obviously she's going through some hard times. She's down here by herself, in this new, slightly bizarre community. And while she strikes me as the type who doesn't enjoy pity, I believe there's a difference between pity and compassion.

At least I hope so, I think, as I climb down and walk toward her when she steps off the treadmill.

When she turns and finds me hovering, she takes a step back in surprise. She doesn't exactly look eager to talk, first just waving without bothering to remove her earbuds. I decide to wait her out and just stand there expectantly. Eventually she caves, removing her headphones and wiping her forehead on the sleeve of her T-shirt. She's actually sweating. I can't remember the last time I actually broke a sweat in the gym as opposed to the parade route.

"Hey, Harper! How are you?"

"I'm good . . ." She answers slowly, eyeing me warily. Then eventually she asks, "How are you?"

"I'm great now. Glad I got the workout out of the way!" I smile brightly.

She studies me for another moment and then says, "Sorry if I'm distracted. I was reading my school's law review, and my thoughts are still wrapped up in it." Harper makes a wry face at the screen of her phone. "I'm missing school way more than I thought I would. And it does pass the time." She looks around at the myriad of cast members surrounding us. "Kinda get the sense that I'm going to be here a lot. It was impossible to miss the stress they put on maintaining your appearance around here. It's hard-core." She lowers her voice. "Talk about making you instantly self-conscious."

"Try not to worry too much." I wave my hand, like this is something I've mastered. *Ha*. "Obviously certain people, the ones playing the Little Mermaid, or princess to Aladdin, they don't wear too much and it's a bigger deal. Our ball gowns, they're more forgiving."

Harper gives me a thumbs-up. "Forgiving. I like the sound of that." She studies me, then points to my top. "I like your shirt. It's sweet."

"Thanks," I answer, looking down at the glittery tank I'm wearing, which reads, CINDERELLA IS PROOF THAT THE RIGHT PAIR OF SHOES CAN CHANGE YOUR LIFE. "It was a gift from my big."

"Your big what?"

So Harper's not a sorority girl. Also not a surprise.

"Oh, my, um, sorority big sister."

Then we stand there, her still panting slightly, and me, quickly running out of small talk. "Well, um, good luck with the rest of your training. Fur can be tough, and the forecast looks relentless."

"Thanks," she says. Harper studies me a second longer. "And thanks for saying hi."

"Of course!" I tighten my ponytail, then offer a quick wave and turn to go.

I think I feel her eyes on me as I leave, perhaps trying to figure me out the same way I'm trying to figure her out.

chapter 5

I SPEND FRIDAY MORNING DOING MEET-and-greets at the base of the drawbridge leading to the Diamond Palace. A long day awaits—I'm working until closing because I'd submitted a request for tomorrow off since some of my favorite Zeta girls are driving up to visit. Typically I don't mind double shifts at the park, but we're experiencing record heat and humidity for the last couple of days of May. By ten thirty in the morning, I'm already suffering. Cinderella's ball gown is even more cumbersome than her dreamy wedding attire—it's made of several layers of silk and taffeta beneath the delicate gold lace filigree. The only (small) blessing is that my hair is upswept and the occasional breeze feels like salvation when it hits the perpetual trail of perspiration running down my neck.

I feel almost guilty about the number of water breaks I request, which will impact my daily guest count that an attendant carefully records with a clicker concealed in his palm. But I'm seasoned enough to know how important it is to stay hydrated. I'd endured several bouts of dizziness and even blinding migraines last summer when I'd tried to tough it out. Today, I have a cooler full of water bottles in the gatehouse behind the castle wall, which I visit frequently.

The added bonus is that the gatehouse doubles as the central first aid station, where Jake is camped out for the day. The walls of the Palace create shadows over the windows, but if I squint, I can see him in there, answering his walkie, joking around with a fellow crew member. His presence bolsters me some.

And he's concerned every time I visit.

"You okay?" he asks solemnly. "You need anything besides water?"

I smile at his businesslike demeanor, his comfort in the caretaker role.

"I'm fine," I assure him. "This isn't even August level heat."

Complaining surely doesn't help anything.

Besides. My dress is heavy, but as I return to my post and see Drako the Dragon lumbering past, I mentally give thanks that I'm not a fur character. Cast members have been known to pass out inside their costumes on particularly scorching days. Drako the Dragon is the character around which the Enchanted empire was built, and he's stuck in one of the worst costumes!

I take my lunch break around noon, deciding to eat at an underground cast cafeteria because one is nearby. Jake's lunch break isn't until two o'clock, so I head downstairs by myself, feeling the instant relief from the heat provided by the dark underground tunnels.

When I approach the entrance to the cafeteria, Snow White in glasses, aka Camila, is standing beside it, talking rapid-fire fast in an unfamiliar language to a ride operator. For whatever reason, she practically scurries away from him when I approach, offering a terse wave in my direction.

I approach her with a smile and ask, "Who were you talking to?" I take a second glance. "He's cute."

"I'm just practicing my Mandarin," she responds, clenching and unclenching her hands at her sides. "That's all."

"It's okay to talk to boooys, Camila," I tease.

She practically glares at me in return, so I let up, gesturing toward the tables inside. "Are you coming or going?"

"I just got here." And still she lingers near the door.

Geez. It's kind of like pulling teeth with her. "Wanna eat together?"

"Oh." It finally dawns on her. "Okay."

We go through the food line, swipe our badges to pay, and then walk toward the back tables, carrying our trays. Mine holds another bottle of water—I feel like a camel—a veggie wrap, and some slices of watermelon since they're practically all water, too. Camila and I sit down with the other princesses present without thinking about it. Because the skirts of our dresses are so wide and difficult to maneuver, the princesses always claim the more appealing round tables with comfortable chairs as opposed to the long cafeteria tables with benches.

I eat my wrap quickly and am finishing my bottle of water while chatting with the girls at our table when I see the Meerkats walk in in costume. The pair are two of the more popular fur characters, because they're hyper and silly and funny, entertaining the masses while they wait in ridiculously long lines to meet the likes of me or ride the newest roller coaster. When they take off their heads and set them down on two chairs to secure a spot, I realize that one of them is Harper.

I wave until I catch her attention and gesture for her to come join us, but she points discreetly toward her partner, indicating she's going to stay put. Smiling in understanding, I wave a second time before she goes and gets in line.

Well, stumbles toward the line would be a better way of putting it. Harper doesn't look too fresh. Her face is bright red, yet she looks a little green around the gills. Her braid is coming apart in pieces and her eyes have a glazed look about them. Obviously, she's struggling with the heat. She returns to her seat a few minutes later with nothing but a pack of crackers on her tray.

Harper sits down beside her partner—I think her name is Kelly—and I notice Yael, Miller's roommate, scooches down to join them. She appears to be filling the Bear role in the Snow White/Rose Red show today.

Camila tells me she needs to get going, and when she stands up to leave, I stand up, too. I grab my unopened plastic container of watermelon cubes. I'm pretty sure someone else needs them more than I do today.

Lifting my full skirt off the sticky cafeteria floor, I carefully make my way down the narrow aisle toward the fur table. I remove the semicreepy bear head from the chair beside Harper and lower myself into it.

Yael stands, reaches over, and snatches the costume head away and grumbles under her breath. "Sure you can sit there. No one was using that chair or anything."

Her face is almost as dark red as her hair, and she glares at me from behind her glasses, but I take a deep breath and attribute the bared teeth and snarling to heat and fatigue. Or maybe an attempt to stay in character.

"Didn't mean anything by it." I try to make a joke of it, patting the bear's head. "I'm sorry."

Yael's face grows redder still.

Okay then. I turn toward Harper instead. "How are you holding up, hon?"

"I'm not so much holding up," she says, puffing out her cheeks. "I don't feel too well."

I nod toward her tray. "I know it might be the last thing you feel like doing, but you really should eat more than what you have there. To drink as much water as you're going to need to make it through the day, you need some food in your stomach or it's going to make you feel nauseous." I set the container of watermelon on her tray. "Watermelon helps. It's actually ninety-two percent water." I shrug. "Some websites even say ninety-three percent."

"Oh. My. God." Yael pokes Kelly. "Straight from the Sorority Girl's Encyclopedia of Useless Knowledge."

Kelly guffaws.

I inhale a steadying breath and keep my attention focused on Harper, who's pushing the fruit away.

"That's nice of you. But I'm already nauseous. I can't really stomach the thought of eating." She looks at me helplessly, like she's pleading to be rescued. "I just keep telling myself, three more hours. Today's my last day in fur."

Kelly's head whips around. "What?"

"Today's my last day in fur."

"I thought someone told me you were staying in fur."

Harper shakes her head weakly. "I don't know . . ."

"I thought you were training," Kelly presses. "You're just doing the requisite five-day stint?"

Harper nods. "I'm starting as a face character next week."

Yael wrinkles her nose. "Really? Who?"

It's not a particularly nice question.

"Beauty."

With this, Kelly actually snorts. She picks up the end of Harper's undone braid and drops it unceremoniously. "Think you need a makeover first, Princess."

"Excuse me?"

"You don't really look the part." Kelly shrugs. "That's all."

Even though her face is still red, I swear Harper's cheeks turn even pinker. "That's kind of rude," she says.

"Whatever." Kelly shakes her head and turns her body away from Harper, toward Yael. "Is what it is. Get over yourself."

Suddenly Harper looks like she's blinking back tears, and I can imagine exactly what she's feeling. Training is no joke, between the heat, the long hours, the requisite daily Enchanted quizzes, and the constant demand to be pleasant and entertaining.

"Hey, give her a break," I insert quietly. I shake my head. "Harper didn't do anything to you."

Kelly turns around again, glaring at me with those glacier-blue eyes of her. Yikes. "It's not *Harper*, per se, sweetheart. It's all of you." She rolls her eyes. "You're all nice and friendly when you're working fur, but once you're promoted to pretty princess, you can't be bothered." She waves her hand dismissively toward the table full of princesses. "You're part of the little clique and that's that." She raises her fork to make a point, but it's inappropriately close to my face. "I'm just as good an actress as any of you. And I know I'm just as pretty. But because I'm a couple inches too tall, I get stuck being a giant rodent and have the pleasure of training a new batch of you girls every few months. Sorry if I'm over it."

"But you don't even know me," Harper protests weakly.

"What the hell's the point? Conversation over." With a loud metallic scraping sound, she pointedly turns her chair, its back slamming into Harper's arm, and positions herself so she's looking only at Yael.

I'm sort of stunned. I mean, I've heard muttered comments about some silly face character–fur divide, this ridiculous idea that we receive better treatment because we're face characters. But . . . really? Is this real life?

I stare at Kelly's ponytail, feeling my nails curling into my palms, the sound of my heartbeat becoming more apparent in my ears. There aren't too many things that make me angry. But I truly hate the practice of kicking someone when she's down. Especially when we're supposed to be on the same team.

So I shove my chair back, march around the end of the table with my skirt dragging, sticky floor be damned, and make my way back down the aisle until I'm standing directly behind Kelly. Then I gently tap her on the shoulder.

With a pronounced irritated sigh, she looks up over her shoulder. "God. What?"

I smile sweetly. "I'm sorry, but . . . conversation not over. There's just really no reason to talk to her like that, okay? Today is hard for all of us. It's awful out there. Do you really think you're helping the rest of the day go smoothly by beating her down? That's not really how we do things around here, at least I hope it's not."

I glance down at Harper, who sneaks me a tiny, grateful smile.

I realize the room has gone quiet around us, most cast members turning and watching the scene unfold.

Kelly stares at me flatly. "Suzie Sunshine. Not really in the mood for the lecture."

"Well," I continue, folding my hands before me, "I'm sure *Harper*'s not in the mood to be insulted and dismissed. We all work hard around here, okay? Have a little respect is all I'm saying."

A few other cast members murmur their agreement, and a cafeteria worker even calls out, waving a spatula in the air, "Preach, Princess!"

"You know what?" Kelly's on her feet before I know it, turning around, her face only inches from mine. Oh my. She *is* tall. Tall and strong looking, like an Olympic volleyball player. She grits her teeth. "I said I wasn't in the mood for this shit." She has the nerve to flick one of the ruffles draped around my shoulder. "*Princess.*"

My mouth falls open in disbelief. "Did you honestly just *flick* me?"

"Yeah." Kelly's chin juts out. "I did."

She's glaring at me, paws on her hips, the crowd is watching in silent anticipation of what's going to happen next, and I . . . well . . . I have no idea how the heck to retreat. I'm pretty sure Kelly's two seconds away from suggesting we step outside and settle the score once and for all, and I have no desire to roll in the dirt in my pristine white gown. Yet I can't look away first, because I just can't concede this one to her. So I'm stuck there, aware of nothing but the second hand on the loud clock overhead ticking by at snail speed. *Crap.*

Craaap.

"Whoa. Hey! Ladies . . . what's up?"

A loud voice cuts into my stupor, muffled as it is beneath a large kangaroo's head from across the room. Then said kangaroo actually hops over to the table in record speed, long tail thumping the ground behind him as he goes. He shoves the table to the side so he has room to make his way toward us and insert his body between mine and Kelly's.

Only then does he remove the kangaroo head and toss it out of the way, and Miller's face appears before me, cheeks flushed, his damp wavy hair matted to his head.

He looks at me. He looks at Kelly. He looks at me again. Then he grins, his eyes going wide. "Seriously? Are you two seriously doing this? How did I just walk in on a character standoff?"

"Miller." Kelly shoots him a pleading look. "You get it. These girls are obnoxious."

"C'mon now, Kel," he says, keeping his voice light. "Relax. I doubt they did anything that egregious."

Yael pushes her chair back, stands, and shoots Miller a look. "*You* are unbelievable, bro." She shakes her head, looks at me, and looks back at Miller. "I give up on you." She turns and leaves. I can't say I'm sorry to see her go.

"Look," Miller says. "We all know management has a very strong zero-tolerance policy about staff altercations. Kelly, I seriously doubt you want a mug shot on record that's half girl, half meerkat."

Shockingly, I see her biting her lip, trying to keep from smiling.

"And Lys, it would tarnish the Enchanted Princess image for years to come and traumatize scores of little girls if they have to haul Cinderella out of here in handcuffs."

Now I'm smiling, too.

Miller circles his paw in the air. "So let's all just dial down the drama a few notches, step away from each other, and get on with our days."

Kelly stares at me for another minute before finally dropping her head. "Yeah. Whatever," she mutters. She sits back down and finally starts eating her lunch.

Miller claps me on the shoulder. "I gotta grab something to eat. I only have ten minutes." He takes a step closer, winks at me before leaving. "See if you can stay out of trouble for a while, okay, Princess?"

I give him a rueful smile. "I'll try." Making sure Kelly's not looking, I mouth a quick "thank you."

Miller leans toward my ear. "You're welcome. She would've pummeled you."

He bounds off toward the food line, and when I look down at Harper, she stands up quickly and we walk toward the door.

"Thanks for trying." Harper frowns. "I wouldn't have expected that to get so . . . um . . . intense."

I have to giggle. "Trust me. Me either." I shrug. "I guess she thought she was making up for all the 'special treatment' we princesses get by treating you like garbage. But it's not right. I had to have your back."

Harper glances over her shoulder. "Really didn't think I was going into a gang war . . ."

She's joking, but she sounds dejected and she still looks like she could keel over at any minute.

"Are you okay to go back out there?" I ask.

"I'll survive. Three more hours," she sighs.

But I'm far from convinced as I watch her go. Her energy

level is reading in negative numbers and she drags her feet, seeming a bit off balance as she walks. She's about to walk out into the most grueling part of the day, and her lunch was far from rejuvenating. I hope these last three hours pass quickly.

THEY DON'T, NOT really, at least for me.

The heat does nothing to dampen the spirit of the crowd, and the lines to meet me never let up. A little boy with a concealed red lollipop gets it stuck in my hair. My *real* hair. I have to find a way to untangle it, while the boy wails about his ruined treat, all while keeping a smile on my face. The fur characters may have their trials, but at least they get to hide their expressions when dealing with something like this.

And last but not least, I get propositioned by a Creepy Grandfather, with just about the lamest line ever, something about how I *must* be Cinderella, because he could "definitely see that dress disappearing by midnight." *Eww.*

When my day shift wraps, I sprint to the tunnel entrance faster than the real Cinderella ran from the ball. My eyes struggle to adjust from the glaring sun to the dim tunnel, but when they do, I see someone up ahead of me, staggering as they approach the top of the stairwell. They're listing like crazy, and I swear they're about to take a tumble.

"Are you okay?" I call, running again to catch up with them.

And just like that, they drop. Luckily they fall backward rather than down the steep stairwell, but my heart reacts as if they had. I lose my shoes and spring toward them, and as I approach, I realize it's a life-size meerkat splayed out on the ground before me. I'm pretty sure I know who it is.

I struggle to wrench her headpiece off. She's no help—she's out cold.

"Oh my God! Harper!"

Hands shaking, I fumble around to find the concealed walkie that's pinned beneath my skirt for emergencies. I twist the dial to the 9-1-1 channel and scream Jake's name into it.

Thank God he's close by.

"Jake! Jake! I need your help in the B tunnel. Something happened to Harper!"

At once I hear a burst of static. Then, "We're en route."

I put my hand to Harper's cheek. It feels like it's about a thousand degrees, but I have no idea what I should do first.

Am I supposed to cool her down? With water? Should I pour water on her face? What if that makes it worse?

I consider taking the rest of her costume off, since it can't possibly be helping. But what if I do some type of damage by moving her? What if she hurt her neck when she fell?

I fall back on my heels, feeling helpless and useless, wondering why the heck I never took a first aid course. When I put my finger to her wrist, I'm a smidgen relieved that I can at least feel a pulse, and I keep calling her name, hoping beyond hope that she'll wake up and answer me.

"Harper! It's Alyssa. I'm here. Wake up, Harper! Help is coming!"

And eventually, thank you sweet Jesus, her eyelids flutter. Then her eyes open all the way and she glances around, still groggy. "Where am I?" she asks hoarsely.

"Harper. Thank God." My hand goes to my chest. "I think you passed out from the heat. You're in the tunnels. You passed out and fell."

She looks confused. And a little bit scared.

"But I paged Jake. He'll be here any second. With the first aid team."

Suddenly she's trying to sit up, but she topples to the side. "What? No, that's okay. I can . . ."

Before she can protest further, I hear people approaching from outside, and when I look up I see Jake and Ron, his partner today, running toward us, heavy first aid kit in hand.

"I don't know if I've ever been so happy to see you!" I greet him.

Jake ignores my greeting entirely, dropping to his knees beside Harper. His partner does the same. Jake takes her pulse while Ron slaps something on her forehead to take her temperature.

Now that someone else is on the scene, I drop her hand and finally have the wherewithal to reach for a spare bottle of water.

I extend it in her direction, but Jake practically bats my hand away. "Don't give that to her!"

I recoil as if I've actually been slapped. "I'm sorry, I was just trying—"

"Didn't mean to snap," he mutters, eyes still on Harper's wrist. "But we have to get her temperature down with cool cloths. Externally. Not internally. Water can make it worse."

I go back to feeling helpless and useless, a bystander, as Jake gently inquires about her symptoms—Does she have a headache, is she dizzy or light-headed, is she experiencing any muscle cramps, has she felt nauseous or vomited?

He still has her hand in his, and he's attentive as always, saving the day, the knight in shining armor.

An uncomfortable awareness dawns—it's like watching an even more dramatic reenactment of our very first encounter, and although I'm sort of ashamed to admit it to myself, it cheapens the memory in some way I don't like.

Jake looks at Ron and me. "We need to get her to a cooler area. Grab some ice packs to help cool her down."

I follow as they move Harper into an air-conditioned office and place some ice packs against her arms and neck.

"Oh my God," she whimpers. "That feels so good I could cry."

"What happened out there?" Ron asks.

Harper, on the floor and propped against the wall, closes her eyes and covers them with her hand. "Kelly was just . . . still riding me pretty hard about the princess thing. I felt like absolute crap at lunch, but she was just so . . . *cutting*. I was even more intent on proving her wrong." She shakes her head. "But she had us running all over the park. She wouldn't let go of my arm, and I had to keep up. She wouldn't let me take water breaks."

"She needs to be reported," Jake snaps.

Harper lifts her hand weakly. "I don't want to cause a problem. I'm okay now. I'll be okay."

Jake raises one eyebrow, unconvinced. "You need to take better care of yourself on days like this, okay?"

Harper won't meet his eye. He *is* a little intense.

"Seriously, Harper." He's gentler this time, and when he says her name, she finally allows her gaze to meet his. "This isn't a joke. Heat exhaustion, heatstroke, it can cause serious damage to your organs."

“Yeah, okay,” she concedes. She stares up at him, biting her lip. “Thanks, Jake,” she whispers.

I find myself looking back and forth between them. I swear I just introduced the two of them the other night, yet they’re talking to each other like they’ve known each other forever, or something. Maybe it’s just that weird intimacy that automatically comes about when someone is providing another person with physical care, leaving outsiders to feel weird standing there watching them.

I clear my throat. “Is she going to need to go to the hospital?”

“Yes”—Jake nods decidedly—“she does.”

Harper struggles to standing. “Please no. I’m sure I’ll be okay. I feel better already.”

“You should be monitored,” Ron tells her. “Looked over by a doctor at the very least. And it’s the safest and quickest way to make that happen.”

“The ambulance is already on its way, anyway,” Jake informs her.

Harper’s entire body sighs, and she turns toward me. “Shit.” Then she glances down at the remaining portion of her costume. “Help me get this off?” she asks me glumly.

Happy I can finally contribute something, I walk around behind her and unzip the outfit. As she pulls it off, I realize her thin white tank is nearly see-through from sweat, her bright pink bra clearly visible. Jake’s cheeks color, and he turns his back at once.

I dig around in my bag and quickly find an old Zeta charity softball game T-shirt and press it into her hand. “Here.”

She looks down, her face colors anew when she realizes how exposed she is, and she tugs it overhead. “Thanks.” Her lips twist wryly. "Never thought I'd be a sorority girl." Then Harper looks around, first at Ron, then at Jake, and finally back at me. Her eyes are serious. "I'm sorry," she whispers.

"For what?"

"For holding you up. I'm sure you want to get out of here."

"No worries. I'm working tonight. I'm not going anywhere, anyway."

Harper looks toward the boys. "Alyssa's been my savior in more ways than one today."

She's relaying the lunchroom story when the ambulance crew—invisible most of the time but never more than a moment away—comes swiftly into the office, hoists Harper onto a stretcher, and carries her away as quickly and quietly as they appeared.

Just before she disappears with them, she sits up and grabs my forearm. "Don't you dare tell Kelly what happened."

I smile. "I won't."

I look at Ron. "Thanks for your help." I turn toward Jake and squeeze his arm. "You were amazing," I tell him.

"It was nothing," he says tensely. "It's just what I do."

Jake doesn't ask to hear the end of the story about what happened in the cafeteria. He stares down the hallway in the direction of his retreating patient. I'm just really not sure what to make of his level of concern. Or the constant weirdness that seems to come about whenever he and Harper end up in the same room.

chapter 6

MY DOORBELL RINGS THE NEXT MORNING at 8:58 a.m. I'm still in my room, zipping up my white shorts, so a second later it rings again. Jogging in that direction, I hear voices calling my name, loudly, from the other side, then fists pounding against the door impatiently.

Inside my apartment, I'm grinning. I've missed my ZTA sisters—their camaraderie, their energy, their noise. Growing up in a house with three younger sisters, moving into a sorority house was a natural choice.

Flinging the door back, I see Lauryn "Y" first. "What up, bi-otch?" she greets me.

Then all four of them burst through, shrieking and sweeping me up in hugs like it's been three years rather than three weeks.

Lauren "E," my "big," which is an oxymoron given the fact she's a shrimp-o, presses her head of springy blond curls against my chest. "I miss you, love!"

"Seriously a lot," Caroline, a member of my pledge class,

echoes, moseying across my kitchen in her ever-present cowboy boots. She's from Tennessee. Plus, she really likes how they make her legs look.

"And we brought pressies!" Blake adds, hoisting a white wicker basket onto my counter.

"You guys didn't need to bring presents."

"You have a new apartment," she protests.

And you have more money than you even know what to do with! I think.

I smile at her, reminding her, "It's just a sublet."

"Still, still."

Blake, our newly elected chapter president, has a generosity problem. Which is really very sweet. I peer into the basket—it contains a ginormous candle from Anthropologie, some expensive Philosophy bath products, and a new navy Vineyard Vines baseball cap with the ZTA letters embroidered across the front and my name across the back.

"Aren't the new hats fetch?" Lauren "E" asks.

"Stop trying to make fetch happen!" I respond on cue. "It's not going to happen."

We laugh together at our running joke about the line from *Mean Girls*, and then I tell her, "But, yes, they're supercute."

Lauryn "Y" impatiently pushes the strands of her short, trendy haircut off her forehead. "Aren't you going to come visit at all? Sigma Nu had this bad-ass slip-and-slide party last night. You're missing all the fun."

"Weekends are the busiest days here. Most weekends, I'm working several shifts a day."

And I'm not really willing to give up what precious little time I have with Jake to drive back and hang out with the girls I get to see the rest of the year. Truthfully, though, it wouldn't be very sisterly of me to say so, so I don't.

Lauryn "Y," however, former pledge chair, total Zeta devotee, isn't above getting a jab in. With one eyebrow raised, she comments, "I'm glad you didn't demonstrate that kind of lackluster loyalty while you were pledging freshman year."

Lauren "E" turns so her back is to her and rolls her eyes. "Wait till you see what we brought to wear to the park," she interjects, taking the hat out of my hands and sticking it back in the basket. She waves at me. "Turn around. Close your eyes."

Smiling at her silliness, I do so, and when I turn back toward them a minute later, the sight almost brings tears to my eyes. All four of them are wearing crowns with the Zeta emblem, and Caro's holding one out for me to take.

"It's my day off from being a princess, you know," I point out as I accept mine, even though I actually love the concept.

"Yeah, but we're going to the Enchanted Dominion," Caroline says. "We *have* to wear tiaras."

Lauren "E" is bouncing about in a way that reminds me of a Jack Russell terrier, her wild curls returning to her shoulders a few seconds after her feet hit the ground. "Can we go now? Please? What are we waiting for? Normally I spend three days at the park, and we only have one!"

Blake slings a heavily bangled arm around her shoulders. "Come on, mama," she says fondly, "we won't make you wait any longer."

We head down the stairs and toward Blake's white Lexus SUV in the lot. It's easy to spot. Not only is it huge, but its rear is covered in colorful ZTA and Vineyard Vines stickers. There's a Hilton Head parking permit stuck on the bumper.

I can barely get a word in edgewise during the drive to the park. My sisters are talking over one another in their attempts to fill me in on campus gossip and personal dramas. I pick up only snatches of stories.

". . . I mean, is he kidding me with that? . . . Put his shit on *blast* on Instagram before he could even . . ."

"Literally, I can't even . . . I mean, it's summer, does she really think we're going to read twelve novels in three weeks?"

". . . felt like she was never going to get better . . . so she goes, 'Eventually I just had to get blackout drunk to rid myself of my sinus headache.' What is wrong with that girl?"

I bite my lip to keep from laughing. The girls are silly, sure, but largely harmless. They don't do much to dispel sorority stereotypes, but they're fun. And . . . I like being part of a group. My mom was in a sorority, so the concept was never mocked in my family when we were visiting colleges. I like walking down College Ave., in my Zeta gear, with sisters on either side of me, knowing I have a place where I belong.

So I'm willing to work my ass off to have that place. In addition to picking up random weekend shifts at the park year-round, which involves some *really* early morning and late night drives to and from, I also work at a popular boutique near campus. I claim it's for the experience in fashion, but really, I need the money. And I need the employee discount, which sometimes still isn't enough. Sometimes I have to be supercareful, having left the tags on a top, knowing I'll have to return it the next morning.

I mean, I knew what dues would amount to, but I hadn't counted on all the additional expenses—the T-shirts created for every last event, the spring break trips, the date parties that also required formal dresses. All the Vineyard Vines stuff. Gifts for my big. Gifts for my little. Everyone else was so lavish in their gifting. So I had to find a way.

My Acura, the one that had been purchased for me in cash right before everything went south, was still mine when I left for college. My parents let me take it as a consolation price for not being able to even consider any out-of-state schools like I'd originally planned. After I rushed Zeta, I traded it in for a tiny used Honda, making up some lame excuse as to why. I needed *money* if I wanted to stay on par with my sisters, which I very, very much did.

It's so worth it. Having a place to call mine. Living in a house with white pillars and landscaping, a campus landmark. After losing the house I grew up in a few years prior and having to relocate to a rental, the Zeta house seemed so *solid*.

Once we park and walk through the gates, needless to say, we get a lot of attention. It's not just the crowns; we'd get a lot of attention, anyway. Back at Coral State, Zeta is known as the "blond" sorority, and also one of the best looking. There's Blake, who passes for a Hollywood celebrity with her long, lustrous hair and regal stature. Lauryn "Y" is a future fitness model, and her body's pretty much perfection. Caroline's long cornsilk hair reaches her waist. And my "big" is just plain adorable. We giggle when we catch a few young dads crashing the strollers they're pushing when we walk past.

Lauren "E" tugs on my arm and makes us stop before the Diamond Palace, where another Cinderella, Kathryn, is ushering excited little girls inside for a show. Chrissi's beside her, and she sneaks a subtle wave.

"OMG, I can't believe you do that all day," Blake comments. "How do you possibly keep *smiling* like that?"

"It's Alyssa," Lauryn "Y" chimes in. "She's always smiling. I'm pretty sure she shits rainbows."

"Very funny," I retort. Then I smile and clarify. "Actually, I shit sunshine."

"Ahh!" Caroline screams. "You're a riot!"

"So what's on the agenda today?" Blake asks. "What's first?"

"We should go hit up all the big rides before it gets too crowded," I answer. I smile secretively. "Then I have a special surprise for lunchtime."

"What is it?" Lauren "E" pesters.

"All in due time," I say. "All in due time."

As we leave the castle to head for the distant reaches of the park, I sneak a glance at the gatehouse. It's not where Jake is working today, but he is in the park. He's supposed to meet us later and hang out for a while. My stomach gives a little quiver of anticipation and worry. I hope Jake likes the girls and the girls like Jake. I want . . . I don't know . . . the different puzzle pieces that make up my life to come together and fit the way they should.

It'll be fine, I remind myself. Jake is sweet enough and . . . Jake's a guy. At his end, what's not to like about four superhot blondes?

I link arms with Lauren "E" and get to the business of making the most of the morning. Thanks to my automatic Line Jumper status, we hit all the most popular rides—Marauders' Mountain, Freefallin', and the Ice Slide—as well as several childhood favorites, like the zip line through the Forest and the hot-air balloons that take you over the walls of the Palace and into its courtyard.

It's the perfect ride to end on, because when I glance at my watch upon landing, I see that it's twelve twenty. We're right on time.

I gesture toward the building. "So we should head inside," I say, all nonchalant. "Our reservation for lunch is at twelve thirty."

Lauren "E" squeals. "We have a reservation to eat in the Palace?"

"Of course." I give a face like it's no big thing.

"But we just decided to come last week," Caro chimes in. "Don't you need to make reservations like six months in advance?"

"Not when you're a princess," I inform her, crossing my arms in satisfaction.

Blake gives me a hug. "You're the best!"

I shake my head. "Oh, it's nothing."

In truth, cast members get only one free pass to dine at the Diamond Palace per season. It's the one opportunity to request to dine there at the last minute, which is a huge deal. Caro was right about how far out you typically need to book a table. The practice of having a last-minute meal at the Palace is known among cast members as "crashing."

I decided to use my pass for my sisters. I know my being an Enchanted Princess gives me this sort of elevated status with the older girls in the sorority, which has a well-defined hierarchy in place. It seems only right to share this opportunity with them. I know they'll be impressed. Everyone always is.

The cavernous dining hall inside the Diamond Palace is divided into ten different pods, one belonging to each of the main fairy-tale characters that "live" within the park—Rose Red and Snow White, the Little Mermaid, the Ice Queen, the Frog Princess, Beauty, Aladdin's Princess, the Twelve Dancing Princesses, the Swan Queen and, but of course, Cinderella. The decor in each is thematic—Cinderella's pod is done up in crystal fixtures that sparkle like her glass slippers. Snow White's pod is done up like a Germanic cottage. The Little Mermaid's pod has floor-to-ceiling fish tanks for walls.

The menu within each pod aligns with the theme. The French cuisine in Beauty's section makes it a very popular choice. The extensive sushi offerings within the Little Mermaid's pod tend to make it less appealing for the breakfast set.

Then, atop one of the rear towers sits the dining pod for the eleventh princess, Rapunzel. It's actually a rotating restaurant that spins you in a slow circle throughout the course of your meal. By the end of your meal, you've been provided the most breathtaking 360-degree views of the entire park.

I got a table in the tower.

We all sit in silent reverie for a few minutes, faces practically pressed against the glass, admiring the view. Last year, of course, I'd opted to eat in Cinderella's pod with Jake before summer ended, the night he gave me the earrings, and so I've never been up in the tower. It's beyond cool.

"Oh my God!" Lauren "E" exclaims out of nowhere.

"What?" Blake asks in alarm.

"I totally forgot! Now I'm having flashbacks to when I was six years old and my parents took me to one of these rotating restaurants by Niagara Falls." She puts her hand over her heart. "I put my stuffed unicorn next to the table, because I didn't know that part of the building was *moving*. I cried the entire forty-five minutes until Majestique made her way back around."

Lauryn "Y" gives her a look as she sits down. "Well, we'll all just have to remember to keep our stuffed animals away from the ledge," she quips.

I bite my lip, because Lauren "E" really is too much sometimes. You'd never guess how high her IQ actually is (127), given her childlike nature . . . and her desire to fit in with a group, one other than her calculus study group, that is.

Despite the creative menu, all four girls opt for the vegetarian option, a salad of mixed greens with citrus fruits, strawberries, and almonds. I do the same.

Then once our server has collected our menus, Blake reapplies her lip gloss and raises one eyebrow. "So . . . ?"

"So?"

"So when are we finally getting to meet Jakey boy?"

"Couple more hours," I promise. "His shift ends at three. Then he said he'd hang out."

"He better," she says. "I mean, he's sort of on my shit list for never making the effort to come down for homecoming or formal or anything."

My stomach tumbles again. *Make a good impression, Jake.*

"Oh, don't be too hard on him. He had a huge test the Monday after formal." I shrug. "And he just doesn't get it. The Greek scene isn't really a big deal at his school. It's not like he's in a fraternity himself or anything."

Caro suddenly grasps my wrist. "Oh my God. Speaking of . . ." She reaches into her purse, fishes around for her wallet, and pulls out a small plastic rectangle, which she waves before me with a flourish. "Ta-da! One superauthentic-looking fake ID for yours truly."

I take it and study it. "This does look pretty good. Much better than that last one."

Lauryn "Y" grins. "Because this one actually has a picture of you, not that random sister with the faint resemblance who graduated in 1989. Her feathered bangs totally gave it away."

I giggle.

"We got ours in the nick of time," Caro says. "You know Jamie who made these? In Sigma Nu? Cops confiscated his laptop and everything. He's officially out of business."

I tuck my brand-new ID away. "Well, only eight months till February. Then I won't need a fake one anymore. But who's counting?"

Our salads arrive, and we take our time eating so that the restaurant can turn a full circle before we're done. We take a lazy riverboat ride around the circumference of the park, then check out one of the newer roller coasters.

When it's almost time to head back to the Palace, Lauren "E" catches sight of a kiosk and points. "I am *so* getting a Dragon's Kiss."

The Dragon's Kiss is a popular, maybe even iconic, park treat. It's got this yummy tart-flavored fro-yo, covered with dragon fruit salsa and cinnamon chips.

"OMG, I can't even!" Lauryn "Y," our resident health guru, practically screams. "Do you even know all the artificial crap that's in there? They try to peddle it as a healthy alternative, but I read this blog post about how it's actually worse for you than Ben & Jerry's."

Lauren "E" considers for a split second and then shrugs. "Whatev. I'm getting a Dragon's Kiss."

She expends so much energy, she hardly has to worry about the calories.

I skip the line with Lauryn "Y" and Blake, happy to have

company. Caroline goes with Lauren "E," but when they sit down on a bench to eat, first she scoops out all the cinnamon chips and then she eats only four bites of hers before tossing it in a nearby Dragon-shaped trash can. I'm sorry about the waste of seven dollars. And such a delicious treat.

Not that I could enjoy it right now, anyway. I glance at my watch. It's almost time.

"Umm, guys, we should probably head toward the gatehouse," I say, butterflies making tight loops in my stomach. "Jake said to just meet him right outside when he's done."

As we walk, I cross and uncross my fingers quickly. *Let this go well.* I nod to bolster myself. *This will go well.*

We're just going to be riding some rides together. It's not like it's an interview or anything.

As we approach the bridge, I see that Jake is already there, waiting for us exactly as I've arranged, looking almost nervous as he leans against a wrought-iron gate. I feel my shoulders relax. I mean, beneath the nerves, I'm proud and excited to finally introduce him to my sisters.

Once I point him out, before I can give any type of appropriate introduction, the girls are all over him like bees to honey, shouting his name and doling out hugs like they've known him forever. He instantly looks overwhelmed in the presence of five sorority girls, and the look on his face screams, "Help me!"

"Jake, we've been dying to meet you," Blake gushes.

"Alyssa has told us, like, everything." Lauren "E" nods. "But you're even cuter than your pictures. Like seriously hot." She tugs on the arm of his corny park uniform. "Even in this getup. Still hot."

Caroline glances down at his kit. "And you're, like, a doctor here? Stop! OMG! Stop!"

"Stop what?" Jake asks innocently.

I bite my lip and whisper into his ear. "It's okay. You just don't speak sorority."

"Thank God for that," he whispers back with a smile.

He looks around at the circle of girls. "It looks like you're having a good day," he assesses. "Nice crowns." He puts one arm around me and squeezes my shoulder. "It's good to see Alyssa having fun. I know how much you guys mean to her."

"Bless your heart," Caro swoons. "You're sweet, too."

"How are you *not* a prince?" Lauren persists.

All Jake manages is a tight little chuckle at their overzealous flirting.

I watch them . . . tentatively relieved. I mean, they're getting on . . . okay.

Blake steps forward and links an arm through Jake's. "So you're coming with us now, right? What ride should we do next?"

Jake takes a step back. "Umm . . . actually . . ." He turns toward me, expression apologetic. "Someone called out sick, and the two people they have on hand haven't gotten official approval to work alone. So it turns out . . . I'm not off duty quite yet." He watches my face, worried about how I'll react. "I'm sorry."

I'm annoyed at once.

The girls already think he's made less than zero effort to come down to campus events. I've always stood up for him, given he's been hundreds of miles away. But now he's in the right state and he still can't seem to be there.

I conceal a deep breath. I don't want my four sisters seeing me get rattled; I don't want to turn this into an argument with an audience.

I force a smile instead. "You might be the most devoted park employee. They should give you a raise." I manage a laugh, try to put a positive spin on his letting me down. "You're going to miss out on a great night, though! I mean, *five* dates in one!"

He looks back toward my friends. "I really do apologize, ladies. It would be much more fun to clock out right now."

Then Jake goes out of his way to give each of them a quick hug, which I know they like, and gives me a kiss and a final apology before ducking back inside the gatehouse. I can't help but think he looks a little relieved to escape their clutches.

Lauryn "Y" stares at his back. "I guess I'll forgive him," she says begrudgingly. She chews on her lips "Because he really is effing hot, Alyssa."

"What's his family background?" Blake asks.

In her world, it's as normal a question as any.

"They're from Connecticut," I say. "His dad has a law practice, and his mom runs this really cool, boho-chic interior design firm."

"Bling bling." Blake smiles. "So when he puts a ring on it it's gonna be *good*, isn't it?" She poses her questions like she's merely confirming the details about a sure thing.

Because that's how I've always talked about Jake. Like a sure thing. Jake had felt like happily ever after from the moment we'd met.

But marriage . . . it's not really something we'd planned together, per se. Talking about it puts a yucky feeling in my stomach.

"I'm sure!" I finally answer. I smile brightly. "So . . . more rides?"

"Actually . . . ," Blake responds slowly. She's staring into the distance and I can see the wheels turning. "We've already managed to get on most of the good ones, and if Jake is bailing . . ."

I try not to react to her negative spin on his unexpected absence. "What are you thinking?"

She gives me a slow, lazy smile, her eyes narrowed. "Are there any bars around here that are lenient enough to test out that new ID of yours? Maybe . . . happy hour?"

"Yes!" Lauren "E" exclaims. "Let's do happy hour!" She turns toward me with wide, hopeful eyes.

I pause. It's certainly not how I saw the night unfolding, but . . . I take a quick side glance toward the gatehouse. Guess there's no sense in sticking around, and if it's what they all want to do . . .

"Actually, I know the perfect spot," I tell them.

BACK AT LAKESIDE, I direct Blake to a parking spot along the block that houses El Barrio. It's a great outdoor gathering spot, designed with the Southwest in mind, complete with giant live cacti, broken clay pots, and a dilapidated fence running around its exterior. There's always live music, outdoor beer pong, and a two-margarita limit that no one enforces.

They don't really enforce IDs, either. If the person at the door knows you're a cast member, they usually don't even ask.

The back patio is already bumping when we walk up, still wearing our tiaras, and I see Miller sitting at the outdoor bar with Yael, having a beer. They're chatting, and she's actually laughing. And *smiling*. Wow.

When he glances up, I wave to him. He gets up at once and

heads over when he sees me, mug of cerveza still in hand. And suddenly Yael's face returns to its normal resting position. Which would be disgruntled.

"Wow, a whole lot of blonde just came up in here!" Miller exclaims when he approaches. He puts his arm around my shoulders, smiling in a way that lets me know he's already had a few. "Holy shit—they cloned you!"

I roll my eyes at him. "These are my sorority sisters. Ladies, this is Miller." Then I point and introduce. "Miller, Blake, Caro, Lauren 'E,' and Lauryn 'Y.' "

"So if I just stick with Lauren, I have a fifty percent shot of getting it right?"

"Pretty much."

He takes a sip from his mug. "Excellent." Then, catching the ZTA logo on Caroline's bag, he bursts into song. One of *our* songs, to be specific. *"This is my personal point of view. That the Zeta blue looks good on you."*

"OMG, I'm literally dying!" Blake exclaims. She slaps his forearm lightly. "How do you *know* that?"

"I'm an honorary Zeta at UD," he grins. "Nah, just kidding. I'm technically considered part of the cheerleading squad, and a lot of the girls on the squad always pledge Zeta. You pick up things."

"You're a cheerleader?" Lauryn "Y" asks. "That's hot."

Miller laughs it off, good natured as always. "Male cheerleaders. Pretty much the epitome of hot. Yes."

"Are you a *prince* at the park, Miller?" Caroline asks.

"Sadly, no. I spend most of my days dressed up as an oversize kangaroo."

"You play Kangzagoo?" Blake asks. "He was one of my favorites when I was little."

Miller nods.

"You should be a prince," Lauren "E" decides out loud. She looks him over. "You totally have this . . . cute lumberjack thing going on."

"Oh my god, Lauren!" I exclaim. "You're not even drinking yet."

Miller merely rubs on his scruff. "It's not the first time I've heard that, you know. I can't say I think the term is spot on, but . . . I'll take it."

"I'm missing the lumberjack part," I say. "He's wearing a Coldplay T-shirt."

"It's the scruff," Lauren says. "That rugged yet boyish face he's got."

"Are you a Coldplay fan?" Blake asks, deftly changing the subject. She's slated for a future taking over her family's multimillion-dollar PR firm. The one that handled the recent presidential scandal.

"Yeah, huge fan," he says.

"Me too." She smiles. She doesn't tell him the part where she flew all of us to London, for twenty-four hours, to attend a concert and meet Chris Martin.

"And how do you know Alyssa? If you're a kangaroo and not a prince?"

Miller still has his arm around my shoulders, and he looks over at me fondly. "You want to tell them the story, or should I?"

"Let me tell it," I insist. "You're gonna make it sound so much worse than it was."

"'Cause you were a total brat!"

"I have a hard time believing that," Lauren "E" says. She points at me. "Usually? Alyssa's shitting sunshine."

This cracks him up. "I like that."

"*Anyway*," I say. "Enchanted Enterprises makes us do these heinous stints in fur costumes as part of the training process. Everyone. No one's exempt. No matter what. And it's torture. My very first day, it was over one hundred degrees and—"

Miller can't help himself and jumps in. "She lasted twelve minutes. Twelve! I work eight-hour shifts in costume, and she started crying after *twelve* minutes. I heard her boo-hooing beneath the headpiece. She was that loud."

"And he was so supportive and sympathetic," I continue drily, and then attempt to imitate Miller's voice. "*Suck it up, buttercup.*"

"You were, by far, the most spoiled princess I'd ever trained. And that's saying something." Miller grins. "So when I called her out on it, put her in her place a bit, that's when she had her real breakdown. It was probably the most pathetic thing I ever saw; I couldn't help but start laughing. And that's when she socked me with her aardvark glove."

"Shut up," Caro says.

"True story," Miller nods. "I'd never been assaulted by a fellow fur character. Angry parent, dipshit teenager, sure. But not another cast member." He glances over at me and smiles. "As soon as she hit me, we both started cracking up at the ridiculousness of it. And I got the feeling, Alyssa here was probably going to turn out okay." He pinches my cheek. "She's just a delicate flower."

Then Miller glances toward the bar, and his arm slides off my shoulder. "Whoa," he says. "Yael is throwing some pretty hefty death stares over there; I better get back." He grins at me. "I don't want to have to break up any more fights on your behalf." Then, "It was fun meeting you ladies." He walks toward the bar, pointing back to our group. "I'm going to send a pitcher over. Go Zeta!"

"Aww," Caroline says, watching him go. "Bless his heart. He is, like, a total sweetheart."

I said it before, and I'll say it again. It's pretty much impossible not to like Miller.

The afternoon turns into early evening. The beers turn into margaritas, and the margaritas turn into shots as we wait our turn on the beer pong tables. There's already a long list of people waiting to play.

More and more cast members show up after work, the crowd gets bigger, the patio is more crowded . . . and it all goes downhill from there.

I see Kellen, Enchanted villain, notorious park playboy, walk in the door. Then I see Caro making out with him in less than ten minutes flat.

Rose stops by with a new cast member for a quick drink, and Blake drunkenly tells her she should enroll at Coral State, because she's "totally hot enough to be a Zeta."

And Lauryn "Y" orders nachos.

Lauren "E" can't wait to call her out. "She's eating *nachos*? Lauryn 'Y' is waaasted!"

I crack up, because my sisters are a *mess*, and they're a hilarious mess. Lauren "E" looks ridiculous, crown now clinging to her head by a hope and a prayer, and Blake has fashioned hers into some kind of choker necklace. Which is pretty much how most nights I spend as part of Zeta turn out.

Finally it's our turn for pong, but Lauren "E" can't retrieve her partner, who's still locking lips with Kellen against a cactus, and Lauryn "Y" won't step away from the nachos.

"Miller!" Lauren "E" screams across the patio, waving wildly. "Miller! We neeed you! I need a partner so we can play!"

I glance up in surprise. I didn't realize he was still here. I smile when he stands, actually walks over to appease her.

But when Miller stands, Yael stands, too.

"Uh-oh," I whisper under my breath. I have a feeling she's not coming over for some friendly competition. And we already have enough players, anyway.

It turns out she just wants to give Miller a hard time. She tugs on the sleeve of his shirt, giving him a pointed look. "We said we were heading out now," she reminds him. "Both of us."

He points to the table. "Just one game."

She looks at him. She looks at me. She looks down at his nearly empty mug. Then she gives him another look, one I can't really make sense of.

"I'm fine," he tells her. "It's fine. I mean, if you really won't stick around, I don't mind walking home by myself, but . . . you should stay."

"Yeah, no. Think I will go." She turns abruptly and huffs out of the bar without a good-bye.

"I like her," I say flatly. "Such a charmer."

Miller chuckles. "It's all good. She'll get over it." He lines himself up across the table from me, next to Lauren "E."

"I will take particular pleasure in sinking my balls into your cup," he calls.

"That's what she said!" Lauren "E" and Lauryn "Y" scream in unison.

"Jinx!" Blake hollers.

Yeah, Blake really needs to start sobering up if she's driving them home tonight.

"'That's what she said' doesn't even make *sense*." I giggle. "You can't just say it anytime someone uses the word *balls*!"

"Are we playing or what?" Miller calls, arm already curved and poised above the board. Seasoned drinking game pros, the girls quickly quit their giggling and get down to business.

Lauren and Miller dominate the game, and at one point she puts her arm around him to "strategize," pulling his head close to hers to whisper to him.

It crosses my mind that she might actually be *flirting* with Miller.

It's not a complete surprise. I mean, I assume Miller gets plenty of girls—he's got that natural charisma and attracts people like a magnet. And he is kinda cute, in that scruffy way of his, in his T-shirt and khaki shorts. He has nice calves, probably from all the hopping he does as Kangzagoo.

But I just can't picture Miller with a girl like Lauren "E." With Miller, I assume, it's girls more like Yael that he's getting.

From the way Yael's acting, I sort of suspect he's already "got" her. Why else would she be so bothered by his behavior around other girls?

But then Lauren "E" rubs the top of his head, the way you would a golden retriever puppy. "You are the cutest," I hear her say. "I want to take you home as, like, our house pet."

To me, it sounds sort of demeaning. Even though she means well.

But Miller is unfazed. "It's cool. Just know I charge for that sort of thing."

They win, and Miller heads out shortly after the game wraps, despite protests from Lauren "E" that they've "got next."

He walks around to my side of the table, puts his hand out, and waits for me to slap his palm. "It was a blast seeing you with your sisters."

"Yeah, they're good girls."

He raises an eyebrow in the direction of Caro and Kellen. "I'm sure." Then he looks back at me, assessing me through narrowed eyes. "I think I prefer you when you're not being a stereotype of yourself, but it's all good."

"What does *that* mean?"

I think I might be offended. I'm just not sure.

"You're like them, but you're not," he says, still staring at my face. "It's like . . . you fit with them . . . but you don't."

I burst out laughing. "That's very profound. You're drunk, by the way."

"Yes, I am," he agrees. "I'll figure it out eventually, though. And I should get home. Catch ya later, Lys."

I watch him leave, pondering his words. But then Blake inadvertently shoves Caro into the table, knocking over several cups of beer, prompting loud squealing all around. I focus my attention on the daunting task of rounding up four drunken senoritas and dragging their butts out of the Barrio.

chapter 7

THE FIVE OF US GOT TO EL BARRIO AROUND four o'clock. It's almost nine by the time we leave, and then make a stop at the twenty-four-hour doughnut and bagel shop so the girls can get some food in their stomachs. By the time I give them hugs at Blake's car, ensure Blake's sobriety, and point them toward the freeway, it's 10:10 p.m.

And I am *so* ready to crash.

I've been up and on the go for fourteen hours and counting. My sisters require a lot of energy when they're in a pack like that. Plus, I'm still more than a little bit drunk. It feels like it takes twenty minutes to climb the stairs, with my legs feeling like lead. I mean, I'm used to *sitting*, not running, around the park. All I need to do is text Jake good night and wash my face. I daydream about face planting into my pillow.

I open my door. I stand and stare. Then I smile. "What are you doing here?"

I feel my heart melting like cherry vanilla over the edge of a sugar cone on a hot summer day. Jake is in my apartment. As a surprise.

"Waiting for you." He smiles back at me. "I figured it was actually okay to put the spare key to use?"

"Of course!"

I fight the urge to leap at him and wrap my legs around his waist.

"I came over as soon as I could," he says. "I felt bad about not hanging out, and I thought maybe I could at least say good-bye to your friends before they left."

Between his presence and this sentiment, any lingering irritation about earlier evaporates. I give him a hug. "I'll tell them that. They'll be sorry they missed you. But it's a long trip to make so late, and they wanted to get on the road."

When I step back, I notice Jake fiddling with a goldenrod padded envelope, nervously flipping it over in his hands. "What's that?"

He stares at the package for a moment before answering. "My mom forwarded it to my apartment. It came to their house." Jake looks up and meets my eye, his eyes hesitant. "It's an introduction to the Child Life Specialist internship. Some background on the program, some personal stories . . ."

I can't help it. I recoil at once.

"You have to understand why I'm not totally excited," I whisper. I half collapse against the counter. "At one point, it seemed like the internship in South Carolina was the definite front-runner. And it's just"—I run my hand through my hair, pushing it out of my face—"I still have two years of school down here, so all we have is the distance thing in the foreseeable future. I was really excited about the possibility of having you close by for a while." I manage a small smile so there's not too much bite in my words.

"Yeah, but Lys," he replies, "the program at CHOP is in the same city as my school. It just makes better sense, establishing connections that could go beyond the internship."

Of course it makes sense. Jake always makes *sense.*

And there never seems to be any sense in giving priority to this relationship.

Jake sighs, then walks around the counter to come to me. "Listen," he says, taking my forearms in both hands. "We said we were gonna work on things, right? That means *working* on things, Alyssa."

I have to turn my face away from his, because I hate these conversations.

But Jake presses on. "Last summer was fun, right? But if we want our relationship to actually grow, I think it would be . . . good to figure out what our common interests are. Or better understand each other's interest, at the very least."

He waits for me to turn back toward him, and his eyes are pleading behind his glasses. "Come on, Lys. I really believe if you watch this, if you see what it's about, it won't just be this big, bad thing keeping me half a coast away. You have the *biggest* heart of anyone I know, and when you see these kids, I know you'll get it."

I stare into his eyes. It feels like if I just keep staring, if I keep being able to see him, this will be okay. He's so genuine, he's trying so hard, and he really wants me to be a part of this. Even if ultimately, I can't.

So I smile again. "Okay. Sure. I'll watch. With an open mind."

He pulls me all the way toward him and kisses me quickly. "Thank you."

So we head over to the couch. In some ways, it's so reminiscent of last year. He's in my favorite Jake postwork getup—jeans and a soft white T-shirt—and he covers me with a blanket when I sit down next to him. He turns off the lights, which makes my eyelids feel about forty times heavier. I physically fight to keep them from falling shut in the dimly lit apartment. I cuddle against him, certain his proximity, the muffled sound of his heartbeat, will keep me alert.

Jake turns on the television, and the image of the children's hospital, illuminated in a rainbow spectrum to make it look less scary, I suppose, fills the screen. "The Children's Hospital of Philadelphia," a cheery voice begins. "Hope lives here."

I suck in a breath, reminding myself not to be selfish. This internship is about something much bigger than me.

Over the next several minutes, while we're provided an on-screen tour of the facility, we learn about the hospital's history and current areas of specialty. A curly-haired woman in street clothes appears after that to introduce the Child Life Specialist program.

Her face is the last thing I remember.

I SIT UP with a start, unsure of where I am.

My eyes struggle to make out my surroundings in the darkness, and then I realize I'm lying down on my couch. The TV screen is a flat, ominous blue, the DVD player no longer running. And I am alone.

Damn, damn, *damn*.

I fly to my feet, instantly aware of how badly I messed this up. Damn.

I notice that Jake's keys are still on the counter and his sneakers are near the front door. My shoulders fall. Thank God. He didn't leave.

I honestly feel like the worst person. He was making this effort, this is something that's so important to him, and I freakin' fell asleep. I may have had my reasons, but in my head . . . *sorority sisters* . . . *margaritas* . . . *beer pong* . . . they sound like little more than lame excuses.

Walking on tiptoe, I ease open my bedroom door, afraid I'm going to find him perched angrily on the edge of my bed. Instead, I find him asleep, facing the wall, snoring softly. I'm not sure if it's better or worse.

Standing there, watching him, I rack my brain for some way to fix this, or at least say "I'm sorry." After a minute, I smile mischievously.

I scamper across my room and bite my lip when I see it. The still-unopened bag from Bare with Flare. I snatch it up. In the bathroom, I shed my clothing and change into the red lace boy shorts and matching bustier. It's one way to apologize, anyway.

Before heading back to my room, I brush my teeth long and hard, getting rid of any traces of tequila. Then I return to him, turning on the soft night-light in the corner, crawling into the bed beside him.

I find his body under the covers and gently kiss his neck. Nothing. I scooch a bit farther and nibble on his earlobe. He wakes with a start, swatting his hand through the air as if a flying insect were in the room. He rolls over when he realizes I'm there, his eyes opening wide when he gets a good look at me.

"Hey." I smile seductively. "Surprise."

But his eyes, now fully open, don't warm a smidgen. "You fell asleep," he murmurs flatly.

I sit up on my knees. "Jake, I'm really, really sorry. It's just . . . I got up so early because the girls were coming, and we ran around all day, and then we went to El Barrio, and . . ." I collapse back onto my heels. "I didn't know you were coming over. I would have . . ." I don't know what I would have. I sigh. "I know this is important to you, and I want to care about it, too."

He narrows his eyes. "You *want* to care about it. But you don't."

I push my hair out of my face. This wasn't how I pictured this going. "That's not what I mean. You know that's not what I mean." I press my body back down over his. "Let me make it up to you. I think it's awesome that you want to involve me in this." I try kissing his ear again. "I get it, and I think it will make us stronger, too." My hand roams over his chest, down to his stomach.

But Jake rolls over, back toward the wall. "I'm tired. I'm not really in the mood."

Abruptly, my throat constricts with the feeling of tears. "Jake . . . ," I whisper. "I said I was sorry."

He doesn't respond for a minute, but then, with a heavy sigh, eventually rolls onto his back. He extends his arm and lets me lie down upon his chest. I try to relax against him, but his body feels tense and unyielding.

Nobody says anything for a while; we just lie there in the darkness, and eventually I wonder if he's gone back to sleep. But then I hear him. He's barely louder than a whisper, and I question if his words are even meant for me to hear. "I guess it's one of the best things about you, how you always try to look on the bright side, hope for the best. But sometimes . . . I wonder if you're doing more than looking at reality with a blind eye."

His words take my breath away. I'm overcome with a sick sense of dread.

Why didn't I just stay awake? I think, tears pricking my eyes. *This night would have turned out good. Perfect, even.*

I lie there, still as stone, until he falls asleep for real.

I know there's no way I'm going to sleep, though. When I hear him snoring again, I lift my side of the comforter and slide out of the bed. I go back to the bathroom, flip on the light, and regard myself critically in the full-length mirror. I spend the next I-don't-know-how-many minutes, hours even, inspecting my flaws, wondering exactly how unattractive he finds me to turn me away like he did.

chapter 8

OH. MY. GOD. I THINK TO MYSELF. *THIS IS the longest parade of my life. And by far the worst.*

As if to punctuate this conclusion, I watch as one of the eight mechanical arms of the Spellbinding Spider, perched atop the float between mine and Harper's, grabs hold of the top of her hair one more time and gives it a crude yank before retracting. I can't tell if its pincer is closing around her wig or her real hair, but if it's her real hair . . . girl's going to have a legit bald spot by the time the route wraps.

If it were funny, which it's not, today's afternoon parade would be a comedy of errors. They're all rooted in some computer glitch that has our individual floats out of sync, starting and stopping in random, jerking motions. Because the timing's all off, the spider is descending when the Beauty and the Beast platform is closer than it should be and Harper has no way to escape its claw.

Poor girl, I think. I'm pretty sure this is only her second time doing the parade. It may be her last. She's probably wishing she was back in fur!

Not that things are all that ducky on my float, either. I'm trying to keep my distance from Josh, today's Prince Charming, while still appearing lovestruck. But his ghostly skin and clammy hand announced his stomach bug even before he did. He keeps being jostled against me, though, because our platform seems to be lurching the worst.

I close my eyes momentarily, envisioning a bathtub full of Purell.

We stop at a corner, allowing some of the fur characters to hop off the cars and dance in the street to the park's theme song. But our car continues to gyrate, and I suddenly realize that the float isn't the only thing heaving uncontrollably. Josh is bent over, and the second we start moving again and our float is angled away from the crowds, he empties the contents of his stomach . . . right into the folds of my shimmering gold gown.

It's not so much the sight of his puke, or even the wretched smell of it, as the sound of his retching that instantly has me nauseous.

But we're coming up on the main corridor now, the homestretch of the parade, so I do the only thing I can think to do to survive. I plaster a huge grin on my face and rearrange the folds of my dress to hide the pile of vomit. "Stand *up*!" I hiss to Josh.

If he hadn't thrown up *on* me, I might be feeling more sympathetic. And we have an Enchanted Moments parade to finish here.

Twelve endless minutes later, Harper, Helena—one of the twelve dancing princesses, and I crack up as we stumble toward the dressing rooms.

"That was such a complete disaster," Harper declares, yanking off her ruined hairpiece and feeling around for patches of exposed scalp. "If I wasn't laughing right now, I'd be crying."

"Hashtag, epic Enchanted fail," Helena agrees. "If anyone was taking video, it's going viral tonight. Worst parade ever."

I blanch as I stare down at my costume in disgust. "Yeah, I'm not even asking for permission. I'm *burning* this dress."

"Someone's getting fired tonight, mark my words," Helena predicts. "Mistakes like that don't fly at Enchanted Enterprises."

"And they shouldn't," I say. "We're better than that."

We duck into our individual stalls and change in record speed. When we emerge, Helena, a smoker, holds her lighter to the hem of my soiled, smelly dress.

"Guess I can't really get away with it," I sigh, then forcefully toss the dress into the laundry chute.

"So much for the glamorous princess life." As Harper ties her hair back from her face, she asks, "Who thinks we deserve Ben & Jerry's? And I'm not talking sorbet, I'm not talking Greek frozen yogurt, I'm talking Chubby Hubby with whipped cream and hot fudge. And gummy bears."

Helena grimaces. "Sadly, I'm working tonight, too. I'm afraid if I leave the park at this point, I won't be able to make myself come back."

Harper turns in my direction.

"I have to work out," I respond automatically. And to be honest, after so many margaritas at El Barrio over the weekend, I can't really afford a trip to Ben & Jerry's. Calorie-wise, I mean.

"Didn't you say you went to the gym this morning?" Helena asks.

"I did. But I do yoga three nights a week. Tonight's one of those nights."

"So skip." Helena shrugs. "Go get ice cream. You deserve it."

"I can't." I press my lips together. She makes it sound so easy.

"You skip once, then you skip twice, then you've skipped for weeks, and then suddenly you're not passing look-overs."

Helena rolls her eyes. "Give me a break," she mutters.

It's always been my opinion that Helena views this job as a joke. So I have no problem answering what feels like an insult. Or ridicule. "You don't have to judge me because I take this job seriously," I tell her, hoping my tone doesn't sound snarky. "That I take the responsibility seriously. Actresses, newscasters, models . . . lots of people have jobs where working out regularly is part of the package. We happen to be some of those people."

Helena digs around in her bag for her Parliament Lights. There are no-smoking areas nearby, so I get the sense she's doing it just to mock my devotion to Princess protocol. "Whatever. If it's that big of a deal to you." She shrugs. "After today? Me? I'd go for ice cream. But I gotta go. I want to grab something to eat before I'm due back." She gives us both a quick hug and dashes up the steps.

Harper is still standing there, a rather uncomfortable-looking bystander. She'd probably side with Helena.

"Honestly, the puke sort of killed my appetite, anyway. And I actually just really like this class," I say as means of further explanation. Then I consider. "Hey, why don't you come with me instead? It's an *amazing* class. The instructor uses all these fabulous beach images projected onto the ceiling and has the coolest playlists I've ever heard. And trust me; it's actually a much better way to forget about this afternoon than gorging on ice cream. You'll feel a lot better tomorrow at any rate."

Harper's enthusiasm is underwhelming. "I haven't really done too much yoga. Just a few Pilates classes."

"It's a beginners' class," I assure her. "Mostly for relaxation." I crack my neck, producing a horrid sound. "I really need to relax."

I haven't been able to, fully, not since Saturday night. I still feel bad about what happened, and although Jake doesn't seem angry anymore, I still have this feeling, like, I bombed a major test. I've been trying not to think about it.

Harper still looks like she wants to flee. But apparently I'm applying enough pressure, because as I continue to stand there and stare hopefully at her, she caves. Plus, she knows *I* know she doesn't have other plans. "Um, okay. Guess I'll give it a try."

Side by side, we walk toward the park's exit, eager to leave this particular day behind us.

I'M GLAD SHE's coming with me, I think, as we climb aboard the Lakeside shuttle and sit down together. When I'm avoiding thoughts I don't want to think, distractions are good. Harper fills me in on how her first show performance went. She gets a little misty-eyed as she recalls a favorite memory from the park with her father, making me think her need to get away this summer has something to do with him. She looks at her phone and groans, explaining that she made the mistake of giving Kellen her number and he's been texting frequently since.

"He basically makes a point of harassing every new princess," I tell her. "D'you know he plays the Jackal? It's like he's really into method or something."

We giggle, and I think we're both doing a decent job of perking back up after the workday.

And then she goes and says the one thing that ruins my mood more succinctly than Josh's vomit did. She morphs from distraction to anything but.

"So when Jake and I were eating lunch yesterday, he told me . . ."

I'm too jolted, too upset, to hear exactly what he told her. I'm pretty sure it was something random and innocuous, but the way she begins her sentence leaves me too dizzy to process.

"You had lunch with Jake yesterday?" I interrupt her.

I guess this is one time when I fail at keeping my emotions off my face, because hers goes sort of pale when she realizes the impact of her words.

"Yeah, I mean . . . no, we didn't have lunch together. I mean, we were in the cafeteria at the same time, and I just ended up talking to him for a few minutes. Filling him in on my trip to the ER. It wasn't . . . it was totally random, and—"

I wave my hand to cut her off and put on a smile so big it actually makes my cheeks hurt. "No, you don't have to explain!" I laugh. A long time. "It's totally cool that you guys had lunch. Why wouldn't you?"

"Oh . . . okay," she stumbles, finding her own hesitant smile.

She returns to the story. I still don't catch a word of it.

Why wouldn't they have lunch together? Why wouldn't they? After all, I've had lunch with countless male cast members during my time at the park, and I'm not the kind of girl who gets worked up every time my boyfriend talks to another girl. I mean, we have a long distance relationship. If I didn't trust him, we wouldn't still be together right now, right?

But . . . he didn't tell me.

We had dinner together last night, we talked extensively about our days, and he didn't tell me. He didn't mention Harper at all.

I stand up before the shuttle even comes to a complete stop, suddenly desperate to get off this bus and into class. Where there won't be any more conversation.

This will help, I think, moments later in the Mind and Body Studio as I sit down upon my monogrammed mat—a gift from Blake—and fold my legs into lotus position. Yoga is all about restoring balance, and inner peace, and positivity. It's one of the things I like about it. The actual process may be kind of miserable, but you can pretty much guarantee you will walk out the door feeling better than you did when you walked in. And that's very cool to me. I would really like to walk out the door feeling better than I did when I walked in.

Just before our instructor dims the lights, Camila enters the studio and settles into the empty spot to my right. She's a regular, but from experience I know she's not here to socialize. She seems to take her practice very seriously. Her focus and precision are impressive. I give her a quick smile, and she merely nods in acknowledgment, her face stoic.

Right, I think, drawing my hands together in front of my heart. *Time to get down to business.*

But class starts off on an ironically bad note. The second song of the playlist is obscure, one you rarely hear on the radio, a bit outdated. It was a song Jake introduced me to, one he'd insisted I listen to on one of his earbuds when I ran into him taking a walk last summer. He'd watched my face while I'd listened, and then kissed me for the first time at whatever he saw reflected upon it, apparently.

"This Year's Love" by David Gray.

The words had held so much meaning in those seconds before our first kiss. *"This year's love had better last . . ."*

The song had instantly broken my heart, how it held so much hope and so much fear, even in the middle of an extremely happy moment. Tonight . . . it flat-out destroys it.

I try, I really do, struggling to concentrate, to "let my mind go blank" as we're instructed, but for the entirety of the class, my body refuses to comply with my attempts to contort it properly. I'm distracted and teary, and my limbs seem to sense it.

Finally, just as I've almost toppled over for the seventeenth time, we're allowed to lie in savasana, like corpses, for several minutes. Our instructor walks behind us, murmuring something about "the good in me honoring the good in you," and after a few "namastes," class is over. We're encouraged to relax in savasana until we're ready to leave, so I lie there for a few minutes, listening to the quiet chimes playing, telling myself I have to get it together before I stand up.

I remain still, on my back, inhaling deep breaths, after everyone else has collected their belongings and left. The room has grown quiet, and through the windows I can tell that twilight has descended. I take a deep breath. *Only good thoughts.* I take another. Then, before I know what is happening, I feel my chest pulsating in some weird way and I'm pinching my eyes shut against the tears threatening my eyelids. A quiet, strangled gasp escapes.

"Alyssa?" Harper calls. "Alyssa. Are you okay? Are you hurt?"

I'd forgotten she was here. Not wanting her to see me like this, I curl into a fetal position, back to her. Away from her.

"I'm okay," I whisper, without looking at her. "I just . . . want to be alone."

She hesitates, lingers. But eventually I hear her gather her things. She stands up and returns her mat to the stack. Then she walks back one last time. "Are you sure?"

I nod.

"I'll . . . see you later?" she says awkwardly.

"See you later," I repeat quietly. I close my eyes until I hear her feet all the way across the room, the door closing behind her. I keep my eyes shut, taking deep breaths, allowing a few silent tears to fall so I can get rid of them and be done with them.

Ten minutes later, when I finally manage to pull myself together and sit back up, I practically jump in surprise when I realize Camila is still sitting beside me, gazing toward the front of the room. Her legs are still folded, and her palms sit atop her knees. She's so quiet I didn't even hear her breathing.

I hastily wipe at one eye with the palm of my hand. "Oh wow. I didn't realize anyone was still here."

"Nothing to be embarrassed about," she says evenly. "It's just physiological. Practicing brings the physical and emotional together. Sometimes there's a release."

"You're probably right." I try to smile. "I do tend to get emotional when I practice. It's weird." I try a little laugh. Then, staring out the windows, I exhale a big puff of air, feeling my entire body deflating. The words come out before I'm planning to let them. "Oh, who am I kidding? It's . . . stuff. It's boy stuff."

I groan. I really, really wanted to avoid all of this. I don't really talk about boy problems. I don't really talk about problems, period, as a rule. *Talking* about a problem does nothing to fix it, after all.

But what Harper said . . . and that song . . .

"I just can't wrap my head around it," I hear myself saying, "or my heart around it, and trying to put it into words . . ." I stop, then try again a minute later. "Last summer, me and Jake just fit.

We had . . . inside jokes, stupid nicknames for each other; a good night was just lying in bed watching stupid reruns."

My throat tightens. Ramen noodles spilled all over my comforter, routinely, and I didn't care. We watched horrible reality TV on MTV, at first as a joke, but then later because we couldn't stand to miss an episode, even if we wouldn't admit it to each other. The memory makes me want to smile and cry at the same time.

I glance over at Camila. "Have you had a serious boyfriend before?"

"No." Her back is stiff, her words immediate.

I smile wistfully. "Well. That's the good stuff. The nothing stuff . . . that's actually the good stuff."

Blowing another lungful of air out my mouth, I keep going. "How can last year be so different from this year?" Tears prick my eyes again. I can't believe I'm admitting this to anyone. To . . . myself. "I'm driving myself crazy, trying to figure it out, work it through, understand it. But there is no equation, no *reason* why things are off right now, and they are. He's trying, God knows he's trying, but I can tell. I can tell he's trying." One more tear falls. "And I know before he didn't have to *try*, so it sucks."

I glance at Camila again. Her face suggests she's struggling, and I have to chuckle. "I'm sorry. I'm probably completely ruining your Zen. I don't know why I'm unloading all of this on you."

Maybe it's partly because I trust that it won't go anywhere. I'm sure Camila would never turn these hidden feelings of mine into gossip.

Her lips are pursed. "I don't mind you unloading on me, if that's what you want to call it," she answers. "We're . . . friends."

Camila shakes her head. "I do, however, mind your completely narrow perspective on the status of your life at this point."

I do a double take.

"I mean, forgive me for being harsh, but there's a reason I find the princesses to be foolish and inane. All they seem to want out of life is Prince Charming." She gestures toward me with her hand. "And look. A lot of good romance does. Oh, the elation!"

"I know there's more to life than Prince Charming." I shake my head. "And I'm not saying relationships are the be-all and end-all," I clarify. "But you don't just give up on them because they bring with them some element of sadness." I shrug. "Without rain, no rainbows."

Camila turns toward me, her expression a combination of amused and disbelieving. Mostly disbelieving. "Did you really just say that?"

"Yeah. I did." I can't help but smile a little, for real. Me and Camila . . . trying to have a conversation about romance . . . it's like watching polar ends of magnets fight their instinct to repel each other.

But I wish she understood.

"I love him, Camila," I whisper. "God, I really, really love him, regardless of this stupid, inexplicable distance between us. And I just want love to be enough to fix this. Love should be enough to fix this."

"Sure," she answers sarcastically. "Love and lacy lingerie."

"What?"

"I mean, clearly, Chrissi's grand plan to make his eyes pop out of his head wasn't a cure-all." Camila rolls her eyes. "Shocker."

"What do you mean?"

Finally, she hesitates. "I should probably stop. I feel like I'm getting to the point where people start finding me offensive." She stands up.

Getting to the point? I think.

"No," I say instead. I narrow my eyes. "I want to hear what you think. Truly."

Maybe a different perspective would be helpful.

"Fine. But you asked for it." She crosses her arms over her chest and stares down at me. "The notion of you parading in front of your boyfriend in new lingerie as a means of relationship salvation is antiquated, demeaning, shallow, and quite frankly, downright laughable."

I wince. Well, boom. There you have it.

"Honest to God, Alyssa. What have you done to impress him from the inside out?" she demands, voice rising in the empty room. "Did you even consider catching his attention with conversation, or discussion about the news, or a lively debate?"

A lively debate?

"I'm not sure I'm exactly debate team material . . . ," I mumble.

The one time I'd tried to connect with Jake's intellectual side . . . I'd fallen asleep after too much Patrón.

And then I'd fallen back on my sexy lingerie.

My shoulders collapse with a sigh.

It's easy to see how Jake's misreading everything. Maybe he really had gotten the message I didn't care about his dreams, or was actively against them, when really I just didn't like the idea of more distance between us. I mean, it impresses me to no end that Jake has the fortitude and wherewithal to work with gravely ill children.

I guess it intimidates me, too, his line of work. I could never do it, and I know it.

Camila is still staring down at me, waiting for a response. It feels like being in the front of a lecture hall before a scary professor, honestly.

I take my ponytail out, run my hands through my hair, then resecure it.

"That part of his world scares me," I admit. "Working with terminally ill kids. Beyond it being something that takes Jake away. It's sad . . . and it's hard, and I don't think I could involve myself in it even if I wanted to. I haven't really actively tried."

"So make yourself."

"I don't know if I can."

Camila raises an eyebrow and regards me coolly. "I got fives on eight different AP tests, a perfect score on the SAT, and graduated from Yale in five semesters."

Her message is clear. She thinks "I don't know if I can" is bullshit.

"My sister . . . Chrissi . . . you . . . you all like to try to push me out of my comfort zone, right?" she says, quieter than she's been. "I'm not trying to be harsh, but if things are no longer so great within yours, it might be time to step outside it."

I sit there, silent, considering.

"Here." Camila extends a hand to help pull me to my feet and offers me a smile, just a small one. "You know what? Forget the test scores and expedited degree. If I can survive playing princess for an entire year, I'm confident you can push yourself to do anything."

chapter 9

WHEN THE E-MAIL COMES THROUGH THE NEXT DAY, I take it as a sign that Camila's words, although biting, were full of wisdom. I mean, it's a *sign*, dropped right into my in-box, complete with a little red flag notifying me of its importance. I can't ignore it, even though these particular e-mails . . . in the past, I've deleted them as quickly as possible. Without even thinking about scrolling down to actually *look* at the pictures of the sick children who would be showing up at the park.

I've never participated in a Make-A-Wish Foundation event before.

The mere thought of it was too much sadness for me to take. *I'm sorry*, I'd thought, *but I'm not your girl*. I knew many of the kids had terminal diagnoses. Their needs eluded my positivity, my optimism. I didn't think I had anything to contribute. And I didn't think I could handle it, anyway.

I really respected the girls who routinely played princess at the events. But I knew better than to think I was one of them.

Today, I take a deep breath and open the e-mail. HR is

pleading for someone to step in for Kathryn, who had to go home for a funeral. A little girl named Kayla had specifically asked for Cinderella, so the list of e-mail recipients was short. Not any princess would do. They needed a Cinderella.

I see Camila's unsympathetic expression and hear her words. *"So make yourself."*

Before giving it any kind of actual thought, I open a "reply" window, fire off a quick response with my availability, and hit send.

Then, I panic immediately. *Oh God, Alyssa . . . what have you gotten yourself into?*

THURSDAY MORNING WHEN I get dressed inside the Palace basement dressing room, I'm the only person down there, and it's a little bit creepy, the changing room illuminated by dim fluorescents on timers. It's deathly silent, and I shiver. I change quickly into Cinderella's breakaway costume. It's one I've never worn before, because typically it's reserved for a stage production I'm not involved in due to the intricate dance routines. When I'm done, I glance in the mirror. I'm wearing Cinderella's patchwork rag dress, and my updo is covered with another rag.

It's still incredibly early when I ascend the stairs and open the hidden door that leads into the park—the gates haven't opened yet and the majority of the maintenance and custodial staff aren't present yet. Glancing skyward, I swear a somber gray cloud is hanging low over the castle, rendering its mirrored panels dark, even though it's probably only my imagination. The sun will soon be high enough to outshine the daybreak clouds, and the familiar sights of the park are sure to be as cheerful as ever. The Diamond

Palace will sparkle. But without the usual scores of people surrounding me, it's easy to get lost inside my own mind, and I realize the truth of the matter is that . . . I'm scared.

What if I fail at this? What if I fall apart entirely? I'll let everyone down.

It's too late to turn back now. I pause outside the Palace. But if I could, I might.

I glance at my watch. *You really should've thought about it for five seconds before signing up.* I'm supposed to be there in eight minutes, and I have no choice but to keep moving forward with the plan.

Besides, I remind myself. *Jake will be there. You're not actually going to be alone.*

I'm pretty sure it was the opportunity to attend Make-A-Wish events that was the actual draw for him to come to the Enchanted Dominion last year. It's consistently one of the most popular requests with the organization, so beyond his aunt's needling about having some fun, Jake knew he'd be able to gain experience within his area of focus by working at the park. Even though he's not a face character, there are plenty of ways for him to support MAW events at the park and interact with the kids and their families. He volunteers whenever the events fit within his schedule.

I smile a bit. He'd been surprised as hell when I told him last night on the phone that I'd be joining him today.

"So I'll see you tomorrow night?" he'd asked, when we were about to say good-bye.

"Actually . . ." I took a deep breath. "You'll see me first thing in the morning. They needed someone to fill in as Cinderella at the event, and . . . I said I would."

"Oh." He was definitely surprised. Then a moment later, "Why?"

"It's a good thing to do. I've always been scared of the idea, but . . . I want to. I'm long overdue to volunteer." I nod decisively, trying to bolster my courage. My voice is softer when I speak up again. "And . . . I respect what you're choosing to do with your life. I want to understand it, firsthand. Beyond a video."

"Oh," he says again. Then I can hear him smiling. "That's nice, Lys. I appreciate that," he says warmly.

IQ scores don't lie, I think. *Camila really is a genius.*

I settle back against my couch cushions. "I could definitely use some advice, though." I never bite my nails but find myself gnawing on a thumbnail. "I have no idea how to mentally prepare for this."

"I won't lie to you. The first day, first time, whatever, it's tough."

My stomach drops. "Okay, not what I wanted to hear."

"But you have to get that first time out of the way," he continues. "Over time, it gets easier. You get desensitized. You're doing a job. You remind yourself, 'I'm doing a job.' That's how you keep from breaking. Remove your feelings from the equation; focus on the task at hand."

I consider. It's a weird concept to me. I put so much heart into being Cinderella. For the kids. To make their experience as authentic and magical as possible. The idea of working with kids and just being . . . clinical . . . it's very much at odds with how I do my job.

But Jake's work is very, very different. It's not all sunshine and unicorns in his world. And what he's saying, I guess it makes sense.

"Okay, I'll keep that in mind," I say. "It will be good to have . . . I don't know . . . a little mantra. Focus on the job."

At the other end of the line, he hesitates in responding. "You sure you wanna do this? It's *not* easy."

"I'm sure," I lie.

"Okay, well, good for you," he finally says. "I'm proud of you."

Bolstered by his advice and his pride, I was hopeful I'd survive.

But now the moment is actually, really here, and walking through the dark and somber castle tunnel, my hands shake at my sides. There are no other princesses on the scene to help shoulder the responsibility. After the early morning carousel ride, where I'll find the rest of the MAW volunteers, I'll join them in the dining hall at the Palace, where we'll greet the guests as a group. But for now . . . it's just me. And I have to get myself to that merry-go-round.

The carousel is only about a hundred yards away when I freeze in place, dropping to the base of the life-size Cinderella statue in a last-minute attempt to both hide and collect myself. I stare up at this portrayal of my idol. She boasts a calm, assured smile. She's looking bright-eyed out over the park. Her expression never changes regardless of what comes her way, thunder and lightning, snowstorms, hurricanes. I rub my hand over her bronze apron for good luck. *I wish I was as resilient as you are. Stay with me today.*

Her presence is comforting, and I know I'll still be able to see her from the carousel once I climb aboard to ride with the children. I feel ready to stand, but as soon as I do, I realize a crowd has started to gather around the carousel. I spot wheelchairs and other heavy-looking medical equipment. I think I see an oxygen tank. I inhale a quick, panicked breath and drop down to the base of the statue again. *Oh God.*

Suddenly a hand is on my shoulder, causing me to startle. I whirl around and look up in surprise, finding Miller behind me. Either he approached silently or I was too caught up in worrying to hear him.

My hand goes to my chest. I study him standing there, looking more put together than I'm used to seeing him, short beard neatly trimmed, wearing a gray polo shirt with the park's insignia tucked into a pair of neat khakis. "What are you doing here so early?"

I ran into him last night, when I was on my way to get my nails done and he was walking home from a pickup basketball game. I know I didn't mention my morning plans, because I'd been trying not to think about them. And he hadn't mentioned a reason for getting to the park this early, either.

"I always do a few of these a year." He winks at me. "My presence causes nowhere near the stir that yours will, but they always need a bunch of volunteers on hand to make sure everything goes smoothly and that the families get everything they could possibly need or want." He shrugs. "I don't mind helping out with it."

Of course he doesn't. I should have known.

I slowly stand up and he nudges me, glancing toward the statue. "What are you doing here, though?" Miller raises an eyebrow at me. "First timer?"

I smooth my damp hands over my threadbare skirt, feeling their heat on my thighs through the thin fabric. "That obvious?" I murmur.

"The first time is the hardest," he tells me. "When you don't know what to expect. But at the end of the day, they're just kids. Back at school, I hung out with the kids at the duPont Hospital for Children every other month or so." He shrugs. "Guess it was always a little easier when I was able to hide behind YouDee, though."

I hear the clock start chiming, and my panic reignites. I'm supposed to be there. Now. "Oh God," I inhale.

Miller chuckles. He squeezes my shoulders once, twice, like a trainer prepping a boxer for the fight of his life. "You got this, Princess." Then he gestures toward the crowd. "I'm late. I gotta run. You do, too. Star of the show and all that."

"Right . . ."

He's already turned to go but glances back at me one last time. "Just be human, Lys. And remember they're human, too. Look them in the eye."

I don't say anything, and he gives me a final thumbs-up before jogging off. "And you'll be okay. You will."

I watch Miller as he joins the group, finding someone with a clipboard who appears to be in charge, standing in the center of the families, and whispers something in her ear. She nods, looking over her shoulder in my direction, and points Miller and two other volunteers toward a stack of cardboard boxes.

Stealthily, hiding beneath awnings and sticking close to shop walls, I follow his path, so I'm within hearing range and can observe what's going on.

I see them passing out sparkling magic wands with long, colorful streamers. Miller appears entirely comfortable as he greets the children, offering high fives and smiles, and seeing him so at ease allows me to feel slightly less panicked.

I crane my neck, searching for Jake. He has a frown of

concentration on his face as he examines levels on some type of oxygen tank or something. I stare at him, sending him a mental message to look up so he'll meet my eye and smile, but all his attention is focused on the equipment.

When every last child and sibling present has been given a wand, the coordinator begins speaking into a microphone. "Helllllo, everyone! We've got a wonderful morning ahead. Who here's ready?"

Not me, I think at first. But then I smile slowly as I realize several kids are bouncing in their wheelchair seats, several others grinning behind oxygen tubes. It surprises me how happy they seem, how much energy they exude. I expected much worse.

The woman glances at her watch. "I've just received notice that Cinderella should be here any moment."

A hush falls over the crowd.

"And when she appears, do we all know the magic words to change her from peasant to princess?"

"YE-ES!" they all shout in unison, already waving their wands.

"Oh, Cinderella . . . ," the woman trills. "Will you join us? Will you make our wishes come true?"

My stomach drops to my feet. That's my cue. I take a final glance in Jake's direction, he finally looks up, and I run out, forcing a huge smile on my face, to the front of the carousel. Then I freeze in position, expectant smile on my face, waiting for what's to come next. *Oh God, please let it work.* I've never handled the breakaway dress, and this could be disastrous.

"Abracadabra, fiddle-dee-dee!" the coordinator shouts.

"Abracadabra, fiddle-dee-dee!" they echo, waving wands and in some cases stomping feet.

I tilt onto my tiptoes. I spin in a pirouette, frantically tugging on the cord that causes my peasant skirt to drop to my feet and the full skirt of my chiffon gown to puff out once it's free. Using some sleight of hand when I'm turned away from them, I quickly tear the bandanna from my head and my curls spring free.

By the time I'm facing them again, I've become a princess, glittery and shiny and grinning from ear to ear. They gasp their excitement and appreciation of the spectacle.

Now my smile is 100 percent genuine, not only because I pulled it off and the transformation was a success, but because their smiles are so huge I can't help but smile, too. I dance among them, waving and blowing kisses. "Good morning, my friends. Thank you, thank you, thank you! Who would like to ride the carousel with me on this beautiful morning?"

Their response is a resounding yes. I throw a quick, triumphant smile in Jake's direction before saying, "Well, c'mon, then!" and ushering the group toward the entrance to the merry-go-round. I wait long enough to see him smile in return.

Getting them all settled on the carousel takes a long time. My heart threatens to break in half as I watch parents transport some of the children, those with fragile, skeletal limbs, as if they're made of glass. There are wheelchairs that need to be secured to the base of the ride. Jake helps with a lot of the heavy lifting, while I watch from my perch atop a shiny white stallion adorned with pink roses.

One by one, the children fill in the horses around me or occupy the canopied benches between rows of horses. I could be horrified, I decide, as I assess them, some with limp bodies, some with sallow skin, some with single strands of hair clinging persistently to their tiny, nearly bald heads. But I take Miller's advice, I look them in the eye, and I realize he's spot on. No matter what the condition of their bodies, their little eyes are so alive, by far the healthiest part of them. Their eyes remind me that at heart, they're just like any other kids who want to enjoy the morning in the park, be enchanted in the presence of a princess.

Just before the ride starts, Miller escorts a little girl to the horse that has been left empty beside me. "This is Kayla," he tells me, still holding her hand. He smiles down at her. "And Kayla, this mare is all yours."

Miller lifts her gently onto the horse, and she turns to me, staring at me with huge glacier-blue eyes, her ears looking too big for her little bald head, which is wrapped in a cheery fuchsia-and-white floral scarf. "Are you the real Cinderella?" she whispers.

I lift my chin, beaming at her. "Indeed I am. And it would be my honor and delight to ride beside you this morning."

The ride starts off, slowly, and Kayla's beautiful face explodes in a smile.

At the base of the ride, her mom is watching her, camera out, camera forgotten. Her mom is crying.

I have to look away. I have to look away, or I know for sure I'll lose it. So I sing instead. I sing Cinderella's theme song, belting it out at the top of my lungs, inviting the children around me to join in the chorus.

Miller holds onto a post nearby, smiling into the distance while still staying close. I'm not really sure if he's keeping an eye on Kayla or keeping an eye on me.

The ride lasts way longer than usual, the children treated to five times as many rotations as the average park-goer. When the extended ride is over, I wait for the children to be transported back to solid ground, and then I move through the line, posing for pictures, talking to the children. I ask them which princess they're most excited about meeting; I ask them to tell me about the best part of their trip so far. Most of them answer quickly. "Everything."

I talk to the parents, too. I look them in the eye. I hug them, because God knows they need a hug, too. I tell them their children are beautiful, because they are. Some of the most beautiful children I've ever seen.

During one of his runs back and forth to the carousel to haul equipment, Jake squeezes my side stealthily and whispers, "You're doing a great job."

He's doing a great job, too, of course, efficient and tireless and kind. But . . . I can't help but notice how he barely even looks at the families as he assists them. He's busy, sure, and hustling around like a man on a mission, and I understand it's part of his philosophy to keep from getting upset. Still the same, there's something about it that seems a bit off.

He's been doing this for a long time. Maybe it's become *too* much of a job.

Feelings are hard, but I'm not sure I'd ever want to turn mine off.

And since I'm not the type to check out, I pull my attention away from my boyfriend and back to the end of the line of children waiting to meet me. Once I've greeted the last of them, one of the other volunteers offers up a second carousel ride for those who are interested, those who can get on easily. I hold Kayla's hand as we board, but she tells me in a soft voice it's okay if I ride next to someone else this time instead, causing my throat to tighten.

I bend down to hug her a second time, noticing that her pierced ears are unadorned this morning. Reaching up, I fumble with the backs of my tiara earrings. I remove them one at a time, carefully affixing them to Kayla's earlobes instead. "These are for you," I whisper to her, my throat tightening. "Take them home with the rest of your happy memories."

She's stunned, reaching up to touch them but stopping just before, as if she's afraid she'll find they're not real after all. Her eyes are popping out of her head. "Really?"

"Really." I nod. "They look beautiful on you. More beautiful than they looked on me, anyway."

I glance around, this time hoping Jake's *not* looking. Giving away a personal item to one of the children isn't exactly in keeping with his philosophy. Plus, I know they were expensive. But in that moment, it feels like the right thing to do, and I'll just have to explain myself later. I never thought I'd find myself in a situation where I'd part with those earrings, but meeting Kayla changed that.

This second ride, every now and again, I glance out into the park, watching the parents pass by in a blur. One mom is wiping at her eyes, trying to hide the hurt while grinning like a maniac. One dad is sobbing unabashedly into the hem of his T-shirt. I feel my smile start to slip at the same time my throat starts bobbing, and I grit my teeth as I stare at the ceiling of the carousel.

Please God, tell me we're almost there.

Tears hover on my lower lashes, ready to fall, until I realize that around me, the kids have broken into a spontaneous round of the EE theme song. Their smiles help mine stay in place.

When the ride ends, I wait for them all to get situated, and as they head in the direction of the Palace for breakfast, I wave both hands overhead. "Good-bye, children! I'll see you soon! Can't wait to have breakfast with you!"

Once they're on their way, I stand as still as stone. I see the clock in the distance. *Twelve minutes*, I realize. *Twelve minutes until you have to be put together and grinning anew inside the dining hall.*

Time is limited. When every one of them has moved beyond the crest of the hill, I dash in the opposite direction, hiding out in the alcove beside the Sleeping Beauty bathrooms. Then I promptly collapse in sobs.

I wrap my arms around my torso, trying to hold myself up, or rather, trying to hold myself together, because it feels like my heart is being torn apart, and as it's being ripped to pieces, it's taking the rest of my body with it.

What I could really use is someone to hold me together. I twist around helplessly, stomach dropping as my eyes fall on Jake's back. It's disappearing with the crowd, heading toward the Palace, as he pushes a wheelchair.

He's not here for you today, I remind myself. *Be a grown-up.*

Be a grown-up, I repeat. Right before a fresh round of sobs rack my body.

This sucks. God, sometimes life . . . sickness . . . it just sucks.

Through watery eyes, someone emerging from the men's room catches my attention. It's Miller, head down, zipping up his pants. Momentarily, he looks embarrassed about being caught coming out of the bathroom, but then concern overtakes his face once he gets a good look at me.

He doesn't hesitate before wrapping his arms around me in a tight hug, pulling me close and running a hand along my back in comfort, shh-ing me. I don't hesitate in collapsing against him.

"Calm down," he instructs me softly. "Take a deep breath."

I try. It doesn't really help. I try again. And again. Then . . . I punch his arm. "You . . . said . . . it . . . would . . . be . . . okay," I sob against his chest.

He takes the hit without flinching. "You are okay," he assures me. "You were more than okay. You were terrific with the kids, Lys. These are just stress tears, an adrenaline crash." He tightens his arms around me again. "And you're going to be *okay*."

I cry in his arms until the tears finally run dry, until my body collapses against his in fatigue instead of need, and I can begin breathing normally again. I settle into his embrace, which is as solid as ever, without any inclination to move.

It occurs to me that Miller has hugged me plenty of times in the past few years. He's thrown his arm around my shoulders more times than I can count, he's wrapped me up in silly bear hugs and actually lifted me off the ground. But this is the first time Miller's actually *hugged* me, and I'm surprised to find how entirely comfortable I feel wrapped up in his arms. Even knowing time is ticking by, it's hard to step away. I linger a few extra seconds, then pull my body off his, abruptly and all at once, like a Band-Aid.

"You're a good friend," I whisper, wiping my eyes and smiling sadly up at him. "Thanks for being you, ya know? I'm sorry I hit you."

It takes a second for Miller's expression to clear when I step away from him. There's something unreadable there before his eyes light and he says, "Again."

"What?"

"'I'm sorry I hit you *again*.' Didn't realize it was an actual *habit* of yours."

I giggle. "Oh, right. Sorry." I rub my hands over my face again, patting my fingers under my eyes in a last-ditch effort to keep them from puffing up. I wave my hands in front of my face, run my index finger under both eyes to get rid of any trails of mascara. "I still have to go to the breakfast. Do I look okay?"

Miller glances somewhere over my shoulder. "Yup. Always."

I squeeze his hand. "I'm sorry I hit you again. Thanks for helping me get it together."

He nods, and I gather my skirts and duck past him, hurrying toward the castle to find Jake and the rest of the group.

chapter 10

WHEN THE BREAKFAST WRAPS, I HEAD OUT, grateful I'm not on the schedule for my usual duties after such a taxing morning. Jake has to stay, but he asks me if I want to get sushi later, at the tiny, no-frills restaurant in Lakeside's downtown. It was a favorite of ours last year, a place we haven't been back to yet this summer. I'm thrilled he remembers it.

The evening feels like some kind of celebration, so I take my time getting ready, spending nearly an hour on my hair and makeup, selecting what I think is one of my hottest outfits. I wriggle into my tightest white ankle jeans that I've paired with a flowy off-the-shoulder white top. I strap on heeled gold sandals and layer several gold necklaces around my neck. I remember my missing earrings and push my hair forward, hoping Jake won't notice their absence.

Jake comes into the apartment without my hearing him, and he finds me in my room, dousing myself with Clinique Happy as a final touch. He comes up behind me, wraps his arms around my waist, and puts his chin on my bare shoulder. "You look hot tonight."

I smile at his reflection. "As do you."

He's not wearing his glasses, his hair is expertly gelled, and there's just the right amount of scruff along his jaw. He has on Sperrys, khaki shorts, and a button-down shirt over a slate blue tee.

We would make really, really cute babies, I allow myself to think for three seconds. Maybe four.

"I'm starving." He plants a quick kiss on my shoulder before stepping toward the door. "Let's go eat."

It's a pretty evening, and we walk hand in hand to Bluefin. Well, he walks. I hobble.

"Those shoes are the worst," he complains.

I shrug, ignoring the way the straps cut painfully into my skin. "Fashion over function, babe."

He grins down at me. "Did you really just say that?"

"It's true! At least for girls, anyway."

Jake shakes his head at me, and we make our way down the center block of the downtown area. I'm smiling at the familiar banter, which there hasn't been much of lately. I decide I'm officially forgiven for falling asleep during the video. I lift my chin. I did good today.

Dinner feels just like old times. Jake tilts his head back and catches the edamame I toss to him like a trainer to a dolphin. We steal bites off each other's plates without asking. We talk about things both silly and serious, and never once does conversation feel stilted. And by the time our check is dropped, the pressure in my chest has lessened.

Jake adds the tip to the receipt and signs his name quickly, closing the shiny black folder with a snap. His foot nudges mine under the table. "You ready?"

"Yeah."

He leans toward me. "Let's go home."

A spark lights within me at his words, the look in his eyes as they meet mine. Tonight, I can feel his attraction toward me, and it feels more than obligatory.

So I stand in a hurry, eager to get home.

Jake's hand is on my back as he leads me toward the lobby, and I'm feeling like his again. As we near the doorway, I sneak a glance at him, flirting, expecting him to glance back at me in return. But he doesn't, his focus elsewhere. I'm looking at Jake, and Jake is looking at . . . a hot girl in a punch-colored dress.

My eyes widen when I realize it's Harper. They nearly pop out of my head when I see who she's with. Kellen. Wearing white linen pants and mirrored shades, *inside.* Definitely Kellen. And *what*?

They don't see us until we're practically on top of them. Harper turns quickly, dropping her clutch, and she and Jake almost bang foreheads when they both reach down at the same time to pick it up. Jake reaches it before she does, and she accepts it from him without a thank-you.

"Oh my God. Alyssa. Jake." Harper smooths her hair back and swallows hard. She gives an awkward little wave. "Hi."

Kellen steps forward, all swagger, to offer Jake a casual handshake and "What's up, man," and I seize the opportunity to give Harper a quick hug. "You caved? You actually said 'yes'?" I hiss into her ear.

I'm half joking, but all Harper can offer me in return is a terse little smile, tugging on the hem of her short skirt. "I just thought . . . maybe I should . . . give it a try. Just, you know, give something different a try."

I sneak a glance at the guys, who are still making small talk, and warn her under my breath, "Just stay in public tonight, all right? I've heard he can get kind of aggressive."

She nods without looking at me, eyes darting over to the guys. She seems really tense, and I hope I'm not out-and-out scaring her.

The hostess is staring at our group, impatience obvious, and Harper steps away from me. "We should . . . probably go."

Kellen grins at us. "We should. I'm in the middle of selling her on staying down south rather than heading back to Philly at the end of the summer." He rolls his eyes. "Pssh. Law school. Who needs it, right? You can't beat the weather down here." He gives a quick wave, puts his hand near Harper's rear, and they're gone.

My stomach turns, and the pressure reannounces itself in my chest, full force.

Heading back to *Philly*?

Jake and I step out onto the sidewalk and I squint at the blinding rays of the sinking Florida sun, feeling off-kilter.

I reach for Jake's hand, hoping to recapture the natural, easy vibe from just moments ago. I pretend I'm not faking it. "So that was weird!" I make a face at him.

But he's looking dead ahead, stride purposeful. "What do you mean?"

"Harper. Kellen. Odd pairing, no?"

Jake tucks his chin. He shakes his head. "Yeah . . . who knows."

So much for easy conversation. So much for any conversation. We both make some halfhearted attempts at small talk as we walk, but the sense of connection I felt during dinner is gone. The pressure in my chest is coagulating, forming itself into a question. And by the time we climb the steps and make it to my door, it insists on being asked.

I pause, key in hand, pressing it against the chipped green paint of my door.

Still staring at the key, the question's out of my mouth before I even rehearse it in my head. "Did you know Harper from before? From Philly?"

Just as quickly, I regret asking. Because if the answer is yes, it means someone is lying. In some way. And the reason for lying is likely something I don't want to know about.

Jake looks semishocked. "No. No! I swear I didn't meet her until this summer. Why would you—"

I stand there still, thinking, bothered, pressing the key into the soft skin of my palm. "I don't know," I interrupt him. I shrug. "It's just this weird feeling. Like . . . I don't know . . . like you two know each other. Like you *knew* each other. Before you were ever introduced." I run my hand through my hair, frustrated, hating this. "It just always feels weird. With you two."

Jake doesn't answer for a few seconds. Then he looks me in the eye. "I promise you I only met her this summer."

Silence settles over us. I can't look at him. I just keep staring at my palm, the dent the key is leaving in my flesh, my hair falling in a curtain over my face.

Then I feel Jake's hands brushing my hair out of the way. His lips find my neck.

"Honestly, Lys . . . why are we talking about other people?" he asks hoarsely. "Or thinking about them? All these questions from you . . . please don't." He kisses me again. "Are you going to let me in sometime tonight or what?"

The key finds the doorknob, and the door falls open before me with a simple twist.

I let him in. I don't want to think about or talk about other people anymore, either. So I lead him into the bedroom at once, craving him in a way I never have, desperately, to block everything else out. I make Jake reassure me physically in a way his words couldn't quite do.

chapter 11

LAST SUMMER, OVER THE COURSE OF THE many hours Jake and I spent together lying atop my bed or between its sheets, we'd watched the entirety of seasons one through four of *The Blacklist* on Netflix. We'd made a deal before season five premiered in early October—we wouldn't watch, and when we reunited this summer, we'd binge watch and get caught up together.

I may have cheated a tiny bit. Turns out Lauren "E" had a thing for Ryan Eggold, so every Thursday at nine, *The Blacklist* was on in the Zeta house. Typically I got home from my shift at the boutique right at nine o'clock, and well . . . it was just so tempting to plop down on the couch with the rest of them. And Ryan Eggold *is* cute. With those glasses, he has a little bit of a Jake thing going on.

The real Jake has no idea, and weeknights when he comes over to my apartment, we've been slowly but surely catching up.

"All the cool kids actually *watch* Netflix and chill," he informs me with a smirk as he points the remote at the screen and navigates to the right episode. "Where'd we leave off? Episode five?"

I squint at the screen, reading the brief episode descriptions. "Yep. We watched that one."

Jake settles down beside me, bowl of Funyuns in his hand. I breathe through my mouth so I don't have to smell them, clicking on another dress option that pops up on my laptop screen.

Jake glances over. "What are you doing?"

"Trying to find a dress I like on Rent the Runway."

"For what?"

I give him an "are you serious?" look. "The *wedding*, of course."

Kallie and Luke's wedding is this weekend. I have to decide on a dress tonight so that it'll arrive in time.

"Oh, right." He studies the screen. "What the hell is Rent the Runway?"

"It's ingenious, is what it is. Instead of having to spend several hundred dollars for a dress you're gonna wear only once, you can rent a designer dress for, like, three days. Then you mail it back to them and they take care of the dry cleaning and all that good stuff."

"It does make a considerable amount of sense," he agrees. "I'm surprised, fashion-wise, you'd go for something so practical."

I don't respond. Instead I click on the next option—a long, flowing watercolor maxi dress—and study the details with intense concentration. I've thanked my lucky stars a million times over for the masterminds behind the Rent the Runway website. There's no way I could survive spring in Zeta without it. Date parties, formals, bid day, graduation . . . the cost to dress for these events would surely have exceeded a thousand dollars and that was a thousand dollars I didn't have to spend. Rent the Runway was a literal lifesaver.

I just had to make sure to intercept the UPS man at the door.

Before Blake, or anyone, actually, saw that I had to *rent* my clothing.

Deciding the watercolor dress is a little too busy for my liking, I go back to the home page and filter my search by color. I'm so used to wearing white, and since that's not an option for a wedding, I might as well look for something bold. Maybe purple.

I glance up when I hear the opening credits playing. Jake turns off the table lamp, as is our custom, and suddenly the light from my computer screen seems glaring. He gives me a pointed look. "Can't you just pick one and be done with it? You know anything will look good on you."

I groan, thinking he's kidding. We don't have any kind of "no distraction" policy when we watch together, and oftentimes I've caught him checking game scores on his phone. "You're such a guy. You don't just *pick* one." I square my shoulders. "It has to be the perfect one."

It has to be the perfect one. The wedding has to be great, and I believe it can be. There's nothing more romantic than a wedding, and this will be a wedding party comprised of our EE friends, set to take place in this old, run-down mansion, complete with a tower for Kallie (formerly Rapunzel) to descend from.

I glance at Jake from the corner of my eye. I've moved past our awkward run-in with Harper and Kellen, but still . . . we could use a reset. I'm counting on this wedding. Thus, a fabulous dress is of utmost importance.

To appease Jake, I devote my full attention to the TV screen, for about three minutes, before letting my attention drift back to the web page. Okay, narrowing the search by purple dresses didn't really help a bit. I mean, it's like a freakin' produce smorgasbord or something . . . plum, eggplant, violet, lavender, grape, mulberry. It's just too much! Shaking my head, I go back to the drawing board. Maybe gold. Gold is good.

My laptop, old as it is, makes a whirring sound as it processes, and I hear Jake give a prolonged sigh of frustration to my left. I ignore it. Because, after all, I'm so very graciously ignoring the smell of those Funyuns.

I scroll through about ninety-seven gold dresses before I find The One. I know it as soon as I see it in thumbnail size; it has Alyssa written all over it. The tank-style top is beaded in varying, dazzling shades of gold, and its short skirt is chiffon. The chiffon is a beautiful color, making me think of caramelized sugar atop a good latte. I mark it as a favorite, and click back on the one other dress I'd marked as a final contender, a bold satin floral print.

I click on the gold dress. I click on the floral dress. I click back on the gold dress.

The gold dress it is, I decide, feeling triumphant. It's better for summer, and I already own shoes and accessories that will coordinate. That seals the deal for me. I verify that they have my size, pump my fist in the air in triumph, and add it to my shopping bag. Or renting bag, or whatever you call it.

But before I can change the shipping address to my summer sublet, the sound coming from the television speakers suddenly goes dead and the screen goes blank.

I look over at Jake in surprise. His mouth is flat, but irritation glimmers in his eyes.

"What just happened?" he asks me.

"What do you mean?"

He gestures toward the screen with the remote. "What just happened?"

I stare helplessly at the blank screen. Shoot. I have no idea.

Jake tosses the remote onto the coffee table and folds his arms across his chest. "We are thirty-five minutes into the show," he says coldly, staring into space. "And you haven't watched a single one of them."

"Yes, I have!" I protest, sounding unconvincing even to myself.

"No. You haven't."

I tilt my head and smile up at him. "Jake." I'm desperately trying to make light of the situation, although my stomach is turning in panicky circles. "Come on. Why are you making such a big deal of this?" I shrug. "Sometimes you have your computer out. Or you text. Or you check what's going on with whatever game on your phone. So why are you so mad at me?"

Jake shakes his head in what seems like a very condescending manner. "It's just a dress."

"It's not just a dress," I correct him. "I mean, it's for our friends' wedding, and for a wedding you should at least put some thought into—"

The explosion seems to come out of nowhere. "It's just a dress!" he shouts, throwing his hands into the air. "I mean, God!"

The anger, or irritation, or whatever behind his words abruptly brings tears to my eyes. I swallow hard to keep them at bay, staring down at the fabric of the couch.

"I am over here, trying to spend time with you, and you—"

My head snaps up. "Thank you so much, for *trying* to spend time with me," I mutter.

"Stop it, Lys. Don't twist my words. I mean, I'm trying to actually be here with you, and you care more about some stupid dress. I don't know. But . . . looking for a dress for thirty-five minutes? Seems *really* superficial to me."

The pressure in my eyes intensifies; I feel them glassing over.

I turn my head and stare over my shoulder, toward my bedroom, because I can't look at him right now. Is that how he really sees me?

He stands up, and I'm afraid he's actually leaving. Over the silliest thing ever.

"Where are you going?"

But he heads to my bedroom instead, not looking back at me as he strides off. "I need a minute. To clear my head."

A few seconds later, I hear the door slam.

I remain motionless, except for grabbing a throw pillow and clutching it to my chest. *Don't move*, I mentally coach myself. *Don't think. Don't feel.*

But the tears that have pooled in my eyes refuse to recede, and I feel them spill over onto my cheeks in a sudden frantic rush, like they, too, are trying to get away from me. A choked sob escapes from my throat, and I press my face into the pillow so I don't have to hear myself cry.

I just can't seem to do anything right anymore, not as far as he's concerned, and it feels like his frustration with me has taken on a life of its own. It seems to be feeding on itself, and things that Jake found innocuous, or even cute or charming, about me before are now these huge character flaws he can't seem to tolerate. While not even noticing any of the good I've been trying to do on our behalf.

I'm *not* superficial, I tell myself, when I'm finally able to sit up and wipe my eyes. It's just . . . it's not just a dress.

For years now, it's been so much more than just a dress.

I REMEMBER THE despair of it, potent as ever, that spring day three years ago, sitting in the car beside my mother in the parking lot of the strip mall. The blue-and-white Goodwill sign, with its happy-face logo mocking me, shines in the distance.

Don't be a brat, I tell myself. *Don't be a brat.*

But I'm seventeen years old, and I can't help it, and the tears fall silently over my cheeks as I consider how much life has changed in only six months. Six months ago, my mom and I had dinner at the Lux Café and then went dress shopping at Lord & Taylor for my winter formal dress. Now, we sit outside Goodwill. We had spaghetti for dinner. Again.

My mom sighs beside me. Her voice is trembling when she reaches for my hand and says, "I'm sorry, honey."

I shake my head, because it's not her fault. It's not her fault that my dad got laid off after twenty-some years of service to his company, because they decided it made good financial sense to hire someone half his age at half the cost. It's not her fault that he had done so well before that she never had to work. It's not her fault that she'd gotten comfortable with the idea, that we all had, that my sisters and I never did the hand-me-down thing, had designer boots, clothes, and purses, riding lessons, and annual trips to the Enchanted Dominion.

But now there's nothing left. No savings, no security. Our lifestyle changed overnight, and it's just a lifestyle, but suddenly I don't know who I am anymore. In a new house, that's half the size of our old one.

Without a prom dress.

Maybe, if I were a grown-up, these things wouldn't mean so much. But now . . .

"We just have to pick and choose," she whispers. "I know you need money for the limo and to get your hair done. So a new dress . . . we can't do a new dress. But Goodwill has a huge selection, and truly, honey, they've only been worn once."

Her words do nothing to soothe me, and the tears keep falling. "But it's Goodwill," I say, like this matters somehow. I shake my head. Something about it feels more pathetic than anything else. Like we are destitute. Paupers. I feel ashamed.

My mom is silent for a minute. Then she sits up straight and puts the car in reverse.

"Where are we going?"

"To a much better option," she says with an authoritative nod. "To Claire's."

I consider, and a second later wipe my eyes and find a smile. She's right, and Claire's is the best kind of compromise. It's an upscale consignment shop nestled among the chic boutiques in town, somewhere my mom has donated piles and piles of clothing over the years. I've been in there with her countless times, and indeed, the atmosphere is much more appealing than the tiled floors and fluorescent lighting I imagine inside the Goodwill store. I don't even hate the idea of finding a dress there.

Which I do. It's floor length, covered in white lace and shimmery sparkles. It fits me perfectly. And it almost feels like someone has made it for me, by adding these delicate straps in a floral lace so that I won't be tugging the top up all night. In the dressing room, with its soft lighting and complimentary Perrier, I don't feel like a charity case. I nod, letting my mom know this is the one, and give her a hug.

Thank you, I whisper to the invisible fairy godmother who put this particular dress in this particular store on this particular night.

When prom rolls around, after getting my hair curled and

pinned up with flower-shaped clips, after sliding my feet into a pair of my mom's old Jimmy Choos, looking in the mirror I don't see the trace of a charity case. I forget all about how life has changed around me so quickly and dramatically. I feel like me again.

Until about an hour into prom.

I notice some of the senior girls from the lacrosse team staring at me. They look a couple of times, their heads coming together to whisper into one another's ears. I notice, but smile and wave, because they're girls I'm friendly with. I'm friendly with most of the girls in my class and the class above me.

Nicole, the captain of the team, comes striding over. She points to my dress. "I like your dress," she said.

"Oh. Thanks!"

She smiles. Then giggles. "I like it a lot. That's why *I* wore it to prom last year."

I don't know what to say. I freeze, feeling suddenly panicked.

I recover as quickly as I can, shaking my head. "It's probably this year's version. Different in some way you can't even tell."

"No." Nicole's unconvinced, reaching out and tugging on one shoulder strap. "I specifically picked out this lace and had my grandmom sew on straps because I couldn't stand the way it kept slipping down over my boobs." She meets my eye. "That's how I know. You found it at Claire's?"

She's not even being mean; she's just asking. Maybe she's even flattered that I liked her dress enough to want to wear it myself. I mean, some girls in my class did borrow dresses from friends. But the idea of admitting it, of acknowledging our financial struggles, seems like the most awful thing in the world.

So I laugh off the idea. "I didn't get it at Claire's! I got it at the mall, with my mom." I can't stand to look at her a second longer. "I'm sorry, I gotta go. I have to pee."

My cheeks are flaming as I head toward the bathroom, and I swear I can hear them talking about me. I feel embarrassed the rest of the night, naked and exposed and pitied.

WHEN THINGS HAPPEN around you, beyond your control, when you're still kind of a kid and you're expected to swallow what life throws at you like an adult . . . it's not easy. And since that night, I've done whatever I've had to do so no one would ever look at me like that, make me feel degraded again.

It's *not* superficial, wanting to look my best and be part of a group and feel good about myself. It doesn't feel that way to me, not after having so much fall apart around me when I couldn't do anything to control it.

You want to hold on to things. You learn to fight for them.

He has no idea, I think, gazing through puffy eyes at the back of my apartment door. *Jake has no idea about any of it.*

And it's not entirely his fault. Jake, with his successful parents and Connecticut upbringing and his security . . . he's someone I would never tell about exactly how and why I take so much care in how I present myself.

So maybe I can't be upset with him for misjudging me. I guess I'd rather have him misjudge me than know the whole truth of the matter. I'm not quite sure what that says about how much faith I have that he'd still love me all the same.

I stand up on shaky legs. I don't want to let Jake in on this part of my life that I keep to myself, but at this point, I don't feel like I have any choice. Maybe, his anger will have lessened and he'll actually be able to listen, understand. Have some compassion.

I creep toward my bedroom and silently twist the doorknob. Jake is standing before my bookshelf, head bent, back toward me.

"Jake," I whisper, "can you just listen for a sec?"

But then he turns around and my stomach drops, because I suddenly sense that I'm going to have to explain a lot more than my sad history at prom.

I'd just been looking at it, the other day, thinking about Kallie's wedding, wanting to distract myself with the fairy-tale idea of it all. I'd meant to put it back in its hiding spot, but now I can't remember if I did, or if I just left it sitting out for anyone to find, on my nightstand.

It's neither here nor there now. Now it's in Jake's hands, wide open, all my girly hopes and dreams exposed. I cringe, knowing how specific some of the ideas are. Knowing I might have slipped a picture of us from last year's Character Ball inside at one point.

"Alyssa." He stares at me with wide, perplexed eyes, and despite how angry he was a few minutes ago, I distinctly pick up on his pity as he presents my wedding binder for explanation. "What the hell *is* this?"

I swallow hard as my throat turns to dust.

Oh *no*.

chapter 12

A MOMENT LATER I'M LUNGING FOR IT, shaking my head, forcing a laugh. "It's nothing! It's really old." I grab the binder from his hands, wedging it into a too-small space on my bookshelf. It falls onto the floor a second later, like it's refusing to be ignored. I cringe because it falls open to a magazine article on how to hold your wedding at the Enchanted Dominion.

I can't quite meet Jake's eye. "All girls think about their wedding day! From like . . . age five."

Jake's staring at the floor. "Clearly, you've looked at it a lot since then," he says quietly. "You . . . you think about the idea . . . getting married . . . a lot."

Twisting my hands, I tell him, "It's not really like that."

He looks at me in this way that lets me know he saw his picture in there. He looks at me in this way that lets me know something really, really bad's about to happen.

Jake's quiet for a long time, staring, expression conflicted, his lips parted. It takes a while for him to finally force the words from his mouth. "I can't do this anymore, Lys."

In that immediate moment, I do not react.

There is the strangest relief in his words, in that first millisecond. When you've been dodging some demon, when you've spent hours, days, maybe even weeks purposely not thinking the unthinkable—"I think I've lost him"—because of how intensely you fear it . . . when that truth is suddenly upon you, and you realize you no longer have to suffer the anticipation of it, there is a millisecond of relief.

Just before the shattering sadness overwhelms you and sucks you under.

I cling to the irrelevant, pin my hopes on a paper-thin scrap. "We just had a fight, Jake," I say, grabbing on to the edge of my dresser for support. "It's just one night. It wasn't that bad."

He presses his lips together before shaking his head sadly. "It's not about one night, Alyssa. You know that."

"Well, there have been plenty of good nights! Why are you only focusing on the rough ones? There have been tons of laughter and smiles and good times between us! Even recently."

They have to count for something; they have to have some power to outshine some darkness. They have to!

Jake hangs his head, chin tucked, and I see his silence as an opportunity.

I stride toward him, grabbing his wrists, ducking down so I can look up at his face. "We've put so much time and heart into this," I remind him. "Don't give up now."

Don't pull the carpet out now. Don't make me start over again with nothing. You can't.

He sighs through his nose, his whole body wilting with apparent fatigue. "I've been trying, Lys. I really have. You have to know that. You know I'm not just giving up."

And this time when Jake looks at me, I realize the wall between us has come down, that all this time it was built out of these things he was not saying, and now that he's saying them, I can see him again. The real him, the person I fell in love with, who hasn't really come around in a long time. It hurts like hell.

"You have a good heart. You have the best heart," he whispers. "And you deserve someone who will be able to give you one hundred percent of his heart. One hundred and ten percent."

With this, the tears come. I struggle to speak through them. "You can't say things like that. You can't say things like that and expect me to believe that this is what you want. What I deserve is *you*!"

Jake doesn't answer me.

I brush furiously at my tears, the problem-solving part of my nature desperate to find a solution to this. To make *this* go away.

"Tell me specifically what it is. Tell me what I need to do to make you feel happy again."

His eyes close. "It's not like that. It's not as simple as that."

"Yes it is," I insist. My hand finds his cheek. "Talk to me. Tell me what. If you care about me like you say you do, then tell me specifically what would fix this. I'll do it."

"I know you would," he says, gently peeling my hand off his face. "But . . . I don't think this can be fixed. I don't think it can."

I take the smallest step back. "What does that mean?"

Jake stalls a moment. Then he raises his head and looks me in the eye. "We're not going to get married like Kallie and Luke. There's not going to be a fairy-tale wedding. There's not going to be any wedding."

His words feel like a bomb launched at my midsection, hitting its mark.

His gaze drops to the open binder on the floor. "Those dreams you have, they're not going to happen with me. That's not how this story is going to end for us." Jake's face crumbles as he looks back up at me. "I know you want that and I'd do anything in my power to deliver it for you, if it was right. But more and more . . . I'm just . . . convinced . . . it's not."

I squint up at him. "Because of me?"

Irritation, or frustration, or something flickers in his eyes. "Not because of *you*. Because of us."

"How long have you felt this way? Honestly?"

I have no idea why I'm asking a question I most certainly do not want an answer to. But I can't stop myself from exacerbating the hurt.

"I don't know," he murmurs, looking away.

"Yes, you do."

"There's not some exact time, Alyssa. I can't pinpoint it like that."

"Tell me," I insist. I step forward and shove at his chest a little bit. "Just tell me."

Jake backs up into my bookshelf. "You want me to be totally honest with you?" He throws his hands up. "I'll be totally honest with you." He takes a quick breath. He shakes his head. "I never really expected this to go past last summer."

Now I falter backward.

My knees turn to Jell-O. "*What?*"

He runs a hand through his hair. "The whole reason I was down here last year. It was supposed to be . . . fun. And it was. It was so much fun being with you." This time when he looks at me, I swear he looks a little guilty. "Then summer ended, and I was going home, and I sort of thought it would fade out naturally."

I shake my head, trying to clear it, trying to make any sense out of what he's saying. "Fade *out*?"

"But you . . . ," he continues. "You were so sure about us. You were so passionate about a future, and I . . . I thought maybe, or, I don't know." He exhales a long sigh of frustration and turns back toward me. "Maybe I was wrong, or maybe I was an asshole. But you were like this . . . butterfly. So lovely and pure and well meaning." He shakes his head again. "No one would willingly crush a butterfly. And I didn't have the heart to crush you, your hopes, your faith in us. Even though I sort of knew"—he pauses—"that you probably weren't the person for me."

"So you just lied to me for a year?"

"I wanted to believe, too! You're an awesome person, and when we were apart, it was hard to tell what was what. Distance relationships are hard inevitably. I let myself think maybe, when I came back down here, it might be different. But . . . it hasn't happened like that. It's sort of been the opposite."

The question is out of my mouth before I can even consider it. "Why am I not good enough for you?"

"For Christ's sake," he grouses. "That's not at all what this is about."

"It has to be. If I'm not the right girl for you, it's because you think I'm not good enough for you."

"Those are two very different things," he says. It sounds condescending.

"I'm not sure they are," I counter. "I've never been smart enough for you, you think my devotion to this job is silly and unimportant, you think my major is a joke, that I'm too worried about my appearance." I manage to lift my chin. "You think you're so damn smart, you're going on to do such important things, and me . . . I'm just not good enough to be part of that life."

His eyes have hardened a bit in response to my little speech. "Don't do this, Alyssa," he warns me. "Don't make it go down this way. It's the last thing I want."

"Stop being nice to me!" I shout in response to a new onslaught of tears. Because this is really happening. "You've been lying to me all year. Stop trying to be *nice* about it!"

"I haven't been lying about caring about you." He steps toward me. He reaches for me, trying to comfort me. "I do. Please know that I do. I know I've acted like a jerk lately, but that was just my frustration with the situation, with holding these things back. It wasn't you."

I shield myself with my arms. "Don't touch me! Don't *you* touch me!"

So he stands there, awkwardly, as I hold myself instead, trying to keep from falling over as the tears threaten to take me under. I sob into my hands, body shuddering, shoulder blades jutting painfully against my skin.

I hear him reaching into his pockets, fiddling with his keys. "Maybe I should leave," he finally murmurs.

I wipe my nose with the back of my shaking hand. "Maybe you should."

Don't go. Please God, don't go.

"I never wanted it to happen like this."

I stare at him through puffy eyes. "Clearly, you did."

Don't go. Then this will be real.

Jake gives me one final sad look. "I'm sorry you're hurting now." He drops his head. "I hate that. I really do."

Then, he actually does it. Jake brushes past me and leaves.

I DON'T MOVE for ten minutes. I can't. I stand there like a statue, clutching my ancient, raggedy Cinderella plush with the missing eye. But she brings no comfort this time, and I realize I'm digging my fingernails into her torso.

This hurts too much, I think. *I can't do this.*

And suddenly I'm darting out of my bedroom. Maybe he hasn't even left yet; maybe he's sitting behind his wheel, rethinking what he did. *Maybe . . .*

I fly through my apartment as quickly as I can, wanting to get away from my bedroom, where I swear our heartbreaking exchange is still lingering in the air. Before I close the door behind me, I catch a whiff of Jake's cologne, the kind he's always worn, and the visceral pain of it pierces my gut. *I can't.* I hurry down the hallway.

I stumble down the stairs, looking toward the parking lot through the dark distance, trying to see if his car's still here. I'll go to his apartment if I have to, but I really, really hope he's still here.

I see it! He *hasn't* left! Thank goodness.

Then, as I reach the bottom step, I see something that yanks me backward, and I cling to the banister to keep from going forward, to keep from inserting myself into a scene from a movie.

My blood turns to ice within my veins.

I'd just been hoping he was still here.

Be careful what you wish for.

He is in the courtyard, shadowed by the high wall that borders it. I can still see him, though.

And I can still see her. Harper.

There's a certain intimacy two people have when they've shared personal space before. Their bodies come closer together; they're oriented toward each other a certain way.

I saw it when he helped her in the tunnel, and I saw it when they were talking at the bar. I saw it again and again and told myself I wasn't seeing anything.

My legs give out, and I collapse onto the step, hands still clinging to the banister like it's a lifeline. I want to run, I want to close my eyes and erase the sight from my memory, but all I can do is sit there and watch.

Listen. The breeze carries their words in my direction.

"Why didn't you come over instead?" she asks him, glancing around nervously. "It's not right being out here."

"That wasn't right, either," he murmurs. "In the same building. With her friends."

It makes me feel sick, them talking about me.

"And I know I said I would," he continues, "but I couldn't tell her the whole story. I just . . . couldn't."

Harper sighs in frustration. "I get it. But she deserves the truth. And I mean . . . we didn't do anything. We never did anything. So we wouldn't feel any worse about it."

All I hear is "we."

The word slices me in two.

We.

And if I couldn't imagine feeling more pain tonight, suddenly I do.

Because I'm staring right at Jake, and he's not even a bit my Jake anymore. He's been transformed into a stranger right before my eyes. He's someone else. He's we. With *her.*

There had always been something weird between them, something that made me suspicious, but it was Jake, my boyfriend, and it was scholarly, innocent Harper, and never in a million years would I have actually thought . . . this. What it was.

I should go out there, I think. I should go out there and let them know I do know, that I did know, and even though they were too chickenshit to tell me, there's no hiding anymore.

I half stand on rubbery legs, assessing my courage, trying to make myself move forward.

He pulls her into an embrace. His hand goes over the top of her head, gently. He tells her, "I just want this part to be over. It sucks."

And she hugs him right back. She tightens her arms at the small of his back. I'm pretty sure I used to do the same exact thing. "Things will work out the way they're supposed to. They will. And it'll be okay."

Her nerve! Like it's that simple. Like I don't even exist.

My foot hits the concrete. Their heads whip around in unison. Harper actually gasps.

I stare at her. I stare at him. They are still embracing, and the sight of them . . . Jake . . . Harper . . . Jake and Harper . . . it makes me want to throw up.

I don't know what I wanted to say, but now all I want to do is go. Go. *Go!* I turn, retreat up the stairs as fast as my legs will carry me, calves burning, and sprint down my hallway, opening the door and then slamming it behind me. I sink back onto my ankles, face falling into my palms, a tight, frantic sob escaping, giving way to an onslaught.

Through my tears, I see my foot, my stupid crystal sandal. I stare at it, crying ugly tears, chest heaving, sliced in half by the pain of the memory of the first day we met, when he slid the shoe back on my foot and I thought it meant something.

Fool.

Look at me now.

Look at me.

All I'd ever done was try to see the best in people, to treat them with kindness, to believe that in turn, people could all be a little more loving and kinder to one another.

I'd believed in dreams, and happily ever after, and believed that *by* believing in them, I gave them the power to come true.

And now I am getting punished for it.

Fool. I'm a damn fool. I'm every bit as stupid as the two of them must believe.

I'd tried and tried, done everything in my power to make things work, and it did nothing for me. Except blinding me to the sad truth of what was really going on.

I remove my shoes and toss them out of sight. I cry into my shaking hands, where I stay until the first sign of dawn insinuates its way through my window.

PART II

the beginning

chapter 13

IT IS TWO WEEKS POSTBREAKUP, AND I AM a Hot Mess, capital *H*, capital *M*.

It's to the point I'm not sure if my hermit-like behavior has caused my hermit-like appearance or if my hermit-like appearance has prompted my hermit-like behavior. Regardless, these days, I make a point of avoiding social interaction at all costs.

After toughing out Kallie and Luke's wedding, solo, in a dress I picked out the night Jake and I broke up, telling lies about his "sudden sickness," I was spent. Since then, I've continued to evade my friends down the hall, despite the fact that in addition to calling and texting, they've left small gifts outside my apartment—a bouquet of daisies tied with burlap, a tube of matte lip gloss—and knocked persistently on my door many more times than that. I hide, motionless, on the other side and wait them out.

Their gestures, their gifts, let me know they know. And at one point, the thought occurred to me, *What if they knew before?* What if Harper had confided in one of them, or all of them, and they'd been in on keeping the secret? What if their gifts were given out of guilt? What if everyone knew what a fool I was while I didn't?

I can't stand to face the possibility. I can't even stand to tell the story of what happened, the true story, not some made-up one, so I dodge them. I show up on set in the nick of time, hiding in my dressing room until I know Chrissi is already in place. I pretend I'm late for dentist appointments that don't exist, cutting her off at her first attempt at conversation postshift, hurrying away from Rose when she appears in the doorway of their apartment. I take random, out-of-the-way paths through the park and avoid the cafeterias.

Which also serves a dual purpose. Of avoiding Jake and Harper. Possibly together. The mere thought kills my appetite straightaway, anyway, so . . . no need for the cafeteria.

One day I make up an excuse for visiting HR and peek at their schedules so I have a heads-up on how to avoid them for the week ahead. So with planning, and care, and a little luck, I can avoid people and avoid reality. I throw all my energy into being Cinderella, and I forget about being Alyssa. I mean, her life kinda sucks right now.

It becomes gym, work, gym, sleep. Repeat. I feel like a ghost of the girl I used to be, and my appearance in the mirror reflects that sentiment. Today, after dressing for my morning trip to the gym, the girl I see looking back in the mirror startles me. I'm fully made up and still look awful. A flash of panic makes my heart pound as I remember something. *Oh my God. I have look-overs on Monday.*

For the first time since I've started working at the Enchanted Dominion, I'm not sure if I'll pass them. Looking at the crown of my head, the line of demarcation is a solid inch and a half past my roots because I haven't bothered to touch them up since . . . I can't remember when. There are a few pimples along my jawline. I still have dark shadows under my eyes, which seem more pronounced because of the weight I've lost.

I lift the hem of my shirt and turn away at the sight of my rib cage. I look downright gaunt, and it's not a good look. It's been anything but intentional. I just don't have much of an appetite these days, and I'm at the gym more than ever simply as a means of filling the hours and staying distracted. I've stopped stepping on the scale because I'm afraid its numbers will be really upsetting. I'm supposed to stay thin, but I'm not supposed to be a waif. And I'm scared of what I might hear on Monday, but the thought of eating a cheesecake alone in my apartment is just too depressing.

I grab my gym bag and step away from the mirror. Maybe if I fiddle around with the weight machines today that will be more helpful, a last-ditch effort to add some bulk to my frame. I leave the bedroom, purposely ignoring my poster of Miss Hepburn. I know I've let her down.

IT'S ONLY SIX thirty when I walk into the fitness center. The early morning crowd is a different one from the group I used to work out with, and I prefer it these days. Fewer princesses, less small talk. The Lakeside residents and cast members working out at such an ungodly hour are focused, here to get in and get out before the day actually starts. No one bothers me.

I stick to my plan and head for the weight machines, but very quickly, and very sadly, I realize I don't have the energy or strength to actually make it work. My triceps and shoulders shake and my hamstrings ache as I try to move the machines, even at the lowest weight setting. Feeling pathetic, I throw in the towel and head back to the trusty row of ellipticals, amping up the resistance as an alternative to the machines.

As I'm programming my workout, from the corner of my eye I see Miller enter the gym. He shrugs out of his sweatshirt and slaps hands with a few of the guys congregated in the weight area. I notice him noticing me, feel the weight of his eyes upon me as his gaze lingers, and I angle my face away from him, furrowing my brow in put-on concentration as I push the buttons. It's not the first time I've seen him here during my early morning stints, and it's not the first time I've done everything in my power to avoid him. My attempt at a happy facade would be weak, and I have this sense he'd see through it. Shoving my earbuds in, I turn the volume all the way up and force my weak body into motion.

Last time, I paused midplaylist, so Ruff Ryders, specifically Eve, blasts into my ears. It's so loud I'm a bit concerned, and embarrassed, that the girl next to me can hear the blaring gangsta rap, and I turn it down, just a bit.

It was the only way I could get back to the gym: Googling breakup playlists and realizing that hard-core rap was the only thing that worked for me anymore. It's ridiculous, I know. I'm this skinny, often-bedazzled princess, whose playlists these days just happen to include Lil' Kim, Da Brat, and Nicki Minaj. The angrier the lyrics, the better. It makes me feel bolstered; I can pretend I'm tough, too. Strong. Bulletproof. I always leave the gym with a little more swagger than I walked in with. Who cares if right now it's only an illusion?

I stay on the elliptical a full hour, until my muscles feel weak and I've finished my thirty-two-ounce water bottle. Feeling dizzy and light-headed when I step off, I hold on to the handlebars for a few extra seconds before wiping down the machine and gathering my stuff. I want to collapse, but the music is still pounding in my ears, and it gives me enough energy to leave the main gym area.

I see Miller again, waving, trying to catch my attention as he finishes a set, but I pretend I don't. I crank the volume back up, stare into the space before me, and head out.

Because it was drizzling when I left my apartment, I drove this morning, and I'm still mouthing the lyrics to "Another" by Notorious B.I.G. and Lil' Kim as I cross the parking lot. The song is raunchy as hell and actually made me blush my first listen, but I've listened to it about sixty-five times since then and now know every word.

It's at the refrain between verses when I collapse into my front seat, so I plug my phone into the auxiliary jack and slam my door shut just in time for Lil' Kim to start laying into her ex who cheated on her. I take a quick glance around the parking lot to make sure no one might be watching before jumping in. Her verse is almost a full two minutes, and I'm proud, and also highly embarrassed, to say I can rattle it off in its entirety without taking a breath.

About a minute and a half later, I'm all in, hand motions and all, jerking my neck with an attitude, and proclaiming "I ain't gonna keep puttin' up with the bullshit" in my best Brooklyn accent . . . when I finally notice that someone's tapping gently on my window.

I realize it's Miller's face, right there, and I jump in my seat, yank the cable from my phone, and promptly blush a deep shade of crimson.

I close my eyes for about twenty seconds, mortified, before I can bring myself to reach over and lower the window, just slightly, and finally make eye contact. And Miller, he looks waaay too happy about this. He's grinning like the cat that ate the canary, while still trying to choke back barely contained laughter.

I put a hand up. "Don't. Just *don't*," I beg him.

But he does, anyway, twisting both hands up into some kind of approximation of gang symbols. "What up, gangstaaaaaa?"

"I said don't!" I cover my eyes with my hand.

"I don't know what you're so embarrassed about," he continues, leaning down, resting his elbows on the door frame so that he can harass me from even closer. "That was truly impressive. I didn't know you had this talent. White girl rapper."

I glance at him, just for a second, then again. I bite the inside of my cheek to keep from smiling.

"I mean, I'm not gonna lie, I *am* kind of appalled at the language." He cocks his head. "Do you kiss Prince Charming with that mouth?"

Damn it. A tiny smile escapes from my grasp. "I hate you," I tell him. I actually laugh. "Damn you."

He's watching me laugh and smile, and abruptly his face changes. The amusement drains from his eyes, and he's studying me carefully. Miller looks down. "No, seriously, though." He knocks gently against the side of my door, twice. "I'm not just here to give you shit. I did want to talk to you." He inhales mightily, as if preparing to deliver a monologue or something. "Can you . . . ummm . . . step out for a minute?" He lifts his face toward the dreary sky. "It's not raining right now."

I stare at him, curious. I can't remember a time I've ever seen Miller look so serious, and what's this about, anyway? "Umm . . . okay?" I finally agree.

Slowly I open my car door and step out, immediately feeling the need to lean against it for support. I didn't eat anything before coming here today. Then I look at Miller, with his hands shoved in the pocket of his hooded sweatshirt, face all hesitant and nervous looking as he stares down at the pavement. I offer a small smile in response to his awkwardness. "So what's up? You look . . . concerned."

He lifts his face at once. "I am."

And then he doesn't say anything else.

"Okaaay. About . . ."

Miller hems and haws for another minute, shifting back and forth on his feet. His sweatpants are a bit too long, probably because most sweatpants are too long for him, and the bottoms are frayed and now damp.

"Don't laugh at me, okay?" he starts quietly.

My eyes widen. What the heck is this about? "I won't," I promise automatically.

He rubs his beard, briskly, a few times before he works up the courage to spit it out. But he still can't meet my eye and stares into the distance beyond my left shoulder instead. "You know how I was technically on the cheerleading squad at UD, right?"

I nod slowly, utterly perplexed.

"I spent a lot of time with those girls. And I started noticing some things that were pretty shitty." He chews on the corner of his lip, his expression looking disturbed. "Every season, at least one girl, sometimes more, definitely had eating issues. And the sickest part about it? Was that some of the girls, the ones who actually ended up needing professional help or checking into treatment programs . . . I started to realize they had help all the way down. People, their closest friends, didn't want to say anything." He pauses and shakes his head. "Or worse. They actually encouraged it. Kept telling the girl how good she looked, even as she was fading away."

Finally Miller meets my eye. But I'm as confused as ever. "All right . . ."

"It's sick," he announces bluntly. "The way people dance around the subject because it's uncomfortable." He lifts his chin. "And I always said I'd never be one of those people, even if the conversation sucks and no one wants to be having it." He looks me square in the eye.

Realization finally dawns, and I shake my head rapidly. "Whoa, Miller, no . . . I . . ."

But he appears to be a man on some kind of a mission. "Trust that I'm not some creepy stalker or anything. But a few days ago, you were working out in your sports bra. And it was your spine that caught my attention." Miller looks sort of sick now. "I could see, like, every one of your vertebrae, and instinct kicked in, and . . ." He trails off and shakes his head. "Something about it . . . just wasn't right.

"God." He winces. "This sounds ridiculous. I totally sound like a creeper. But . . ." He squares his shoulders a final time and looks at me, his cheeks pink. ". . . I know there are a million and a half girls around here who wouldn't say a damn thing. And I may be botching this big-time, but I will be the one person to say something, just in case you actually want someone to say something. To notice. To care." He swallows hard. "Are you having issues? Do you need someone to talk to?"

I don't know if I've ever been so stunned in my life.

I stare at Miller for a long minute. I want to hug him. So I do.

"Miller." I press my forehead right into his damp T-shirt and wrap my arms around his roundish middle. "Oh my *God*."

Then I step back and put my palms to my cheeks, still figuring out what to make of all this. I shake my head. "You are . . . that was . . ." I give up and start over again a few seconds later. "First off, thank you. That was awesome. That was really, really awesome."

And he was spot on. About the way girls encourage one another . . . all the way down. How no one will ever say anything to someone's face, even when it's evident as anything that she's suffering.

I reach for his hand and give it a quick squeeze because his cheeks are still pink and there's no reason for it. "Don't feel dumb. You're right. And more people should do what you just did."

I think he relaxes slightly then.

"I don't have an eating disorder," I assure him. "And I'm being totally honest with you." But I can't help but remember my appearance in the mirror this morning and my head drops. "That being said, I do know I look like complete shit right now."

"That's not what I—"

I smile wryly. "I thought we were being honest here, Miller."

He doesn't try to refute me again.

I wait until he'll look at me so he knows I'm not trying to cover anything up or dodge his concerns. "I do have some . . . personal stuff going on. It's been a rough couple of weeks," I whisper gruffly. I start nudging at my overgrown cuticles with my thumbs. "I haven't had much of an appetite, but trust me, that's not something that I want. At this point, I'd kind of give anything to actually feel like eating again. You know, *enjoy* a meal."

I look up and we kind of stare at each other, uncomfortable. Miller and I have always been friends, but it suddenly occurs to me that this might be the first serious conversation we've ever had. Usually we're laughing together, not really . . . talking. I feel like he's seeing me naked or something.

And I think it's likely the end of the conversation. Miller is a total sweetheart, and his approaching me like this . . . it was a real stand-out move. But I highly doubt he wants to stand around listening to me boo-hoo about everything that's messed up in my life right now.

I smile at him. "Thanks again for checking in on me. Not too many people would do that. It was supercool."

I open my door again, preparing to get back inside.

"I bet you I could make you a meal you'd enjoy."

I pause, midway inside, and glance over my shoulder at him, eyebrows raised in surprise. "What?"

He shrugs. Finally he's smiling again, that goofy, self-possessed Miller smile. "I bet I could make you a meal you'd enjoy."

"How's that?"

"I make a mean steak. A *mean* steak. And I'm gonna go out on a limb here and guess that you don't allow yourself a whole lot of red meat, but"—he raises an eyebrow in challenge—"if you want to try something different to get out of this slump of yours . . ."

My eyes narrow. "You're offering to cook me dinner?"

"Well, yeah. Provided the idea isn't offensive to Jake or anything."

My fingers curl around the door frame in response to the

internal assault. "The idea won't be offensive to Jake or anything," I assure him quietly, swallowing hard.

I wait until I regain my composure, till I'm sure my eyes are clear, before looking up at him. His offer is so nice. It's the nicest thing I've heard in about . . . forever. The truth is, I'm not at all sure he can deliver on his promise, but these past few minutes, talking to him, have been some of the most tolerable minutes I've had in the past two weeks.

So even if I don't have an appetite, the prospect of having dinner with Miller isn't terrifying. It sounds like a relief. A relief from the isolation and sadness I've been cocooned in.

"You're really offering to make me dinner?" I clarify again.

He nods simply. "If you'd like." He winks. "I feel fairly confident."

I nibble on a fingernail. "I need to get some meat back on my bones. I have look-overs on Monday."

"I'm not sure you're going to pass."

His honesty concurrently floors me and makes me crack up. "Kick a girl while she's down!"

"Hey, I'm just trying to reiterate the necessity of you eating a decent meal." He pulls out his phone and scrolls through his calendar. "No time to waste. You free tomorrow night?"

"Yeah. I'm done at three."

He shrugs. "So come over tomorrow night. I'll fatten you up in time for Monday."

I can't help but laugh again. "You make me sound like a prize heifer."

"Yeah, sure." Miller taps on his phone again. "I'm texting you my address. Come over anytime after six."

“Okay.”

I hear myself officially accept the invitation.

“Cool.” He turns around and saunters off. “See you then, Lil’ Kim.”

I don’t have time to think of a retort before he disappears inside his truck.

chapter 14

I HEAD OVER TO MILLER'S APARTMENT AT 5:59 p.m., because apparently I've been craving social interaction more than I realized. I've changed into a tank top and skinny jeans that now fit loosely, and before I leave, I grab an old, washed-out hoodie and zip it up. I don't really want to catch Miller noticing how thin my arms have gotten.

Because he lives clear across the complex, I decide to drive. I didn't hesitate before accepting his invitation to come over for dinner, but along the way there, random concerns pop into my head.

I should've brought something, I think. *Where are my manners?*

Is Yael going to be there? That would be awkward.

I mean, her attempts to hide her dislike for me are . . . nonexistent.

But it's too late to seriously rethink any of it, so I just keep driving, arriving at his building five minutes later. Theirs is a second-floor apartment, so I climb one flight of stairs, find his door, ring the bell, and wait.

I really wish I had a plate of cookies, a salad, anything . . . in my hands.

But I relax the second Miller opens the door wearing a wide, easy smile. He's recently showered—the back of his collar is damp and he smells like soap, barefoot in jeans and a mossy green T-shirt that brings out some green flecks in his warm brown eyes.

"Welcome, Princess." He ushers me inside.

"Hey." I tuck my hair behind my ear and walk past him. "Thanks again for inviting me."

He nods. "Of course."

I check out the entrance to their apartment, its dark red walls covered in framed black-and-white stills from the various Enchanted Enterprises movies. The decor doesn't surprise me. Yael seems like the artsy type.

"Cool walls," I comment, running my hand reverently over one of the stills. "I love all the EE stuff."

"Right? Would be cooler if they were originals, but the reprints are good, too."

I wander a bit farther, coming to stand in front of the image of Enchanted's Cinderella running from the ball, her lost slipper in her wake, the Prince chasing after her. A pang of sadness hits me. Prince Charming. If only he actually existed.

But I'm quickly distracted when I catch sight of the small kitchen area, its countertops covered in multiple cutting boards, a collection of prep bowls, and a whole lot of sharp knives.

"Whoa." I smile over my shoulder at Miller. "You're not messing around, are you?"

"I do know my way around the kitchen," he admits. "But it's safer to say I excel at the basics as opposed to being a gourmet chef." He walks behind the counter and uses a large fork to flip over some marinating steaks. "Beef is simple. But preparation is key, letting it sit out at room temperature awhile, making a decent marinade. Then all you have to do is toss it on the grill." Miller selects a knife out of the dozen and deftly chops a pile of mushrooms.

I watch him, bemused smile playing on my lips. I don't know too many guys whose kitchen skills extend past popping a DiGiorno in the oven or whipping up ramen in the middle of the night. "I have to say . . . I'm rather impressed with this secret talent of yours."

He glances up to give me a quick smile before returning to his mushroom business.

I . . . well, I linger awkwardly on the other side of the counter. I'm not entirely sure where to sit. It's been a while since I shared personal space with a guy who wasn't my boyfriend. Miller seems to notice and without looking up, nods toward a stool against the far wall. "Grab that if you want. Make yourself comfortable."

I position the stool at the side of the counter so I can watch him work. I'm kind of fascinated.

"My family owns a butcher shop back in Jersey," he tells me. "This isn't a self-taught skill or anything like that. I was just raised with more information about various cuts of beef than you'd ever want to possess." He switches from chopping mushrooms to chopping tomatoes, wiping his hands on a dish towel in between. "My family's very carnivorous. It's all about the meat and potatoes." Miller looks up and grins. "That's really all I know. In case you hadn't noticed."

I smile but shake my head at him. I think his tummy suits him.

"Do you have any allergies or anything?"

"No," I answer.

"Okay, good." He looks at me for a few seconds, hesitant.

"And you're aware the menu is going to far and away exceed your typical daily caloric intake, but that's what we're going for, right?"

I take a deep breath. I consider my skinny arms. "Right."

Miller stares down at the platter bearing two huge steaks, his eyes lighting up. He comes over to me to display them. "Look at these; look at that marbling. It's pretty, Alyssa, it's so *damn* pretty."

I giggle.

"The grill's already warmed up, so I'm going to go throw these on." He gestures toward the patio. "You wanna sit outside with me while they cook?"

I stand. "Yeah, sure."

I follow him out to their small deck, reaching past him to open the sliding door for him. Seconds later, the steaks hit the grill with a loud hissing sound and Miller closes the lid. When he does, I notice the grill is hand painted with an exact rendering of Drako the Dragon. His snout covers the grate, so as smoke escapes, he's literally transformed into a fire-breathing dragon. So cool!

"In the meantime, I'm gonna have a beer," Miller announces as he steps back. "Can I grab you one?" He offers me a few choices, name brands I don't recognize.

"I'm not much of a beer drinker." I shrug. "I guess just pick me out something that goes good with what we're having?"

"The porter. Porters go well with steaks, but they're less malty than stouts." He grins. "It's a vanilla porter, too. Nice and girly for you."

"Thanks." I nod, settling into one of the rickety wicker chairs surrounding the small table. When Miller ducks inside, I study the horizon, exhaling a deep breath, relaxing. The sun is descending in the sky, at the perfect position to still warm my face, and the faintest of breezes is ruffling the palms and carrying the aroma of cooking meat past my nostrils. My stomach rumbles in anticipation.

Then Miller reappears, an open bottle dangling from each hand. "I would've gotten something classier, red wine or whatever, but I didn't want Jake to think I was trying to be a little too smooth in having you over for dinner, right?"

Miller's all smiles, waiting for me to laugh the situation off right along with him, and so I force a smile and nod in his direction so that he'll turn back to the grill and flip the steaks.

But once he does, I find myself staring down at my thighs, conscience protesting.

I'm pretty sure I should force myself to say the words. It's been more than two weeks now. And I haven't said them aloud to anyone but members of my family. I need to start working on accepting reality.

I fiddle with my zipper, running it all the way down. I pull it back up. Run it back down.

"Jake broke up with me," I blurt out.

There. I said it. And I didn't just say it, but I stated the whole truth about it, without sugar coating. I didn't weasel out with "we're no longer together"; I didn't say *we* broke up. I tell Miller what happened. Jake broke up with me.

Miller's surprise is evident. He pauses, with his beer halfway to his mouth. "*What?*"

"Yeah, umm . . ." I go back to fiddling with my zipper. "Those problems I was referencing the other day at the gym. They were of the really ugly breakup variety." I take a long sip of the porter, which isn't half-bad. Sort of tastes like coffee. "So . . ."

"I'm sorry," Miller tells me. He looks me in the eye. "You don't deserve that." He adjusts the temperature on the grill, staring down at the dial when he asks, "Are you okay?"

I consider before answering him. "Yes. No. Maybe somewhere in the middle."

There is a part of me that is tempted to spill more, to throw Jake and Harper under the bus for further evidence of exactly how undeserving I was. But I keep quiet, because there's a bigger part of me that sees no point in it. A part of me that imagines how I'll sound and doesn't want to sound that way to Miller.

But I do want him to understand something. "There are some . . . extenuating circumstances surrounding the whole mess," I tell him. "It's been . . . really hard reaching out to some of my other friends." I smile weakly. "I've kind of been hiding out. So"—I start peeling the beer label off the dark brown bottle—"I really appreciate this. It's nice of you."

He shrugs. "Of course," he says again. Miller clears his throat. He looks at me. "I'm sorry I brought it up."

I wave my hand. "It would've come up eventually." I laugh. "And I know I need to get my appetite back. This is so much better than being the girl eating an entire cheesecake by herself alone in her apartment."

"As luck would have it, I got a cheesecake for dessert. I'll eat more than my fair share, and you won't need to feel the least bit pathetic."

"Thanks, Miller," I say quietly as he spears the steaks and sets them on a clean platter.

He covers them in foil, sets them on the table, and says, "I'll be right back with the rest." He glances around, looks toward the sky. "We should eat out here, right? Tonight is perfect."

"Absolutely," I agree. I start to stand. "Can I help?"

"Nope." He disappears before I have the chance to insist.

My butt falls back into the seat. *I bet Miller treats his girls really well*, I decide. He cooks and he's sweet. Without even really trying to be.

It requires two trips before everything is arranged on the table—several large bowls, our plates and silverware, and fresh beers. Miller plops into the seat across the table and points to each of the dishes. "Potatoes, with onions sautéed in a *lot* of butter. Salad with egg and full-fat ranch dressing. Bread. More butter. Use it."

I point toward a small pitcher filled with a reddish-purple sauce. "What's this?"

"It's a cabernet goat cheese sauce for the steak."

I lean toward it. It smells like I imagine heaven must. I look at the spread again. "Are you trying to fatten me up or give me a coronary?"

"It's just one meal," he retorts, tearing a chunk of bread from the loaf and smearing it with butter. "You'll be all right."

The meal smells too good to even consider any further protest. I pour the wine sauce over my steak, cut off a sizable piece, and pop it in my mouth.

"Oh my God," I moan around it a few seconds later. My eyes practically roll back in my head. "Oh my God." I tilt my chair and stare heavenward. When I can actually speak again, at least with any kind of manners, I tell him, "Hands down, this is the best steak I've ever had."

A huge smile lights his face, and he bows at the waist. "Thank you. Nothin' but the best. I felt it was very important to deliver."

I try everything. The potatoes are almost as good as the meat, and even the salad tastes decadent. Everything tastes rich and full, but then again I can't remember the last time I ate something that was, as he called it, "full fat."

I point toward my plate with the tongs of my fork. "You definitely have a talent, Miller Austin."

"Ah, it's just genetics." Miller finishes chewing and leans back in his chair with his beer. "It's a family business," he tells me, taking a sip. "My great-grandfather started it. I'm the oldest male child, and for a while the expectation was that I would take over the shop. My dad doesn't have the greatest business sense, and the store hasn't been doing so well, and not because of any lack of quality. He just doesn't get the business side of things."

Miller squints toward the horizon. "I was first one in my family to go to college. So there was a lot of pressure for me to put my fancy 'book learning' toward turning things around."

I chew my bite of steak. "But . . ."

"But . . ." He smiles and raises his bottle in the air. "My brother saved my ass. Cheers to him."

"What do you mean?"

He shakes his head. "The butcher shop wasn't my future. At least, it wasn't the future I wanted. My brother is into business, and even though he's only a sophomore at Rutgers, he's already started taking things over, getting them back on track." He shifts in his seat. "And now my plans can get back on track, too."

I spear another bite of steak, circle my hand in the air. "Do tell."

He looks back at me, a little sheepish. "I told you I had an agenda for this summer. And I do." Miller jumps out of his seat and runs inside without further explanation. He returns a moment later with a sketch pad in hand, which he lays down before me.

Curious, I flip it open. My eyes widen. The cartoons it contains are phenomenal, detailed and lifelike and whimsical. They're beautiful. They're huge and fill the pages; they practically jump right off them. A lot of them are renderings of Enchanted characters, but some must be originals, too.

Miller's still hovering over my shoulder, and I glance up at him. "You draw."

"Yes."

I flip a few more pages. "You draw really, really, really well."

This time, his smile splits his cheeks, and he reaches past me to carefully remove the tablet from the cluttered table. "Thank you," he says, tucking it close to his body. "I changed my major from business admin to art and animation a couple of years ago." Miller inhales a deep breath. "Before I knew my brother would be stepping in. All I knew was that I couldn't."

I stare at the cover of his sketchbook. "Good choice!" I tell him. "Your work speaks for itself." I glance at him. "It's your calling, huh?"

He nods, looking way more serious than I'm used to seeing him. "I want to do animation, and . . ." He takes a deep breath. ". . . I'm planning to stay down here and try to get in with the movie studio. You can apply for internships, and I've submitted my application." Miller shakes his head. "I'm not going back to Jersey. I want to stay here, hopefully work for EE."

My eyes widen suddenly. I stare back at the grill. I point. "Did *you* do that?"

He looks down, bashful. "Uh, yeah."

"That's amazing! It's spot on. You should sell those! You'd make a mint."

He chuckles. "Oh, I just did that for the fun of it." Then

Miller's running his fingers over the cover of the sketchbook. "I love this place, Lys." He shakes his head. "I mean, I love my family, too, but I could never get excited about the prospect of meat hanging from hooks. So . . . I hope I get to stay put. I know the brood at home is a little bit bummed, but I hope they also understand."

"The brood?" I ask. "How many of you are there?"

"I have three younger brothers and one baby sister."

"I have three sisters."

He looks at me. He laughs. "That doesn't surprise me." He shakes his head. "Your poor dad."

"At least the cat's a boy."

Now it's my turn to be serious. "My family . . . ," I tell him, meeting his eye. "I think they're probably also a little disappointed about my devotion to the park. My mom especially. She didn't go to college, and I know she came to regret that." When she couldn't help keep us afloat. When finding a job to support a family of five wasn't terribly easy.

"She's always preaching about how us girls need to always be thinking ahead, making smart decisions about our futures." I roll my eyes. "I'm sure she thinks the practical thing to have done would have been to find an internship, in Manhattan or somewhere, if I'm truly going to pursue something as 'frivolous' as fashion merchandising. Instead of just working at a theme park as a full-blown adult. But. I had my reasons."

"Jake?" Miller guesses.

"No," I say, shaking my head rapidly from side to side. "Not just Jake. I love the park, too. The magic that exists here. I'm not ready to give that up." I shrug. "I know I can't play princess forever. That one day I'll outgrow it way before my heart ever does. So right now I just want to stay here." I finish my second beer. I look down, gently kicking the table with my foot. "I mean, we can't all be brain surgeons or physicists or . . . *lawyers*. But maybe I do lack serious aspirations."

"Really?" he asks, sounding genuinely surprised. "What better aspiration is there than finding a job you actually love? A job you actually look forward to going to day in and day out. Personally, I think very few people can say that about their jobs." He lifts his shoulders once. "Hands down, you're the winner in that equation."

I consider. "That's probably the best way to look at it that anyone's ever given me."

Miller flashes me a quick smile. "I'm gonna go put this back inside. Grab another beer."

I sit in the quiet of twilight while he's gone. My hand comes to rest on my belly. It's full, jutting out between my hips. It's also very, very happy with me. Probably because I haven't given a single thought to sucking it in, adjusting my posture, and attempting to press it against my spine. I can't recall the last meal I've eaten where I've been at ease like this, where I haven't been concerned about who I'm with and what kind of impression I'm making. And I am just really, really grateful to have Miller Austin as a friend.

I'm still patting my belly when he returns. "I think your reverse Weight Watchers program is a total success." I refuse the third beer he's brought me. "Although I should probably quit when I'm ahead with the drinks. I'm sure I'll do even better at look-overs tomorrow if I stumble in hungover." I roll my eyes.

"Alyssa." Miller plops unceremoniously into his seat and gives me a "come on, now" look. "Yes, I gave you shit about being a mess at the gym, but you know it would be impossible for you to actually look *bad*. You on a bad day is still better than most girls at their best. C'mon."

"It's an internal thing more than anything else," I say, remembering how sad I look in the mirror nowadays, sad from the inside out. "I need to turn my mood around more than anything else. And . . . I'm having fun, Miller. So thanks."

"Yup."

I stare back into the dark interior of his apartment. "Is Yael working tonight?" I ask suddenly.

"Yeah."

"I don't think she likes me very much."

"She's just prickly. Like a hedgehog. So it's mostly all bark and no bite."

"I think she might be one of the leaders in the gang wars," I tell him.

Miller cracks up. "*What?*" he asks, leaning forward.

I sit up straight. "That scene you walked in on in the cafeteria? That was no joke. And a second before you saved my butt, Yael was totally backing Kelly up. Egging her on, even. I'm telling you." I nod knowingly. "Leader in the gang war."

He laughs so hard he sprays some of his beer.

"Anyway, at the very least, she has totally prejudged me," I conclude.

Miller wipes his mouth with a piece of the paper towel we're using as napkins and raises an eyebrow. "Alyssa, you rolled into a bar with a posse of blond sorority princesses, all wearing *tiaras*. What did you expect?"

"I expect not to be stereotyped!" I insist. Then I have to laugh, too, because it *is* funny, imagining what we must have looked like to Yael.

I stand. "I'm going to go use the bathroom."

There are more cartoon stills in the hallway, and it occurs to me Miller probably provided the decor rather than Yael, as I'd first assumed. In the bathroom itself, there's a huge framed Coldplay concert poster.

I comment on it when I return to the patio, where Miller is now sitting with clean plates and a boxed cheesecake before him. "Nice Coldplay poster you've got in there. You really are a megafan."

"Pretty much."

"I love them, too. Always include them in my top-five-bands list."

"Really . . . ," he drawls slowly, devilish grin dawning. "See, I would have assumed they were *way* too white bread for you, homegirl."

My eyes bulge out, and I make a warning face at him. "I thought we were never going to speak of that again!"

"I never agreed to that."

"You're a pain in the ass. Just give me my damn cheesecake."

Miller laughs. He obliges me, opening the box and cutting a slice, transferring it to my plate, and topping it with a generous portion of whipped cream from the spray can. Then, without any warning, he leans across the table and shoots the spray of sugary foam right into my mouth.

I recover quickly, jumping up on instinct and grabbing the can from his hands, reversing its direction, and pointing it right into his mouth. He's attempting to dodge me, laughing, and I miss my mark, spraying whipped cream all over his beard.

"Holy shit!" he cries as he futilely attempts to wipe it off with a paper towel. It just rubs it in further, and I crack up in victory.

Giving up on his attempt, he pounces without warning, pinning my arm behind my back and wrestling the can away from me. Next thing I know, I feel a nest of whipped cream settling atop my head. My piercing scream echoes in the quiet night.

It's ten minutes before a truce is sought, before we collapse, sticky, tired, and bent over from laughter at the table again to finally eat our dessert. I'm still laughing so hard my bloated stomach hurts, and I'm practically crying.

Somehow I still manage to cram the entire piece of cheesecake in.

When I'm done, I push the plate far, far away. "Roll me home, Miller," I groan. "Just *roll* me home."

We've ended up sitting side by side. I'm beer buzzed and food drunk, and I let my head fall onto his shoulder. It's so easy to let it stay there.

Things were so tense . . . for months . . . I've almost forgotten what it feels like to relax with someone. To laugh. To smile without trying.

These snippets of thoughts spin drunkenly in my head, my eyes falling closed as I rest against Miller.

I don't know how long it is before he nudges me. "You still awake? Or are you in a food coma?"

"Maybe," I murmur.

It takes a physical effort to lift my head, and when I do, I'm surprised to find how close his face is to mine, how my eyes are drawn right to his in the darkness that surrounds us. Miller swallows hard before glancing away, and suddenly I'm aware of the slight awkwardness inherent in the situation.

Platonic relationships are never completely without some degree of awkwardness.

I push my chair back and force myself to stand. "I should probably go. Before I do pass out entirely."

Miller shrugs. He reclines in his seat, his hands coming to rest behind his head. "Stay as long as you'd like."

It would be so easy, to stay longer. But it feels like a slippery slope, being this happy and relaxed. "I should go. I have to get ready for tomorrow. If there's any chance of it going well." I start piling plates, gathering silverware.

"Don't do that." Miller quickly pulls my hand away from the table. "Don't do that."

"This was amazing. I owe you. It's the least I can do."

This time I insist, making several trips inside and back, loading his dishwasher, even washing a few pans in the sink. When I'm wiping down the counter, a Post-it note catches my attention.

We're doing breakfast tomorrow, right?

It's signed with a heart, the letter *Y* next to it.

Huh.

Not very hedgehoggy.

Miller appears inside just as I'm finishing.

I walk over to him slowly and give him a big hug. "This was the best night I've had in two weeks," I tell him. I squeeze his shoulder. "Thanks for that."

His face remains serious. "Well, I've known you for a long time. And you deserve to smile."

And I am smiling as I leave his apartment.

I'm smiling enough to stop at CVS and buy a touch-up kit for my roots and a clay mask treatment for my face so my pores will look as small as possible at look-overs tomorrow.

It's time to start picking myself up, time to get back in princess shape.

After the meal at Miller's apartment, I actually have the energy to start thinking about making that happen.

chapter 15

I SLEEP WITH A PLASTIC WHITENING TRAY in my mouth and an avocado green clay mask on my face, crossing my fingers that the building doesn't catch fire in the middle of the night, forcing a group evacuation with me looking like a monster. Then, the next morning at eight o'clock sharp, I throw my shoulders back and stride into the HR office with a pretend confident smile on my face.

I'm disheartened when Diana does a very obvious double take when she glances up from her computer, her brow furrowing, mouth agape.

My own smile wavers.

"Sorry . . . good morning, Alyssa." She stands, takes a hurried gulp of her coffee, and waves her hand. "Don't mind me; it's been a morning. I had to let Vivienne go." She rolls her eyes heavenward. "A nose ring! A *nose* ring! Please tell me"—Diana walks toward me, iPad in hand—"what self-respecting Ice Queen has a nose ring?"

It's kind of her, trying to cover her initial reaction, but I know. I'm definitely not "first chair" these days.

She barely meets my eye as she snaps the pictures and records all the numbers. It's such a crappy feeling, taking data on all of it, having my hard times calculated, captured, and recorded on various devices. Look-overs feel brutal in a way they haven't before, and I find myself engaging in this visualization exercise where I'm back on Miller's patio, having whipped cream sprayed into my mouth.

When she's done, Diana sets the iPad down and removes her glasses. She looks me in the eye. "Sweetheart, you okay?"

"I'm okay." I stand up straight and try to keep any internal pain from reflecting in my eyes as I meet her gaze. "I promise."

Please don't take this away from me. I can't lose this, too.

She hems and haws. Then, "Okay. I'm clearing you." Diana flashes a small, sad smile. "But go and eat a sundae when you're done today, okay? You're withering away."

If only it were that simple.

Before she can change her mind, I thank her, collect my things in a hurry, and fly out of the HR office.

AS I CHANGE into costume and get into character, I give myself a mental pep talk. I know I passed look-overs only by a hope and a prayer, and I have meet-and-greets on the balcony next. *Wow them*, I say as I secure my hairpiece. *You need to knock this out of the park.* It's not just about convincing HR, but convincing myself, that I haven't lost my touch.

Balcony meet-and-greets are a big deal. More than at any other post, your stats on how many guests you greet are critical, and more than that, it's a super big-deal part of a lot of little girls' visits. Many of the princesses, they're easy to come by, more visible, public personas in the park. Cinderella is "the" coveted meet-and-greet, and even though there are stomach-dropping roller coasters and dazzling shows with two-hour waits, a lot of parents use Line Jumper credits to avoid waiting in line on the balcony of the Palace.

It's time to step it up. Hopefully, high numbers and maybe even a few glowing guest reports shared via the computer system at the exit gates will put Diana's mind at ease.

I dress in the basement of the Palace, and then take a dark, hidden stairwell up several flights to the balcony. Cinderella's throne is on the left side; a second purple velvet divan is on the right side. Cinderella is a constant for balcony meet-and-greets, but a second princess is always present, so guests who endure the wait get two princesses for one. The other princess varies day to day and could be anyone from Sleeping Beauty to the Frog Princess to . . .

I push open the balcony doors and step outside. My stomach falls to my feet.

Shit . . . shit . . . shit . . .

. . . to Beauty.

She's standing in front of the divan, arranging her dress so it lies prettily when she sits down, but she freezes, hovering halfway to her seat, when she sees me, eyes turning panicked.

I freeze as well, muscles turning to lead, unable to take a single step forward as I stare back at her.

I was so busy worrying about look-overs, I'd forgotten that Monday was the start of a new week, meaning new schedules were posted. I'd forgotten what else I was supposed to be worrying about. Now it's too late, and it looks like today I'll be costarring with none other than Harper.

She tries to smile, but it doesn't reach her eyes. I stare back at her evenly, and beneath her thick, creamy foundation, I see her go pale. But Harper doesn't look away, I'll give her that much. Guess she has more of a backbone than Jake does. She lifts her skirt, marches right over to me, and stands before me. "I have something to say to you," she begins determinedly.

I look at her one second longer. I remember how alone she seemed that first night I met her, when she'd been in Florida only for days, when she'd teared up in the girls' apartment.

I felt sorry for you, I think to myself, feeling the lump rise in my throat at my own foolishness. *I hated the idea of you feeling alone.*

I can't do this right now. I need to focus. And right now, it would be a helluva lot easier to be Cinderella than to be Alyssa, anyway. Noticing the attendants unhooking the velvet ropes, glimpsing the first set of eager faces behind the glass doors, I shake my head. "No, you don't," I whisper, plastering a sweet smile on my face before visitors catch any other type of expression lingering there.

The attendants open the doors, and a group of tentative little girls, many of whom cling to their parents' arms, wearing Enchanted tiaras, step forward. "Good morning, darlings!" I call brightly, focusing on them, offering my warmest smile.

Princesses are pretty and lovely, yes. But more important, princesses have dignity. Princesses are resilient.

Harper may have taken one love from me, but no way I'll let her take another. I will not let her ruin this.

So I tune her out, putting 110 percent of my heart into talking to each of my little visitors, asking them questions beyond the perfunctory ones, complimenting their smiles, their manners, their humor. I'm direct and efficient, mindful that there are other, just as eager, children in line behind them, mindful it's part of my job to please everyone. I give good hugs, worrying little about germs or sticky hands or random goo that goes with the territory.

And for a few minutes, I get to forget about her.

But at the end of the first session, we're required to come together, to pose as a pair with the group, to put our arms around each other's waists and smile.

A little blonde turns and looks up. She's missing her front teeth and has a sunburned nose. "I think you're the prettiest," she says.

"No, I think Belle's the prettiest," her sister, a brunette, chimes in.

"Yeah, Belle's prettier!" a chorus agrees.

"Cinderella!" another protests.

The photographer is snapping away, my body is pressed against Harper's, and . . . I want to be just about any other place in the world at that moment.

Stay in character, I coach myself.

"Beauty shines from the inside out," I remind the gaggle at my feet. "And every little girl has her own beauty that comes from her heart. It doesn't look the same, and it's certainly not a contest."

I squeeze the little blond girl's shoulder.

And I'm pretty sure I hear Harper exhale a trembling breath beside me.

I look at the camera and smile.

The group photo wraps, we wave madly at the girls as they're ushered back inside, and for a five-minute break, we find ourselves alone on the balcony. I retreat to my throne, as far from her as I can get on a stone ledge several stories above the ground. But I swear from the corner of my eye, I see her wiping swiftly at hers.

"Was that a dig?" she whisper calls to me.

My head whips around. "What?"

"Beauty shines from the inside out," she repeats. She swallows hard again. "I'm not a bad person, Alyssa. We're not bad people."

It takes a minute to register. "That wasn't about you. I wasn't being snarky. I was just telling those little girls the truth." I look away again.

But the attendants have stepped around the corner to take their break, and since I'm not Rapunzel and don't have yards of hair to toss over the edge and climb down, I can't escape her voice, even though I'm turned away from her.

And Harper is insistent on being heard.

"We were on the same flight down," she says. "Our seats were in the same row."

My head snaps up before I can stop it.

Then, I consider in retrospect. And in retrospect, I don't know why I'm surprised. It's like looking at the lid of a puzzle and suddenly having it make so much more sense how the pieces sitting in a useless pile fit together. When he arrived at my apartment, Jake was superdistracted and said something about "we" when telling me about the taxi ride. The very first time I met Harper, Chrissi mentioned "this guy" Harper met on the way down. And then there was the way both of them had acted when they came face-to-face with each other during their supposed introduction.

"We just . . . we had this really intense conversation. It felt like we'd known each other forever. I was feeling really emotional about some family issues, and I just felt like . . . I don't know, like he had been *put* there."

Something else occurs to me. My lips fall apart, and I say it out loud. "He didn't tell you about me. He didn't tell you he had a girlfriend."

"No. He didn't. Not when we talked, not when he . . . kissed me."

I'm too stunned to speak, and Harper seizes the opportunity to continue.

"Then I met you, and of course found out he did very much have a girlfriend, and I . . . liked you so much. *Like* you so much. He'd obviously lied to me, was a total jerk, and I had no interest in ever seeing him again."

So what changed? I can't help but wonder.

She's quiet for a few seconds. "But then I did. See him again. And again. We kept running into each other, even though I was trying to keep my distance. We kept finding ourselves in these bizarre situations. Like when I passed out, and another time when we ran into each other in the grocery store, and it was like . . . I don't know . . . fate."

I cringe at the word.

"We're both from Philly. We had all these connections. We talked like we'd known each other forever. It was impossible to keep believing he was a jerk, no matter how hard I tried. That connection, the one neither of us really wanted, was still there." Harper pauses. "So we decided, why not be friends? That we could try to be friends. And no one would get hurt. I even tried dating Kellen, hoping something, anything, would help."

All of this was going on behind my back. No wonder Jake was always so distracted. No wonder Harper was so hesitant around me.

"But. That night we all ended up out together, at the restaurant. It was like . . . something was being thrown in our faces. Something we couldn't ignore. Like we were being told we had to step up and face the truth, even if people would end up getting hurt. Because this was *supposed* to happen."

The attendants reappear at the same time I feel my fingernails digging into my skin. I rise, for a second time pushing my own feelings way deep down beneath the surface so I don't hurt the feelings of these little people who have waited so long to get up here.

"None of this was supposed to happen," I reply, and then put my smile back into place. "Things like this are not *supposed* to happen."

I never want them to leave, that second group. I want to sit with them at my feet, commenting, "Oh my, you have the brightest smile I've seen all day!" and "You've traveled all the way from Belgium! How delightful!" I feel bolstered with the little girls at my feet. I envy their innocence; I want to soak it up as long as I can.

The second group photo is no easier than the first, especially when some dad, who clearly thinks he's being really clever, calls out, "Two princesses. Hey. You two ever fight over that one Prince Charming dude?"

I put my hand on my hip and wag a finger at him. "Princesses never quarrel," I quip.

When they depart, desperate to avoid further one-on-one conversation with Harper, it's me who walks around the corner this time, hoping I'm making my point clear, that I don't want to hear any more.

But she follows me, speaking to my back, apparently insisting on getting it all out to her satisfaction. Which is really rather selfish, I think.

"I have one last thing to say, and then I'll be done with it," she promises. I hear her inhale a long stream of air through her nose.

"If I could've controlled things, none of this would have ever happened."

I grit my teeth and wrap my hands around the stone railing. More "beyond their control." More "fate." *Blah, blah, blah.*

"But I am sorry that it did, that this aspect of my life caused someone else pain." She's quiet when she speaks again, the tears in her voice evident. "I know what it feels like to hurt. I know what loss feels like. And I am so, so sorry that this thing inflicted that pain on someone else." She takes a minute to steady herself before finishing. "You were my friend. Without hesitation. Without expecting anything in return. And I am so sad that I hurt you."

My lips start trembling despite how hard I'm working to control them. I feel the tears pooling in the corners of my eyes. I swallow and swallow and swallow, until they recede.

I never thought there was anything she could say to make me soften.

She is being so honest, and her apology actually sounds more heartfelt than anything Jake offered me.

She is on point. She is saying sorry in the right way. And it's hard to hate her, to fully fault her, in that instant.

I glance over my shoulder, almost ready to look at her.

But then she goes and says it.

"I so didn't want any of this, Alyssa. I didn't want a boy; I didn't want a relationship. The last thing I was looking for was some big dramatic love story." She sighs and her shoulders fall. "All I wanted was to get away," she explains wearily.

Her words flip a switch inside my heart. As quickly as I felt myself softening, I feel myself turning bitter again.

She got my fairy tale. She got my fairy tale . . . and she doesn't even want it.

The least she could do is want it. If she was going to go ahead and take it, if all along he was meant to be hers more than mine, the least she could do is want it!

I turn my back again.

"I'm sorry," I hear myself calling to her, my voice cold. "But I can't accept your apology. So please . . . just stop. Just stop and let me get back to work."

It's not like me to say something like that. It's not like me to feel it. Beginning-of-summer Alyssa always accepted apologies. It's called having grace. It's the princess way.

But she didn't even want it.

She acts like this is a burden. To her.

The idea makes me so angry, I can't bring myself to look her in the eye and feign forgiveness. Right now, I just can't.

And even though I've always meant every word I've said to little girls about extending a hand to one another and always showing kindness, I brush past Harper, leaving her to collect herself, by herself, in time for our third group's arrival.

Her attempt at an apology has done nothing to mend any fences, but at least I have my answers. At least I don't have to devote any more attention to wondering. She told me the story, and now I can close the book on both of them.

chapter 16

I'M NOT REALLY SURE WHAT POSSESSES ME to step into the boxing room at the gym. I don't know what the room is *really* called, but that's what I call it, the small exercise studio with red matted floors and retractable rows of long, narrow punching bags hanging from the ceiling. Maybe I'm driven by some lingering resentment from my run-in with Harper. Maybe I've been listening to too much angry rap music.

Whatever the reason, I find myself walking in, the room empty, its lights still off. My motion activates them, and the space is immediately bathed in bright light. I slowly turn in a circle, taking it all in—the mirrors, all that red and black equipment I'm unfamiliar with, the chains hanging from the ceiling. It feels like I'm in a room designed for torture more than anything else.

But I don't leave. Because I'm overcome by my desire to punch one of those big bags. *Hard.*

Taking a quick look over my shoulder to make sure no one's watching, I stride over to the bag at the end of the row. I curl my hand into a fist, thinking it'll be just like the movies, satisfying and gratifying and effortless. My hand meets the bag with a dull thud, and I wince, the word *ow* forming silently on my lips. Yeah, it's not like that at all. It's like punching a brick wall, and it *hurts.* Pain vibrates through my fingers and into my wrist. And the damn thing doesn't even budge.

I shake my hand out and try again. And again, and again, and again. There's a burgeoning frustration in my gut that's fueling my punches, despite the pain, but no matter how hard I hit it, the bag won't move.

The frustration turns to anger. It's making me mad, that I have no power or control over this stupid inanimate object, that no matter how hard I try I can't make anything happen, and before I realize what's happening, I've resorted to wrapping my arms around it, pressing my forehead against the foul-smelling rubber, and pounding the crap out of it in small little bursts from both fists while grunting and cursing.

He has to shout for me to hear him. "What the hell are you doing?"

I spin around, see Miller in the doorway, and lose my balance, collapsing against the bag, which is as unyielding as ever. My chest is heaving uncontrollably, and I bend over in a useless attempt to catch my breath. Eventually I manage to stand up. And make a face at him. "Do you have some sensor that allows you to catch me at my absolute most humiliating moments?" I have to ask.

"Actually," he says, glancing over his shoulder, "this time it wasn't just me. You were attracting quite the crowd, because a class is about to start across the hall. I scared them off, though."

I cringe, feeling my cheeks heat up. I must've looked like a crazy person.

"So, seriously, what the hell are you doing?"

I look back at the bag. I hate it. "I just wanted to . . . move the damn bag," I tell him, throwing my hand in the air. "It's refusing." I give it a little kick for good measure. Still nothing.

Miller is very evidently biting his lip to keep from laughing at me. But he does manage to contain it. "Okay, well, first thing," he tells me, coming into the room, walking to the corner, and selecting a pair of pink-and-black gloves with the Everlast logo on them from the shelf, "you need these." He holds them up, then comes over to me. "And these ones are pretty and pink." Miller raises one eyebrow. "Otherwise, at this rate, you're going to break your hand, okay?"

"Right. I forgot that part." I take the gloves from his outstretched hands.

A hint of a smile plays on his lips. He ducks his head to hide it, reaching past me to grab a roll of something that looks like colorful gauze. "You might as well wrap your wrists while you're at it."

"Seriously?" My brow furrows. "I just wanted to throw, like, one punch."

Miller looks at me and raises an eyebrow. "If you're gonna do it, do it right. Plus"—he glances back toward my nemesis—"that looked like more than one punch." He gently taps the back of my right wrist with two fingers. "I'll do it for you. Put your hands out."

I put the gloves on the ground and extend both arms, and Miller snorts, then pantomimes the way my hands are dangling limply from my wrists. "Not like that." He extends his hands so they're lying flat and spreads his fingers. "Like you mean business. C'mon."

I comply and he nods, satisfied. "Better." He hooks the end loop of the wrap around my right thumb and circles the wrap around my wrist about three times. Then he pauses, gently sliding his thumb inside the wrapping, running it back and forth across the underside of my wrist, right where someone would take my pulse. "Not too tight, is it?"

It takes me a second to answer him, because I'm startled by the unexpected intimacy of the subtle motion of the pad of his thumb tickling my skin. "No. Don't think so."

Miller continues, concentration focused on my hand, slowly and carefully wrapping the tape around my thumb and then winding it around each of my fingers. Meanwhile, he coaches me. "You've gotta put your body behind your movements, too. You were only using your arms, and your stance was all wrong. You were way too close to the bag to get any momentum."

He finishes with my fingers, then doubles back to my hand, taking the tape in diagonal paths until he reaches the end of the roll and secures the Velcro tab near my wrist. He taps the back of my left hand. "Next up."

The process is repeated, in silence this time, and I'm hyperaware of his breathing as he stands within my personal space, head lowered as he wraps my hand, which lies in his. In turn, I become aware of my own breathing, which automatically starts to sync up with his. A giggle makes my torso tremble, and Miller glances up, his eyes going from focused to amused. "What's up?"

"Nothing." I hold the finished product up for examination. "I'm officially a mummy."

"Go like this," he instructs, tightening his hands into fists and then releasing them. "Feel okay? Not too tight or like it's falling off?"

"I think we're good."

"Good stuff." He bends to retrieve my gloves and slides them on my hands. Then Miller gestures for me to step back and away from the bag, coming around behind me and guiding my hips into proper position. Just like that, his breath is back in my ear. "Are you a lefty or a righty?"

"Righty."

"Then you're going to want to throw the first punch with your left hand." He quickly tugs on a pair of black gloves and models the correct ready position. "Throw the punch in a direct line from your chin. And keep your hand relaxed until just before you make contact, then make sure it's fully clenched."

Miller moves in front of the next punching bag in the row and demonstrates the proper technique, throwing three punches, making his bag swing. He nods toward me. "Now try."

I bring my fists up to my chin. It's silly, but just wearing the tape and the gloves makes me feel more capable, and I concentrate on the bag before me with renewed focus and determination. I think through everything Miller told me and put my weight behind my movements as I step forward and extend my arm.

The bag moves half an inch.

"Better," he tells me.

I throw a few more punches, stepping back each time, eyeing up the bag. Even though my hands feel ten pounds heavier, I'm making more headway.

I look over at him and smile. "Yeah, it hurts a heck of a lot less this way," I admit.

He chuckles, then crosses his arms over his chest, gloves still on. "I have to ask, though . . . why all the heavy equipment? I thought you were one of the elliptical girls."

"I was. I am." I shrug and look down at the ground. "I just wanted to."

Then I chew on my lip, studying the red mat beneath my feet. "He called me a butterfly," I murmur.

"What?"

I look up and meet Miller's eye. "He called me a butterfly. Jake. He said he never thought our relationship would go past last summer. But that I was too delicate, this happy-go-lucky *butterfly* that he couldn't stand to crush. So he led me on for an entire year instead."

Miller cracks up. He laughs and laughs, shaking his head as he pulls his gloves off. "I'm sorry. Jake and I always got along okay, but . . . that's the lamest breakup line I've ever heard. Man."

"It didn't feel lame. It felt really hurtful." I stare at my reflection in the mirrored wall. "It made me feel so weak," I admit. "I guess I wanted to feel . . . stronger, but this bag is mocking me. Proving his damn point."

Miller slowly walks back over. He gives me a small smile and easily closes his hand around my bicep. "Well, you are kind of weak. You're skinny-girl weak, but that's something that can be fixed." He raises an eyebrow in challenge.

I look at him in question.

"They have an awesome power hour class in this studio. Friday mornings. You should come."

The idea makes me laugh out loud. "I didn't really last three minutes with the bag. I'm not gonna last an hour."

Miller shrugs. "Eh, maybe not at first. But everyone works at their own level and there's no pressure. I'll save the pretty pink gloves for you if you come."

I shake my head. "It's not for me."

"Too much of a butterfly?" I glare at him, but he's unfazed. "Come on. Prove him wrong. Just show up."

I do kind of like the idea of proving Jake wrong. So a minute later, I hear myself saying, "I'll think about it."

"Hey, if you come to class, I'll start calling you Laila Ali instead of Lil' Kim."

I giggle. "That alone might make it worth it."

Miller glances toward the hallway. "I gotta go." He points at me. "Friday morning, okay?"

"I said I'll *think* about it."

AND I DO, think about it, briefly, but by Thursday night, the idea seems silly again. Riding home on the last shuttle after a full day being Cinderella, I shake my head. I stare down at my glittery, pale pink manicure. I'm a princess, not a fighter.

Then I see the gift bag in the hall, sitting atop my doormat. The bag is bright pink and nondescript and doesn't have a card, but I know at once that the girls down the hall have resumed their gifting. I remove the nest of black tissue paper and pull out a T-shirt. Holding it before me, I smile wryly. This pick has Rose written all over it.

It's an off-the-shoulder gray T-shirt, and looks about two sizes too big. Black block letters run across the front. CHIN UP, PRINCESS, OR THE CROWN SLIPS.

I stare at the message and can't help but think it's some kind of omen. It's the perfect shirt to wear to the boxing class tomorrow morning. Someone, or something, is encouraging me to go. And while I have a love-hate relationship with the idea of fate these days, I have to admit it: I'm inspired to follow the sign.

So the next morning at six o'clock I pull the baggy T-shirt overhead and then tug on a pair of tight black shorts, my sneakers, and a headband. I get to the boxing room fifteen minutes early so I don't have to walk into a full room of onlookers. Still, as the first few attendees saunter in, long before class even starts, already I feel silly. Some of the guys look like Olympic athletes. Most of the girls have visible biceps and look like they would cream me in any type of real fight. I really, really hope there's none of that. Miller didn't say.

Speaking of . . . where is he?

He shows at the last minute, with Yael in his wake, which surprises and intimidates me. Her face says it all, and she thinks my being here is a joke. She rolls her eyes when she reads my shirt and makes no attempt to hide it. She busies herself wrapping her own wrists.

But Miller, to his credit, doesn't look surprised. He just gets me my pink gloves, as promised, and helps me get my hands ready, although the process is more rushed this time than last. "You need these during warm-up, too," he explains simply before returning to the only free space left in the room, beside Yael.

"All right, people," the instructor, Jarred, announces, stretching his quads and then clapping a few times. "Let's do this."

The hour that follows is possibly the most grueling of my life. By the end of the warm-up, which consists of jogging in place, jumping rope, and high kicks, I'm already past the point of being out of breath. Directly in front of me, Jarred looks like a machine, his body a walking anatomy chart of the muscular system, his long dreads flying wildly as he leaps into the air or throws punches.

The bag work that follows provides little relief. We're allowed only short breaks between combinations so that our heart rates stay up. The combinations, even the simplest, make me feel unco-ordinated and silly, and no matter how hard I try, I can't get my limbs to coordinate. But Jarred is a patient teacher, and he doesn't let me feel like an idiot. Or give up.

By the time he retracts the rows of bags again, my limbs are shaking visibly and I'm sure class must be over. Why oh why isn't there a clock in this room? As it turns out, class *isn't* over, not at all, and the rigorous mat work that follows nearly breaks me. There are endless sequences of crunches and push-ups, and something really, really god-awful called a burpee.

I struggle. I falter several times, nearly face planting on my mat.

Jarred drops down beside me and whispers to me. "There's a difference between pain and effort, Alyssa. Effort is about your brain telling you you want to stop. Pain is your body telling you you *should* stop. We practice effort, not pain, in this class. Listen to your body."

I know, beyond the shadow of any doubt, that my body has crossed the threshold from putting forth effort into experiencing pain. But no one else in the class has stopped, not even Yael, who doesn't *appear* to be all that fit, and I refuse to be the only one.

Finally . . . mercifully . . . blessedly, Jarred announces, "That's all she wrote, folks," and we collectively collapse on the mat for cooldown and stretching.

My heart pounds furiously. My lungs beg for air. My body is alive and *working*.

Ten minutes later, class is over. I literally crawl over to the side of the room and find my water bottle again. I down what's left in it.

Miller appears before me a moment later, looking sweaty and disheveled. He doesn't make a big deal out of my finishing. He just brings his gloved hand down to mine and gives me a pound.

"Think you'll come back next week?" he asks, wiping his forehead on his shoulder.

I wait to see if I can physically stand, which I can, after some effort, before answering him. "It may take me that long to recover. But . . . I'd consider it."

I've never left the workout center the way I'll walk out today. It's the first time I feel like I've actually accomplished something other than crossing my workout off my daily to-do list. I've worked my body a million times without ever feeling like I've actually engaged it. Today, I feel like I've run a marathon. No. I feel like I've completed a freakin' Ironman. And I'm pretty proud of myself.

Miller smiles. "Good. Hope you do."

He starts walking back toward Yael, who is holding his sweatshirt for him, but he turns and looks at me one last time before he goes. He nods toward my torso. "I like your shirt. It suits you."

Miller holds my gaze a second longer, and suddenly it occurs to me that maybe it wasn't Rose who left it outside my door, after all.

chapter 17

THE FOLLOWING WEEK, I TEXT MILLER AHEAD of time to let him know that I'll be making it back to boxing class. He offers to pick me up on the way, and remembering how useless my legs were after my first class, I accept immediately.

Miller lingers in the hall after class, which irritatingly didn't feel even the slightest bit easier than my first class. He's talking to a friend, something about an extra Coldplay ticket, and I'm mentally begging him to hurry up because I'm about to collapse.

Finally we're on the way to his truck. He stops and snaps, turning to me. "Hey, you like Coldplay. We have an extra ticket because one of my buddies can't go now. You want it?"

I struggle to climb into the cab. "When for?"

"The last Wednesday in July. July twenty-something."

I don't know why I asked. My social calendar is free and clear these days. "Umm, yeah. That's pretty much too good an offer to pass up."

I'm seated beside him in the cab of his truck, and I think how it would have been a tight squeeze for three people.

"Where is Yael today, anyway?"

"She picked up an opening shift at the park. Apparently she was out of bed and on her way without my even hearing her."

Miller stops at a red light at the central downtown intersection and glances over at me. "Whatcha up to this weekend? Rejoicing at the day off like everyone else?"

He's referencing the fact that tomorrow the park is technically closed for the huge, annual I Bleed Enchanted event. The central feature of the day is a half and full marathon and blood bank that raises funds and donations for the Red Cross. The Red Cross is the charity closest to the heart of Martin E. Everly, the founder and CEO of Enchanted Enterprises.

"A Saturday off is a rare gem around here." I shrug. "But I'll probably join the finish line contingency at some point. It was cool last year."

It's tradition for cast members to man the celebration tent at the race's end point, handing out balloons, medals, and water bottles bearing the park's emblem on their labels.

"Me too." He grins. "It's a good opportunity to break out my cheering skills one last time."

"I'll probably donate, too," I tell him. "The artistic team always comes up with the cutest tank tops to hand out at the blood bank."

This makes him laugh, even though I wasn't really kidding.

He parks in front of my building. "So I'll look for you at the finish line tomorrow." He nods toward the apartments. "Are you going over with Chrissi and the gang?"

"No," I answer succinctly, glancing down at my lap.

Miller's looking at me. "What's up with that?"

"Nothing, really." I shrug. "I just haven't talked to any of them in a while."

I can't tell him why. Well, I can't tell him why without bringing Harper's name into the breakup mess.

Thankfully, Miller doesn't press the issue. "All right. Well . . . I'll keep an eye out for you."

"Thanks for the ride," I tell him as I hobble out of his truck. *Ow.* "I'll see you then."

SATURDAY MORNING DAWNS the perfect day for a run. We're getting a break from the humidity; there's cloud cover and a hint of a breeze. It will be hot by early afternoon, but most of the runners will have finished long before then.

There's a festive feeling surrounding the event that extends all the way to the Lakeside complex, reminiscent of homecoming or big game days back at Coral State. The shuttle lines are long early, and people settle for standing room between the aisles in order to get to the park as quickly as possible.

When the shuttle arrives at the Enchanted Dominion, the initial impression is that a theme park has sprung up outside a theme park. There are striped tents and food trucks, people running around in costume, bounce houses, balloon artists, clowns on stilts, and a stage for speeches and performances. Lots of big-name celebrities have been Red Cross ambassadors over the years—the Manning brothers, Demi Lovato, Penn Badgley, and Miley Cyrus—and there's always excitement surrounding which celebrities will be spotted, usually with their families in tow, inside the park on event day.

I Bleed Enchanted is an absolute park-size party, like none I've ever seen since the park celebrated its fifteenth anniversary. It's noisy and chaotic, with blasts from bullhorns, staticky announcements, screams from the rides, and plentiful laughter and music. It's one of my favorite days of the year, and my spirits are high as I bounce toward the park entrance, even if I'm arriving solo this year.

And it doesn't look like much will change about my solo status. As I approach the entrance and begin pushing my way through the masses toward the finish line, I decide there's no way I'm going to find Miller. The park is absolutely swarming with people, a group as loud and frantic and busy as an actual hive of bees.

On my way, I do, however, run smack into Rose. Literally, our shoulders bump, and when she looks over her shoulder to offer a quick apology she stops in her tracks and instantly causes a ten-person pileup.

Before I can disappear into the masses, I feel her hand closing around my forearm and she drags me out of harm's way, right into a cluster of artistically trimmed shrubs.

"Hey, stranger." She looks at me pointedly. "Long time no see."

"Hey, Rose." I glance toward her shirt, a gauzy white top printed with vines and tea roses. "Your shirt is sweet. Does it have a name?"

I knew it. She can't resist. "Yes," she tells me, tossing her hair over her shoulder. "The *rose* less traveled."

I grin. "*Très* apropos."

She doesn't smile back. "Nice try. But you're not going to dodge this conversation."

I hem. I haw. I look at the ground. Finally I sigh. "It's *awkward*," I admit. "The whole situation . . . it's just too awkward."

"Get past it," she tells me bluntly. "The summer's more than half over, and to hell if I'm going to let you ignore us for the rest of it. We're friends," she reminds me. "Chrissi's a wreck. She thinks you're mad at her."

I look away, feeling guilty for the first time about my behavior toward the girls. "I'm not mad. And I wasn't ignoring you. I just . . . wasn't ready to be cheered up."

"Next time I call you, answer the damn phone."

"Okay." I nod. "I will."

She reaches out, her pinkie finger raised. "Pinkie promise."

I giggle. "You don't have to make me pinkie promise."

"Do it," she orders.

I roll my eyes and oblige her, intertwining my finger with hers. "I pinkie promise that I will pick up the phone next time you call."

"Good. I gotta go." She wags her finger at me before moving on. "Answer your phone!"

She disappears into the madness in seconds, and I continue on my course toward the cast member tent. People are spilling out of it—hundreds of employees are on-site—and again I consider how unlikely it will be that Miller and I are here in the same area at the same time. Then two seconds later I find him, front and center, holding a bullhorn.

"Get up here!" he bellows over the crowd when he spots me. "I was saving a spot for you."

Smiling, I grab a bunch of rainbow-colored balloons from the helium tank and push my way through the bodies to Miller.

And no wonder he was able to secure the spot he did. His energy is as high as I've ever seen it, and his enthusiasm never fades. He cheers the loudest when runners cross the line. He approaches those who seemed to struggle the most in the homestretch, putting a hand on their backs and personally congratulating them. He makes a point of thanking active military personnel for their service.

Sometimes I have to stop and watch him. His excitement is

so genuine, and it's impressive. It's impossible not to get caught up in his spirit. A few runners even move me to tears with their tears, at what an accomplishment this is for them, or the person they're running in memory of, a photo on their shirts.

The finish line of the marathon is alive with triumph and joy and emotion. I love being a part of it, love that it's one more wonderful aspect of being a cast member at the Enchanted Dominion.

Around ten forty-five, in the middle of the pack, a runner crossing the finish line catches my attention. Hands poised midclap, they fall still, and the smile slides off my face.

It's Harper. I take a step back, even though there's little chance of her seeing me anyway, as caught up as she is in finishing. She collapses to her knees in the soft grass and pumps her hands in the air as someone comes over and places a medal around her neck. It's one of the specially designed ones, honoring EE employees who actively participate in the marathon.

I rub my throat, trying to swallow back the bitter taste in my mouth. Harper just successfully completed a marathon, and I'm merely standing on the sidelines, playing cheerleader. I was so proud to be here, had been feeling so proud about finishing my stupid boxing classes, and now . . .

Insult is promptly added to injury. As soon as she gets back on her feet, Jake appears. He wraps her up in a hug, lifting her off the ground.

I watch them, for no other reason than it's impossible to turn away. It's numbing, watching them, the idea that I *ever* felt like I knew either one of them.

They're moving on. They're happy. I was merely a bump in the road to their future together.

I find myself backpedaling, away from the finish line, the

cheers, the time clock. I work my way to the outskirts of the crowd and lean against a low wall. But I can't get far enough away, and I still see them.

Miller appears in my peripheral vision a few moments later. He's bounding toward me, still pumped, huge smile on his face. It falters as soon as he sees the look on mine.

"Whoa, what's up, Ali?" he asks me. "Where'd your spirit go?"

I'm not in the mood to joke around. I point toward Jake and Harper. "It went right over there."

If they're not hiding it anymore, then I'm not going to hide it for them.

Jake bends down to kiss Harper.

Miller seems to pale a bit. "Holy shit," he mutters. He looks at me worriedly. "Did you know about that? Or . . ."

I nod quickly. "That's the reason he broke up with me. Her. But . . . I wasn't really expecting to see that today." I shrug. "Really, it's nothing more than the final nail, seeing them together, but still"—I screw my face up—"not my idea of a good time."

Miller doesn't hesitate. "Do you want to go?"

If I stay, running into them, directly, seems almost inevitable. They, too, have access to the cast-only areas.

"Yes," I decide at once.

Miller nods, drops his bullhorn on a table, and looks around. He takes my hand and leads me through the crowded pavilion to an open area of the parking lot beyond it. He drops my hand when we've cleared the crowd, and we walk in silence around the perimeter of the lot until we've looped back to the shuttle depot, the huge, red blood bank tent set up beside it.

Miller looks hesitant as he broaches the subject. "Did you still want to donate or . . . just bail?"

I stare at the tent for a long minute. Honestly, I just want to get out of there.

But man, I hate feeling weak these days. Leaving feels like such a cop-out.

Chin up, Princess, or the crown slips.

I actually lift my chin. I came here with the intent to donate, and I still should.

I make a face at Miller. "Oh, why not? I just had my heart crushed . . . the blood should be plentiful."

"And you need to get your shirt."

"Right. I do need my shirt. They *are* in fact supercute this year."

I lead the way into the tent, where we stand in line to register and show ID, and move on to answer some questions about our medical and travel histories and have our pulse and temperature taken. After some volunteers take a small blood sample to test our hemoglobin levels, we're directed to semicomfortable chairs for the actual donation. The insertion of the needle isn't that bad—just a quick prick—and then we're told to relax for about ten minutes until they've collected what they need.

Miller and I sit side by side during the draw, lost in our own thoughts, until the nurses reappear to remove the needles and take away the full blood bags. I never like to watch that part. One nurse places a piece of gauze over the red spot on my arm and tells me to hold it in place. I do as she says, collapsing against the chair back and applying pressure with my fingers.

"You wanna grab some lunch when we get out of here?" Miller asks. He deftly removes the gauze and slaps a small Band-Aid on to his arm.

"Yeah, sure."

"You look worn out," he says with a smile. "You should eat something so you don't pass out."

I exhale slowly. "Not sure if it's so much the blood donation or . . ."

He scoots his chair over and slings an arm over my shoulder. "You'll be okay," he says.

I allow myself to feel comforted, for a few seconds, before I feel the need to refocus. To stop wallowing and redirect.

"You were a real great cheerleader out there," I tell him, standing up. "I'm sorry I pulled you away."

Miller rises, too. "It's cool. I was there for a few hours before you showed up, anyway." He smirks at me. "The cheering comes naturally. You do know I actually won the UCA National Mascot Championship this year?"

I stop in my tracks. "Shut up."

"I'm serious. I was down here, in Daytona, in January for the competition. The cheerleading squad as a whole placed second. But in the mascot competition? I took top honors."

I slap his forearm. "Why didn't you let me know you were down here in January? I wouldn't have missed *that*." I consider the missed opportunity of seeing Miller run around in front of thousands in a giant chicken costume. "Man, I am *bummed*."

"No worries. There's video evidence, obviously."

"Can I watch it? I have to know what it takes to win a national giant chicken award. Is it on YouTube?"

"No need for YouTube. I have the DVD at my apartment. Come over now." He shrugs. "We can just order pizza instead of going out."

* * *

FORTY-FIVE MINUTES LATER I'm back at Miller's apartment and a pizza's on its way. I'm sitting on his couch, staring at his television screen in fascination. The segment is from ESPN, and I recognize the commentator hosting the championship. The crowds fill a huge stadium, divided into segments by school colors, and the energy is palpable.

Then Miller's front and center, turning backflips and leaping from trampolines, all while dressed in a six-foot-tall bird costume with a huge plumage behind him.

"OMG," I proclaim, accepting a cold bottle of water from Miller, who comes to sit down beside me. "This is no joke. I can't believe that's *you*."

"Cheerleading is in fact a sport," he jokes. "And YouDee has a very proud history. He's been a national champion several times over and is only one of seven college mascots inducted into the Mascot Hall of Fame."

"The Mascot Hall of Fame?"

He provides no further explanation. "Several guys who have been YouDee went on to be mascots for NFL teams. The guy who turned over the feathers to me is now Swoop for the Philadelphia Eagles."

I giggle. "You didn't share that aspiration?"

"Yeah, no," he says, taking a drink from his water bottle. "Even I knew that was taking it a bit too far." He rolls his eyes. "My parents would've been happy, though. I would've been just across the bridge instead of a coastline away."

He glances at his watch, which I notice is authentic Enchanted gear, with a hand drawing of Drako on its face. "Speaking of . . . shit." Reaching below the coffee table, he produces an iPad. "I'm supposed to FaceTime with them in about five minutes. It's my brother's birthday."

I start to stand. "Should I step out or something?"

Miller waves the idea off. "No, stay. It's all good. Trust me, you'll probably get a kick out of them."

He's right, and the members of Miller's family are every bit as entertaining as he is. They're loud and boisterous, all talking over one another and physically pushing into the frame. His mom inadvertently disconnects the call three times, proclaiming, "I hate technology!" each time she reappears.

His brothers are smaller, nonbearded versions of Miller who tumble off the couches and pummel one another between snippets of conversation.

"Wait, Ry wants to talk to you before you hang up!" his mother calls when Miller starts saying good-byes.

"Who's Ry?" I whisper.

"Ryder. She's my little sister. She's eight." He grins. "And now that you've seen my brothers, you'll understand why she's the way she is."

"How is she?"

"Tomboy and a half."

Seconds later, a fierce-looking, unsmiling little girl appears on the screen. At first I don't know what to make out of her expression, but then I realize she's in costume, dressed as Rey from the latest Star Wars movie. She's even brandishing a lightsaber.

"Hi, Ry!" Miller greets the screen with a friendly wave. He blows her a kiss. Then he gestures toward me with his thumb. "This is my friend Alyssa."

She doesn't bother to greet me. She just points the lightsaber at the screen.

"I like your costume, Ryder," I tell her, leaning toward the screen. "Very cool. Are you coming from a party?"

"No," she answers me blankly.

"She wears that every day," Miller says. He looks back at the screen. "Alyssa likes to dress up, too," he tells his sister. "She's Cinderella at the park."

I smile, waiting for the inevitable oohing and aahing that will follow.

"Princesses SUCK!" Ryder shouts. She swings her lightsaber over her head and down and across in a fierce slashing motion. "Prepare to suffer, Princess!"

I scoot away, somewhat concerned, and Miller can barely end the conversation his face is so red from trying not to laugh at my reaction.

When he finally says good-bye, I look over at him, wide-eyed. "I never thought I'd say this about a little girl . . . ," I begin slowly, ". . . but oh my God. I think your sister might be my mortal enemy!"

Miller, who was finishing off his water, starts laughing so hard I think he's choking.

And I can't do anything but join in. I start laughing so hard my sides hurt and I collapse against the arm of the couch. My abs are still sore from yesterday's class, and it *really* hurts.

"I think she just tried to *smite* me with a lightsaber!"

This only makes him laugh harder.

I'm laughing so hard, so long, that I have no idea when it is that he stops laughing, until I look over and catch him regarding me seriously. I sit up straight and wipe my eyes. "What?"

"Nothing. It's good to see you laughing again." He pauses. "It sucks when you're sad."

"Well, duh. Being sad *sucks.*"

"No. I mean it sucks when *you're* sad." Miller scratches at his beard. "Admittedly, I was fairly wasted that night I ran into you with your sorority sisters. But I *did* have a point."

"A point about what?"

"When I told you you're like them but you're not."

He stares at the blank TV screen; he taps his fingers on his thighs.

"You have this . . . light about you, all right? You're nice. Below the surface, you're nice." He shakes his head. "Most girls, especially ones who look like you do, it's not like that."

I glance down, embarrassed at the compliment.

"So from a third party's perspective? It'd be a damn shame to see that . . . I don't know . . . go out. A little moping, that's understandable. But . . ." He struggles, at a loss for words. "It's just good to see you laughing again."

The doorbell rings, and Miller stands to go retrieve our pizza.

chapter 18

ROSE WASTES NO TIME IN CASHING IN ON my promise. She texts me at eight o'clock the next morning.

Are u working today?

I'm still lying in bed as I text her back. *I have to be in at 1:30.*

Prrrfect. She includes three cat-with-heart-eyes emoticons. *We'll stop by to pick you up in an hour.*

I smile and shake my head. She's sweet, trying to leave it at that, but . . . I dial her number.

"Hello?"

"I'm going to need a *few* more details."

"Chrissi, Camila, and I are working today. They need to start prepping by noon, and I'm in at two. So before that, we're crashing breakfast at the Diamond Palace and stopping by wardrobe for a preliminary search. The Character Ball is only a couple weeks away. Come with us."

I hesitate. The Character Ball means little to me anymore, but there's no way I'm passing up a meal at the Palace. Rose was probably well aware of this in making her invite. *Sneaky, that one.*

But ultimately, a pinkie promise is a pinkie promise, and I'm still upset that Chrissi's been thinking I'm mad at her. And even though I've been avoiding them . . . I'm glad they still think of me as the fourth member of their party.

"Okay," I agree. "I'll be ready in an hour."

"Yes, I know," Rose says coolly, before hanging up.

Because we're having breakfast at the Palace, I dress in a sundress and cardigan before packing my bag of things I'll need for my afternoon shift. Then I wait for the girls.

When my doorbell rings a few minutes later and I open it to reveal the twins, at first glance I realize how much I've missed them, this incongruous pair. Camila's hair is parted down the middle, her face is free of makeup, and she's wearing a drab green dress. Rose is wearing a wild floral-print sundress. She has perfectly painted red lips, and her hair is arranged into two curly pigtails. Rose's look screams for attention, while Camila's begs to fade into the background. I smile widely. "Morning, sisters. Thanks for letting me crash with you. Where's Chrissi?"

"I'm right here!" I hear her before I see her, and then she's pushing her way between Rose and Camila, using her elbows, trying to reach me. "I mean, I know I'm short, but I didn't realize I was completely invisible." She raises her eyebrow; it gets lost beneath her messy bangs.

Then she wraps her arms around me in a vise grip. "Thank you for coming out." She steps back and squeezes my hand, staring at me intently. "We *miss* you."

Rose links her elbow through mine and hauls me out of the apartment. "Yes. More on that later. For now, we've got to jet. We have a nine forty-five reservation. If we're late, you know they're not letting us in."

We hurry to the shuttle, and upon arriving at the gates hurry some more, down the main corridor, and over the drawbridge to the entrance of the Palace.

As Rose hands the hostess her computerized employee card to scan, I ask in a hopeful voice, "Did you get the Mermaid Cove? That's the only pod I haven't eaten in yet."

"No, we're in Aladdin's Dunes," Camila answers.

"I heard it's the best food," her sister adds.

The hostess leads us inside, and as we pass the aquariums, Camila sort of shudders. "I'm glad we didn't end up in there," she comments. "It's way too early for sushi, in my opinion."

"It's not all sushi. They come up with all these supercool presentations for the kids," I inform her. "I looked at pictures online. Like, they carve grapefruits into octopuses and make pancakes shaped like starfish. And they make these jelly doughnuts rolled in coconut that they shape like sushi rolls and slice into bite-size doughnuts!"

She doesn't seem to get my enthusiasm for doughnut sushi.

Neither does her sister. "That's what you do in your spare time?"

I shrug. "So?"

"So we let you hide out in your apartment way too long."

After we're led to the large tented section that belongs to Aladdin, we're encouraged to sit on the oversize damask pillows that serve as chairs around the low table that sits in the middle of them. Our server immediately pours us cups of rich Turkish coffee and presents a platter of fruits, sugared dates, and nuts.

I glance around the room, and my heart smiles at the sight of all the little girls dressed in full princess regalia, too excited about being here to actually eat their breakfasts. I love these rare opportunities to visit the park as a guest and watch the magic unfold through the little princesses' eyes.

"Thanks again for the invite," I say as I smooth a colorful silk napkin over my lap.

"You're allowed a party of four, so of course," Rose answers. She glances at her sister. "I'm sure Camila's relieved you accepted. Otherwise, I was going to make her invite her 'friend.'"

"Camila has a 'friend'?"

I've missed a *lot*.

"God, Rose," Camila huffs, slamming her small porcelain coffee cup down. "It's nothing. I simply like practicing my Mandarin with him. He's only here on a work visa. He'll be gone at the end of the summer, as will I, and"—she shrugs—"there's absolutely no sense in thinking about it beyond that."

"You really are a trip," her sister says. "I can't believe spending the summer here hasn't instilled the smallest bit of romance in you."

"Man plus woman does not automatically equal romance," she states firmly. "And besides . . ." She trails off, giving her sister a look that I think is *supposed* to be subtle.

I stare down at the fruit platter. "Oh, just go ahead and say it. Not every story that goes down here ends in happily ever after."

"Yes, let's talk about that," Rose says, pouncing on the opportunity. She draws her hands together, tenting her fingers.

"Oh, do we have to?" Chrissi asks nervously, fingering the edge of her fringed napkin.

"Yes." Rose nods decisively. "We need to clear the air about all of this. So we don't have to keep dancing around the subject." She narrows her eyes at me. "Please explain to us how what happened with Jake translated into what felt like a breakup with *us*."

I inhale a sharp breath at her bluntness.

I'm saved as our server delivers and describes the various components of our rich Middle Eastern breakfast—hot loaves of bread we're to tear apart and dip into bowls of salty goat cheese, bowls of something that resembles porridge and is called *hunayua*, and some sweet, sticky concoction called *knafeh jibneh*, which we're directed to douse with some kind of hot, thick syrup.

Her spiel takes several minutes, but the second she departs, before taking a single bite, Rose is back on me, refusing to eat until I give her *something*. "Well? What *happened*?"

My shoulders sag and I sigh. I'm assuming nothing short of a real genie appearing in a puff of smoke from the huge golden lamp in the corner of our pod will distract Rose.

Over the courses of our meal, I fill the girls in on my version of the story. I sort of assume they've heard another version. I try to tell it without infusing a lot of emotion or blame into it. I don't bash Jake. I don't bash their fourth roommate. And I consider this progress, being able to talk about what happened without feeling like I'm coming apart in pieces.

Even though Chrissi's eyes actually fill with tears when I get to the part of the story about actually seeing them together moments after losing Jake.

"Why on earth did you keep shutting us out?" she asks, shaking her head and wiping at her eyes. "I mean, that is big. That is huge! I would've . . . I would've . . ." Eventually she throws her hands up. "Oh, I don't know! But the point is, I would have. Done whatever I could've to make you feel better."

"I was in a bad place," I admit. "And I was . . . embarrassed. Embarrassed about what happened, the way it felt like I had . . . failed at something. The way . . . they . . . had made a fool out of me.

I couldn't come knocking, or anything. She was still your roommate, and it was just too awkward." I manage a weak smile. "I guess I just wanted to wallow, and maybe I guess I knew you wouldn't let me."

"Well, there's no reason not to come to our apartment," Camila tells me. "Harper's never there, anyway. We barely *have* a fourth roommate."

Rose jabs her in the side, but it's too late, and I get the subtext. Harper's practically living with Jake. The way I was last summer when we first got together. But the realization doesn't pain me the way I expect it to. I mean, I saw it before my eyes the other day at the marathon.

"I think I'm done hiding out, anyway," I say, trying to get the conversation back on a better track. "And I'm sorry I was a crappy friend while I was. I should've explained, or something. Not just checked out entirely. But . . . I just couldn't. Not then."

"You don't have to apologize," Chrissi says at once. "Pretty much any postbreakup behavior is excusable." She rolls her eyes. "If I can excuse myself for keying Body's custom Harley two years ago, I can certainly excuse you for screening a few phone calls."

I can't help but giggle.

"Seriously, though," she continues. "As long as you're on your way to feeling like 'you' again, all else is forgiven. Jake is a dipshit douche bag, and losing yourself would be a much greater tragedy than losing him."

FORTY-FIVE MINUTES LATER, when we exit the Palace and step into the morning sun, I suddenly feel very full.

Beside me, Chrissi echoes my sentiments. "Ugh. I'm going to pop. Why didn't we go to costuming before we had breakfast?"

"Timing didn't work out," Camila says.

"Besides, I wasn't really planning on trying anything on today," Rose adds. "I'm just going for some . . . initial inspiration. I want my makeup to be epic. I need to thoroughly inspect all the costumes available so I know which direction I want to go and can begin planning and trying some things out."

"Are we required to go to the Character Ball?" Camila asks.

"Oh my God, what is *wrong* with you?" Rose asks, stopping in her tracks and putting her hands on her hips. "No, we don't have to go; we *get* to go. And I might add, it's your last weekend down here. You will go. Bring Ji."

"No."

"Yeah, you don't skip the Character Ball." Chrissi actually laughs at the concept. "Everyone gets really into it."

That's putting it mildly. The Character Ball is a grand fete thrown by the park for its cast members every August, as a thank-you for a busy summer season. It takes place at the Diamond Palace, at midnight, after the park closes. It gives cast members a chance to do something most of us secretly dream about—dressing up as an Enchanted character different from the one we usually portray for an evening.

So it's no wonder that Chrissi and Rose react as if the Pope's announced he's converting to Buddhism when I turn to Camila and say, "Well, I'm skipping. If you end up needing company."

"*What?*" they squeal in unison.

I keep my eyes trained on Camila. "I'm not going."

"But you adore the Character Ball!" Chrissi protests. "Last year you had a virtual countdown on your computer! You were the first person in line to reserve a costume the first day they began taking requests! You *are* the Character Ball."

I look away, because she's right about all of it. She's right that I lived for the Character Ball, that I actually took pride in the fact that both Cinderella's ball gown and her wedding dress were among the most popular requests, that I tried on every single princess costume last year before deciding on Rapunzel.

Last year.

When I'd gone with Jake, when it had been every bit as perfect as the Character Ball should be, even if he'd whined about dressing up in prince garb and opted for a boring old suit.

If the Character Ball wasn't going to be magical and spectacular, then I didn't want to go. I didn't want to half-ass it. I didn't want to tarnish it that way.

I raise my eyes to Chrissi's, hoping she gets it, hoping she'll stop harassing me about my decision. "You said any post-breakup behavior was acceptable," I whisper. "And I just don't want to go."

"Can I go and not dress up?" Camila asks her sister, playing on her phone. "That would be the biggest thank-you management could give me. Not making me dress up for a day."

Rose shoots daggers at her sister. "I absolutely loathe you today."

This actually makes Camila smile. *Sisters.*

It makes me smile, too, and also promptly changes the subject from my attendance, or lack thereof.

And when I'm convinced that Rose and Chrissi are over their initial shock and aren't going to try to coerce me, I decide it's safe to follow them inside and keep them company as they check out the costumes.

I feel a sharp pang of regret as we make our way down the row of princess dresses. God, they are collectively stunning! I guess I might as well *look*, maybe weigh in on possible selections the other girls make. I can't resist lifting the lacy sleeve of Snow White's formal gown. As long as I'm here . . .

Rose stops in her tracks, and I nearly bump into her. "You know what? I just got a flash of brilliance," she declares. "I don't want to go as another princess. I want to go as a villain!" Her eyes light up, and I can practically see the ideas firing across her brain at lightning speed. "They have the best makeup, anyway, but I could take it to a whole 'nother level! I could do an awesome Evil Empress. Or better yet, be one of the male villains. But I could put this cool, bad-ass feminine twist on it."

Even Camila has to admit, "That actually sounds pretty cool."

"Done!" Rose decides with a firm nod. She claps. "I can't freakin' wait to get started."

It turns out she really can't wait, and after impatiently twitching and hemming and hawing for another fifteen minutes as Chrissi and Camila consider costuming, she finally erupts. "Okay, I have to get out of here!" she exclaims, popping off the old armchair in the corner of the warehouse and grabbing my arm. "Walk over to makeup with me? Please? If you're not looking for a costume, anyway?"

I square my shoulders, turning my back on the gowns. "Sure. No reason not to. I'll come with."

"Thanks," she gushes. "I need to try out some ideas on another person before I can transfer them to my own face. And today I'm here and I have a few hours to kill."

I do, too, so it looks like I just signed up to be her canvas.

THE ENCHANTED DOMINION "makeup studio" is really more a stockroom than a studio. Since as part of our training we're taught to do our own makeup, there are no spinning chairs or makeup artists on hand to make us beautiful under soft lighting. We pop into the studio only to replenish our stock of heavy foundations and dramatic eye shadows and black mascara when we're running low. The space has an impressive organizational system, however, rows and rows of cabinets adorned with visual guides for creating each character's face, and corresponding step-by-step application procedures within the drawers. They're not something I need to reference; I'd gotten Cinderella's makeup down pat before I even had my first shift.

Despite the no-frills atmosphere inside the studio, Rose is perfectly at home and as happy as I've ever seen her, humming as she adjusts some lamps to provide adequate lighting and drags some stools over to a shabby table to set up shop. She ransacks the supply closets, selecting various color palettes and enhancements from multiple villains' sets.

She studies my face, then quickly gets to work applying some sort of base with her fingertips. "I want to try my female take on the Jackal idea first," she murmurs.

Rose doesn't talk as she works; the only sound in the room is that of her breath, which I also feel on my cheek. Periodically she gives orders—"Close your eyes" or "Flutter your lashes." And then several minutes later, she says, "Now look straight at me," as she brushes something on both sides of my nose.

I stare at her, because given the intense look of concentration upon her face, I almost forget it's Rose I'm looking at, the resemblance to her sister is so strong.

I giggle.

"Don't giggle," she says.

"I'm sorry," I say as I try to keep my lips from moving. "But you look like you're performing brain surgery."

She finishes the task at hand. "Not brain surgery," she says, blowing some powder off the bristles of a brush. "But . . . it's work that makes me happy. You should have work that makes you happy, right?"

"Yes, you should," I agree, remembering a similar conversation from Miller's patio.

Then Rose rolls her eyes. "And I know, to my sister, writing code is actually work that makes her happy. That she's actually itching to get back to it. It's something I will never understand, not in a million. But it does, and that's good. Even if we'd make for such an interesting study of nature versus nurture."

"What do you mean?"

"You know Camila and I were adopted from Vietnam when we were toddlers?"

I nod.

Rose throws her head back and laughs. "Considering what I know of traditional Asian parenting, I doubt our birth parents would have been cool with my choice of schooling after high school or my sidetracking Camila from her more appropriate path." She shrugs. "But our parents are American, and they're supercool. They support what I do. And actually encouraged Camila to come along for the ride. Bribed her with the fancy high-tech new computer she wanted. There was something so backward about that!"

"Anyway," she continues, as she leans over, considers several dark shadow palettes, and eventually selects one, "I wonder if Camila would have a lot in common with our birth parents, because I'm definitely a product of our upbringing. Our parents aren't particularly academic; they're artsy types. And so am I."

Rose makes a face. "When Camila and I came over from

Vietnam we had to wear these awful thick glasses because our eyes were crossed. We had this thin hair that was practically falling out from poor nutrition. Endured what seemed like a decade of braces when we got older. My point is, I don't feel at all superficial for wanting to feel like a princess for a little while. For long term wanting to do a job that allows people to feel beautiful, to find the features that make them beautiful." She shrugs. "Even if it isn't world changing in the *grand* scheme of things."

I like it, and I smile. "Good for you," I say, twisting my back, which is starting to get stiff. "I respect that."

"And to be honest, sometimes I think it actually can be life changing."

I raise my eyebrows, waiting for her explanation.

"After all, makeup's not just this mask to hide behind. You make someone look more beautiful, more together, more confident, when they're in need of a boost, it can almost transform a person from the outside in." She smiles sagely. "They can internalize the illusion. They can believe it. Even if it's not real. And that can be powerful."

I sit there quietly, something nudging at my conscience as I consider Rose's words. I can't figure out why I'm bothered, because I get what she's saying, and she's right, in this sort of "see it, then be it" kind of way. But . . .

Before I can fully process my thoughts, Rose is whirling me around to reveal the finished product in the full-length mirror behind me.

"Holy crap!" I almost fall off the stool. "How did you create that in fifteen minutes?" I ask, leaning forward as I touch my face, because I'm not really sure it's mine anymore. It's practically three-dimensional.

I'm the Jackal. I have his hollow cheekbones, his dark, haunting eyes, his signature scar marring his right cheek. But with the proper shading and lipstick and contouring, Rose has made the look sexy and alluring, like some kind of predator of man.

"Wow . . . ," I murmur. I can't stop staring.

Behind me, she shrugs, but I can tell she's struggling to stay humble. "Just a little bit of this, little bit of that," she says.

She pulls out her phone and instructs me to turn around so she can take a picture to help her remember what she did. Then she glances at her phone again. "Do you think you have time for me to try one more thing? After looking at the costumes, I really want to see what I can come up with for the Sea Snake."

"I have time," I assure her, hopping off the stool. "You're so quick."

"Here." Rose hands me a clean cloth and some kind of heavy-duty makeup remover. "You're going to need both of these. And probably the regular face wash, too." She giggles. "Maybe, like, three times. Again . . . many thanks."

"Yeah, sure," I mumble, walking away, feeling distracted.

Something is still nagging at me, and until I can figure out what it is . . . I'm going to be preoccupied.

I lock the bathroom door behind me, turning on the light and staring at my reflection.

Her words keep turning over on themselves in my brain.

Internalize the illusion . . . internalize the illusion . . .

I pour some of the makeup remover onto the cloth and swipe it over the left side of my face. The sexy Jackal disappears at once. She vanishes like that; she was never real. There's no trace left behind.

And that's the thing about illusions.

I put the cloth down, figuring out why her words got to me.

Sometimes internalizing an illusion is a good thing.

And sometimes it's not.

Today marks four weeks since Jake broke up with me. But the truth is, our relationship was over a lot longer than that. Because our relationship was an illusion, one that I wanted to believe in, one that I had internalized, because I so badly wanted it to be the real thing.

I loved the idea of Jake. I loved that we started out as a fairy tale, and that my fairy-tale prince was good looking and stable and on his way to an honorable career. I loved the illusion.

Beyond it . . . I stare down at the sink, feeling particularly foolish. Beyond it . . . I'm hard pressed to remember the last time Jake had made me feel more happy than nervous in his presence, the last time he gave me a sense of security rather than a fear of loss. The last time we felt like pleasure rather than work.

So I guess . . . sometimes . . . Rose is right. An illusion can be empowering. But sometimes an illusion can be debilitating.

You stare at an illusion for too long, you stop looking for something real. Maybe you stop even remembering what it feels like.

chapter 19

I GROAN, COLLAPSING ONTO A MAT AND leaning heavily against the mirrored wall behind me. It's dirty from handprints, so I'm not concerned about resting my sweaty body against it. Three minutes of heavy breathing later, I extend my arm in Miller's direction. "Come onnn," I plead. "Help me up."

He shadowboxes in front of me, bouncing from foot to foot. *Seriously, where does that energy come from?* "Help yourself up, lady."

"What is it with you and Jarred?" I wonder aloud, struggling, mightily, to my feet. "You both seem to think a few weeks automatically turns me into a seasoned pro." I point to myself. "Still struggling here!"

"I'll buy you a protein shake, how 'bout that?"

"That, I will take," I agree. The chocolate-strawberry ones actually taste like a chocolate-covered strawberry. And I feel like I actually recoup some energy a bit later when I drink them.

Miller turns around and tosses his arm around Yael's shoulders. "Ya-ya, you wanna come to the juice bar with us?"

I glance down at my sneakers. I guess I'm not surprised he has nicknames for her, too. I guess he probably has nicknames for everyone.

"Nah, I want to do fifteen minutes on the bike to cool down," she says, zipping up a sweatshirt. "I'll catch up with you at home."

She doesn't bother to say good-bye to me.

Miller laughs at me when, in the hallway, I stab mightily at the elevator button. He tugs on my arm and pulls me toward the stairwell instead. "We're going down! We're not even going *up*!"

"Come baaack!" I call longingly in the direction of the elevator as I see the button turning green.

I more or less let gravity carry my limp body down the stairs and fall onto the first available stool at the juice bar counter. We order our shakes, then chat over the whirring blender noises in the background.

Miller studies my face. "You look different today," he says.

"What do you mean?" I ask, instantly self-conscious.

He moves his hand in a circle in front of his face. "I don't know . . . just different. Au naturel, or something."

"Maybe I'm just glowing from all the sweat," I say.

I don't tell him the complete truth, that I've finally given up on wearing full makeup to the gym. Friday power hours just make a complete mess of it. Today, for the first time ever, I skipped the concealer, mascara, and lip gloss. I'm wearing just a *dab* of foundation and a *hint* of bronzer.

Two tall Styrofoam cups are placed before us, and after we both take a long sip of our shakes, Miller asks, "So how'd last night go for you?"

I roll my eyes at once. "Oh my gosh."

Last night was Drako the Dragon's twenty-fifth birthday celebration. There'd been a huge princess dance party, a sixty-thousand-pound, reptilian-shaped cake, and giant LED birthday candles handed out to guests. There had also been a near riot when guests stormed the blockades that were meant to grant dance party access to guests with tickets *only*.

"Consider yourself lucky that you were at one of the satellite parties," I say. "Did you hear what happened at the Dragon's Lair?"

Miller nods.

"It was absolute insanity. I think it was the first time I actually felt scared inside the park. Chrissi and I got separated, and when the guests broke in, it was just like a tidal wave of people coming toward the stage. Of course security was focused on getting One Direction out of there ASAP, so we were left to our own devices for a few. Finally an attendant just *grabbed* me and practically carried me over to the next party quadrant."

"Chrissi get out okay, too?"

"Well, my plan was to wait for her," I tell him, taking another pull on my straw. "But when they dropped me off near the Palace, they didn't think anything about logistics. I look up, and I see another Cinderella, like, fifty feet away."

The panic I felt in that moment had trumped the worry I felt when the crowd had been rushing toward me moments earlier. Because basically, the first cardinal rule of Enchanted Princesses is "*Never be seen at the same time in the same place as your Enchanted double.*"

"You would have died if you saw me, Miller. Most people had

their heads up because the fireworks were starting, but a few little girls . . . I was watching their eyes go back and forth between the two of us. Ready to tug on their moms' shirts and everything."

"So what did you do?" he asks.

I shrug. "I did what I *had* to do. I dropped onto my belly and basically army crawled to this row of shrubs that wasn't too far away. I hurled myself into one and hid there for about half an hour."

Miller cracks up, shaking his head. "Only you, Alyssa, only you."

My eyes go wide. "It's *cardinal rule* number one!"

"Yes. Even in the middle of a near prison riot," he deadpans.

"So anyway, then I find out from Rose that things were even wor—"

I'm interrupted by his phone ringing loudly, and when he pulls it out to see who's calling, I think I notice his face go a little bit pale. He stands at once. "Uh, I'm sorry, Lys, normally I wouldn't, but . . ." He holds up one finger. "Just give me a sec."

Then he darts around the corner, and I hear him nervously answer his phone a second later. "Hello?"

I sit there, nearly dying of curiosity for several minutes. I finish my drink; I consider ordering a to-go wrap.

Then, when I've almost given up on his return, all of a sudden he comes bounding around the corner, jumping up and down, pumping his fist into the air. "I got the internship!" he yells.

Weary body forgotten, I'm off my stool at once, running to meet him halfway, throwing my arms around him. "Miller! Oh my God! Congratulations!"

His grin is the definition of *cheek splitting*, and he's spitting the story out as fast as he can manage. "They said I was a 'shoo-in.' That my portfolio was a standout and had an impressive level of attention to EE detail. Coupled with my devotion to the company, they didn't think twice after reviewing my application."

I laugh. "All that Kangzagoo time paid off."

"I can start as early as two weeks. They're even willing to coordinate with my park schedule if I still want to pick up shifts since the pay isn't that great."

"I'm so happy for you!" I pull back, still holding on to his arms, and study his face. "Seriously, Miller, I am so, so happy for you. No one deserves this more than you do. Like, as both a person and an artist."

I bring him back in for another hug. I mean every word, and I'm thrilled.

We linger there for a minute, embracing, and it's Miller who ultimately steps back.

His cheeks look a bit red, and despite his excitement he's suddenly a bit subdued. "And uh, I definitely want to hear the rest of the story." He glances toward the stairs. "But I promised Yael I'd let her know the second the call came in this week, so . . ."

I step away and wave him off. "Yeah, yeah, sure. Of course." I tighten my ponytail, feeling a bit silly, like maybe I let my enthusiasm get the better of me.

"I'll be right back," he says, already jogging toward the stairwell, wide, excited grin reemerging on his face.

I sink back onto my stool, my excitement draining quickly, wondering why that's the case. Of course he's going to share the news with others; it's not like I should be feeling . . . possessive of this moment. Miller has other friends, lots of them, and I just happened to be the one sitting next to him when the news actually came in.

To busy myself, I pull out my wallet and slip my credit card inside the black bill portfolio, covering his drink and asking the server to put one of the small, gluten-free cupcakes they sell inside a box for him as my official "congratulations."

chapter 20

I WORK THE PARK THE DAY OF THE COLD-play concert, so I change into my concert-appropriate tank top and ripped jeggings beneath the Palace and catch a bus downtown. There's a stop pretty close to the amphitheater, and it's a short walk to the parking lot. I know Miller, Yael, and her friend are already there, probably already camped out around the small charcoal grill among the rows of cars.

I text Miller to let him know I'm on my way, and he answers immediately, letting me know where they're set up in the ginormous parking lot. Section B6. Glancing up at the signs above me, I turn around, and reroute. Eventually section B comes into view.

As I walk, I realize I'm nervously clenching and unclenching the straps of my shoulder bag as I approach them. It's kind of a foreign situation—I'm not used to feeling uncertain when making an appearance. I mean, I make grand appearances, every single day, for a living. I'm used to having all eyes on me. I'm used to attracting attention when I'm with my Zeta sisters; I'm used to getting stares when I walk down the street by myself.

But . . .

When Miller had walked away from me at the juice bar, it was like . . . I don't know what it was like. It was, like, I hadn't wanted him to go, some weird sense of loss as he ran off to share his big news with someone else.

The sensation was unsettling and kind of surprising. These past few weeks, getting used to being alone, without the girls around all the time, without a boyfriend . . . it was just a weird sense of lingering attachment.

But despite this weird bit of awkwardness regarding Miller that I can't quite shake, days later, at least he smiles when he sees me approaching. He waves enthusiastically, friendly as ever, making me feel welcome and like nothing has changed between us.

Yael . . . her demeanor isn't nearly as inviting. I swear her spine stiffens as I walk up, and her lips are moving behind her soda bottle like she's mumbling something to the girl beside her. I smile in their direction when I join the group, because I don't want her poor attitude to put a damper on the night. I love outdoor shows.

"Hey." I squeeze Miller's arm in greeting as I approach, finding myself struggling to meet his eye, which bothers me. Why am I being so bashful? I force myself to look at him, but then feel heat infuse my cheeks when my eyes find his.

I glance away quickly, turning to Yael instead. I say hello, trying to be nice. It takes a lot of effort, because she's still scowling. Also because she's wearing one of those loathsome T-shirts with an image that portrays EE's Little Mermaid covered in tattoos, smoking, wearing hipster glasses and a ripped Jack Daniels T-shirt. In my personal opinion, those T-shirts are sacrilege, but I put my personal opinion aside in an attempt to keep the peace.

Really, I just want her to know I'm not evil incarnate just because I'm a park princess.

"Hey, Yael." I reach into my bag and produce a thin envelope with some cash, which I extend in her direction. "Thanks for offering up the extra ticket. I was superexcited to get it."

Her mouth is a flat line as she takes the payment and stuffs it into the back pocket of her denim shorts. "Yeah, well, it wasn't really me who offered it up," she says.

Miller chuckles. "Put your claws away, Yael. We're all friends here."

I tried, I think, then turn toward her friend instead, reaching out to shake her hand. "Hi. I'm Alyssa."

"Hey. Daniella."

When I get a better look at her, I narrow my eyes, pausing. "I know you," I say.

At once I can tell she's more pleasant than Yael, even if that's not sayin' much. There's amusement in her eyes when she tells me, "Probably. I used to work at the Shimmy 'n' Shake Shack."

It's a popular smoothie stand, right off the main path near the Diamond Palace. I'm sort of a regular.

"That's it! I thought you looked familiar." I study her for a second longer. "Guess it's the hair that threw me."

It was white blond before. It's ombre turquoise and indigo now.

"It threw HR, too." She laughs, running her hand through her short locks. "I got fired."

To say that Enchanted Enterprises has a strict policy about staff member appearance, even for those who don't portray its characters, is putting it mildly.

Daniella sticks out her tongue, revealing a piercing in its center. "So I figured might as well put this baby back in, too!"

Yael sighs. "I love the hair, but I still think it was foolish. Where are you going to find another seasonal job at this point?"

Daniella shrugs. "It was a job making *smoothies*. I'm sorry, I just wasn't willing to be a bland, carbon-copy park employee in the name of family values. It's antiquated. What kind of message are they sending to all the parents who visit the park with colored hair, or tattoos, or piercings? They're basically saying they're unfit parents if they don't look like Mr. and Mrs. Brady."

She ends her soapbox and takes a quick swig of her drink.

And I see why she and Yael get along. So anti–EE establishment . . .

I glance toward Miller for some kind of rescue before Yael starts getting some digs in about how I so wholeheartedly espouse Enchanted dogmas or something, but he's busy setting up the grill, squirting lighter fluid between the grates.

Daniella nods in my direction. "Is this your first Coldplay show?"

"No, I saw them a couple years ago when they toured in the U.S. And last year in London, actually."

"London? Did you do a semester abroad or something?"

"No, umm . . ." I tuck my hair behind my ear, thinking Yael won't appreciate a mention of my sorority sisters. "I went with a friend."

I leave out the part about the company jet.

"It was this supersmall venue. It felt like a private performance. It was amazing."

"Yeah, but they put on a fantastic show when they go all out, too."

"Yeah, they do," I agree. When I saw them on tour, it was more an experience in color and sound and love than a *show*.

Yael crosses her arms over her chest and stares at me defiantly. It's like any pleasant conversation I'm having with *anyone* she has to put a damper on. "Didn't think this would be your scene," she tells me.

I just keep smiling and gratefully accept a cold water bottle from Miller when he comes back over. "Well, I adore Coldplay. Do you have a favorite record?"

"I like their older stuff. Their latest album is too pop for me. I kind of think they've sold out, but . . ." She shrugs.

"Oh, I think they've just evolved."

I see Miller from the corner of my eye, his gaze ping-ponging back and forth between me and Yael as we debate the merits, or lack thereof, of the latest album. His grin keeps widening; he's obviously getting a kick out of us going at it, duking it out like oil and water.

But when the debate ends and Miller removes a pack of hot dogs from the cooler, I notice the way she subtly steps closer to him, inserting herself between the two of us. And suddenly I remember that there's another reason why Yael's not so quick to warm up to me. I don't know what their status is exactly, but all signs point to something beyond friendship.

And I don't particularly like the idea of feeling like a third wheel.

So when I'm scanning the crowd of tailgaters surrounding us and spot a girl wearing a Coral State T-shirt, I go over and introduce myself, make polite conversation. It's conversation that comes much easier than my attempts with Yael and Daniella, and we uncover common friends and acquaintances.

By the time I've returned, Yael has set up bottles of ketchup, mustard, and relish atop the cooler, and Miller is doling out dogs.

"You hungry, Lys?" he asks me.

"I'm okay. I grabbed something at the park on my way out."

He raises an eyebrow at me. "You sure?"

I nod and smile. "I'm sure."

I don't want him thinking I'm not eating again. Truthfully, I don't readily eat hot dogs, because the ingredient list kind of creeps me out. But otherwise, I realize I can't remember the last time I've been weird about food in front of Miller. I shared the pizza with him without it even crossing my mind not to. And another day inside the park, I agreed to have lunch with him at the barbecue stand instead of trying to drag him over to the salad station. I hope he's not still worrying.

The rest of them eat some dogs and some chips and salsa. I accept a light beer, still trying to drown this lingering sense of unease as Yael keeps managing to insert herself between me and Miller. *If I was so unwelcome, why on earth did she agree to let me take the ticket?*

And despite her best efforts, when we finally head inside and find a spot on the grassy hill, Miller sits down beside me on one of the old blankets. He tosses an arm around my shoulders, just as he's always done. "Having fun?" he asks, smiling down at me.

"Absolutely."

"You ready for this? You're not going to actually *stay* on the blanket, are you?"

"Hell, no!" I assure him. "That would be a waste of a ticket."

As the front man of the band, Chris Martin pretty much demands audience interaction and enthusiasm. There are usually elaborate stage layouts that bring him right out into the crowd, so concertgoers can absorb that infectious energy and beaming smile of his. You don't sit at a Coldplay concert.

And right on cue, the colorful lights start twisting in the air, bathing the hill with beams of pink, purple, and orange; the mic checks go into high gear; and rhythmic pulsations start pouring from the speakers. On the large screen above the stage, the members of the band come sauntering into view, and the crowd goes nuts, everyone jumping to their feet at once. Miller grabs my hand to pull me up, and it's the last time that night my butt sees the blanket.

We dance, we sing, we scream. Apparently my fake ID works here, too, and we take turns grabbing the occasional draft beer from the stand at the top of the hill. As I sip mine, it becomes easier and easier to become part of the collective vibe of the amphitheater and feel like I'm one with the crowd. The mood is euphoric yet chill, a pervasive cloud of dense smoke hovering over us. Even if I don't actually *see* a single person smoking.

Anytime my energy starts to drop off, Miller refuses to let it, throwing his arm around my shoulders and belting out lyrics in my ear, appearing before me and doing some goofy dance or playing air guitar. I inevitably smile and find myself joining him again.

And when the sun has finally descended below the stage and a few stars have come faintly into view, I hear the opening strains of "Adventure of a Lifetime." It's the faster stuff, the stuff I personally love, and Miller's arm is still around me as we sway back and forth. Balloons, every color of the rainbow, are released as if from the sky itself. The colorful lasers are pulsating in time with the rhythm, in time with my body.

I feel the lyrics from the inside out.

"I feel my heart beating . . . oh, you make me feel like I'm alive again . . ."

Miller's temple finds the top of my head. I feel the weight of it there, for a moment. Then I turn to look up at him. Our eyes meet, linger together, and he takes a step to the side, hurriedly downing his beer.

Before I even know what's happening, he's gone. Yanked away, very pointedly by Yael, even if she covers the expression on her face a second later with a silly grin, as she pulls Miller in for some maniacal dance.

But I caught a glimpse of it before she turned away from me, and it read something like . . . *shame on you.*

She is definitely his something. She must be.

I sink down onto the blanket, wrapping my arms around my knees, suddenly feeling so out of place there.

And with her look . . . I *do* feel ashamed.

I feel ashamed because I'm suddenly remembering a very particular night not so very long ago, inside Bluefin, when I was in Yael's shoes. When I was watching some girl getting inappropriately close to my boyfriend, conscience screaming at me loud and clear despite my desire to ignore it.

My head drops, and I close my eyes.

The last person I want to be is some girl.

The last thing I want to do is make someone feel the way I felt that night, even if it's someone I'm not particularly fond of.

I want to tell her what Harper never told me, couldn't tell me.

We're just friends. Miller and I . . . we're just friends. He's yours.

Miller is just a friend. A friend with a girlfriend. I squeeze my knees. And that is that. I will respect the boundaries.

No wonder she's always so cold to me.

I sneak a glance in their direction, my eyes immediately going to that wide, easy smile, those effortlessly cheerful eyes, and suddenly I'm swallowing hard over the lump in my throat, feeling a painful tightening within my chest.

My hand goes to my heart at the shock of the sensation, the confusion surrounding it.

What is with you? You didn't drink that much. You're not getting your period. Why are you so emotional?

Maybe it's because the band has moved on to "Fix You" and the stage lights have turned a morose shade of indigo. Maybe that's why I'm tearing up inexplicably. I stare into space the remainder of the song, trying not to feel.

I try to inhale a deep breath of cool night air but find myself choking instead. I look over at my group again, confused. Right to my left, Yael and Daniella have huddled together, squatting right above the ground, and are holding a lighter to the end of something. Okay, so maybe that's why I'm tearing up. The breeze is carrying the smoke right in my direction, and every time I try to breathe, it chokes me, making me cough.

Miller's all into the music, standing by himself now, shifting ever so gently during the ballad, but he turns when he hears me struggling.

He drops down before me, placing a hand on my shoulder, looking into my eyes. "You okay?"

I stare into his eyes. I still have a little bit of a beer buzz. Everything feels a little bit hazier than it did a few minutes ago, and I'm just really . . . confused. I tell him as much. "I'm confused." I giggle. "I'm just . . ." I feel my brows drawing together; I'm staring at him intently as if trying to impart something really deep. "I'm just . . . really confused."

Miller tilts his head, still smiling. "What's wrong? Are you drunk?"

"No." I giggle again. "I'm not drunk. I only had, like, two-point-seven beers." The concept is hilarious, and I'm giggling again, even though I don't mean to be. I cover my mouth with my hand, trying to stifle the giggles, but they escape like helium from a balloon.

Miller can't seem to help but laugh along with me. "What are you laughing about?"

"I really don't know . . ." I giggle. Then I'm laughing so hard, ridiculous tears are suddenly pooling in my eyes, which seems even funnier.

Miller glances to his left, a look of astonishment taking over his face as he looks back toward me. "Are you *high*? Did you smoke with them?"

"No! There's just . . ." Giggle, giggle, giggle. My stomach is starting to hurt. I wave my hand through the air. "There's just . . . a lot of smoke."

Miller's suddenly nodding. He laughs out loud. "Because you weigh ten pounds. You weigh ten pounds, and now you have a freakin' contact high."

The idea is so ridiculous that I fall over sideways laughing at it.

And of course, it's Miller who steadies me, righting me, eventually helping me to my feet and letting me lean against him so I don't topple over, at the same time chastising Yael and Daniella for smoking so much, so close, and rendering me helpless.

Please don't, I want to tell him. *Don't stick up for me. Don't be a good friend. Don't make her feel disregarded.*

Don't make me feel like this.

Don't make me feel . . . sad . . . wistful . . . heartache . . .

Jealous.

Don't make me feel jealous.

The emotion announces itself in my consciousness at the same time it announces itself in my gut, finally coming to fruition.

I am jealous. Of Yael. Over Miller.

The naming of the feeling stuns and confuses me. I've never been jealous of a girl who's anything like Yael. I've never been jealous over a guy like Miller.

I am jealous over Miller. What?

But I am. It dawns and grows in a sudden force, clenching my heart as I inhale the soft cottony scent of his shirt, as I sneak a glance at his profile in my peripheral vision. I miss the encore entirely.

Oh my God. I have feelings for Miller.

I have feelings for Miller.

And I need to get away.

From this night, from them, from him.

I need to go home. I need to get as far away from these feelings as I can. Nothing good can come from them. For anyone involved.

The hurt caused by Jake and Harper's betrayal has been fading, and the last thing I want is a new kind of hurt to stake claim inside my heart. I need to get away from this.

Problem is, they're my ride home, and there's some late-night construction inside the complex blocking the route from their building to mine. Miller offers to walk with me, an offer I know I can't accept, and besides . . . after a night of avoiding the atrocity of portable toilets, my bladder is certain there is no way it will hold up during the walk home.

So instead, when Miller parks Yael's car, I follow him toward their apartment, dashing up the stairs past him, and bounce outside their door until he finally, blessedly, turns the key in the lock and I can dart past him, into *their* home, and to *their* bathroom. "I'll be quick!" I promise as I dash.

I'm not quick, not really. I swear I pee for a solid three minutes. Then I find myself staring at my reflection in their mirror, first trying to make some kind of sense out of my tangled hair and then just staring at my face.

Don't feel this way.

You can't feel this way.

Okay?

Don't feel this way.

I stare down at the two toothbrushes, side by side, in the holder. One blue, one orange. They live here together.

You said you wouldn't feel this way!

With a heavy sigh, I turn off the light and walk back into the living room.

Miller is sitting on the futon, his head resting against its back, his eyes closed. They open when he hears me approach, and he gives me a small, tired smile, patting the open cushion beside him.

I don't take another step in his direction. Glancing around the apartment, I realize that Yael hasn't come up. "Is she actually waiting downstairs for me to leave?" I ask.

Miller looks confused. "Huh?"

I swallow hard and glance away. "Miller, I don't want to cause any problems," I whisper. "You're a good friend, and I know you mean well. But if she . . ." I hang my head. "I don't want to cause any problems."

Miller stares at me for a long minute. Then his eyes light up, and he bites back a grin. "It's so nice out. I was waiting for you on the balcony. You know why I came in here, into this oven, broken air conditioner and all?"

I shake my head, utterly confused.

Miller stands up, grabs my hand, and leads me toward the small balcony. He leads me over toward the railing, then points in the direction of the courtyard. I have to squint to make out what he's looking at. It's dark. And sort of far away. But finally they come into view.

Yael and Daniella. Sitting side by side on the old green wooden bench. Kissing like there's no tomorrow.

My mouth falls open. "Whhhhhh . . . ?" is all that comes out.

He turns toward me and raises his eyebrow. "Yael said she was gonna"—he puts his hands in the air and makes finger quotes—"walk her home. Guess that's what the kids are calling it these days. Anyway . . ." He runs a hand through his hair. "I didn't want to be a voyeur. So I came back inside."

I'm still staring. Daniella's hand is now snaking under Yael's T-shirt. I turn abruptly. "Inside. Right. We should go there."

I fling the door open, march inside, and collapse onto their futon, staring ahead, eyes wide.

Miller plops down beside me. "I mean, you knew she was gay, right?" Miller studies my face for a minute, then laughs. "No, okay, the look on your face . . . you did not know she's gay."

"No . . . I mean . . . that's cool, but . . . I thought . . . you two . . ." I wave my hand in the air. "She leaves you love notes. You said something about her being 'out of bed before you even heard her.' And she, like, hates me . . ."

He looks confused for a second, and then his eyes widen. "Love notes? What? No! We're just friends." He shrugs. "Largely because I find her perpetual surliness kind of entertaining, but yeah. We're just friends." Miller looks down at me. "You thought that all along?"

"Yeah."

He doesn't say anything for a while.

"Why didn't you ever say anything about it? Or just ask me?"

I stare into space. "I guess . . ." I hear myself admit the truth. To myself, at the same time I admit it to him. ". . . it got to a point . . . I wasn't sure I wanted to hear the answer."

Miller inhales sharply. "Why not?"

I glance up at him. His face is so close. His eyes are locked into mine. I'm pleading with my eyes.

Come on, Miller . . . don't make me say it.

So I don't.

I kiss him instead. It's just easier.

And I shock him. I must, because it takes several seconds for his lips to get the hint and for him to kiss me back. But eventually, he does. Miller kisses me back.

Oh my God, I'm kissing Miller! It sort of surprises the hell out of me, and it is weird, and different, but . . . not bad. Not bad at all. A good kind of weird.

My hands find his face, so he doesn't stop kissing me, and like this gives him some kind of permission he was waiting for, he deepens the kiss.

It works for me. I end up with my back pressed against his futon cushion, kissing Miller. And I'm giggling again, because I'm kissing Miller, and also because his beard is tickling the crap out of my cheek and neck.

He pulls back an inch. "What?" he whispers.

"Your beard. It tickles."

"You want to stop?"

"No." I kiss the tip of his bearded chin. "I want to make out with you for a little bit."

I pull him closer and kiss his ear, which makes him shudder against me. "Do you want to make out with me for a little bit?"

I can hear the smile in his words. "I want to make out with you for a lot bit."

Then his mouth is back on mine in record time.

That's when things get a little bit crazy.

Somehow, I collapse onto the futon and he shifts his weight, making room for me, and then twisting around so that he's hovering above me.

I kick off my shoes, hear them land on his carpet, and put my arms around his back, encouraging him closer still, his body coming to rest atop mine.

Kisses are landing everywhere as we get situated . . . necks, faces, foreheads. And even though the futon is narrow and uncomfortable, we line up perfectly, our feet twisting together, our mouths just right.

Miller's hands tangle in my hair, and my hands roam his back, and he's still tickling me, and I'm giggling again, which makes him laugh right into my mouth.

Yet every time, as soon as the laughter starts, it stops, our lips coming together again with renewed urgency. The truth is, Miller's kisses feel even better than Miller's hugs, and before I know it, I'm sweating beneath him, and his T-shirt is damp. *It is hot as hell inside this apartment!* We're twisted together trying to find purchase on the narrow futon. My legs are caught between his, and we're rolling around, and the next thing I know . . .

. . . I'm falling off the futon, taking us both down, and we tumble right onto the carpet, narrowly dodging the coffee table.

And I'm giggling again, my hair fanned out around me on Miller's carpet, because I'm lying on Miller's carpet beneath Miller, and I'm kissing him, and I just found out that I *can*, and I really, really like it.

He's watching me laugh, laughing, too, and I reach for him, so he'll come all the way down here with me and kiss me some more.

"Come back," I whisper, tugging on the bottom of his shirt. My eyes fall shut against their will.

When they open, for the first time since I started this, I see hesitation reflected in his.

I struggle onto my elbows. "What's wrong?"

He doesn't answer for a minute, staring past me to the wall. "Nothing's wrong, just . . . you were drinking tonight, and then you were . . . practically *high* or whatever . . . and so . . ." Miller actually winces at what comes out next. ". . . we should probably call it quits for now, okay?"

"Miller." I groan. I kick him playfully and pout. "Boo. Booooo."

"Okay, thanks for proving my point."

"I'm not high!" I protest fervently. I think for a minute, blowing my hair back from my face. "If I were high I would . . . I don't know!" I circle my hand through the air, considering. "Ask you if you *always* have spray whipped cream in your fridge. Or another cheesecake."

He grins. "No cheesecake. But I do, as a matter of fact, currently have spray whipped cream in the fridge."

I stare at him. "As a matter of fact, that sounds freakin' delicious. Go get it."

I mean, dinner was seven and a half hours ago at this point.

Miller cracks up. "Oh my God, you are still high," he mumbles. Still the same, he goes over to the kitchen, produces the trusty red canister with the white top, removes it with a flourish, and leans down to spray a thick stream directly into my mouth.

I stare up at him. He's so damn cute.

I can't help but grab his collar, trying to pull him in for a sugary whipped cream kiss.

But he pulls back, giving me a firm look. "I'm not making out with you anymore tonight."

I swallow the whipped cream and frown.

Then, "I'm not kicking you out, either," he says, a bit more gently. He kisses my lips once more. "It's too late to go home. Why don't you go sleep in my bed? I'll crash out here."

I twist my neck and stare at the futon in horror. "That thing is, like, illegally uncomfortable. I bet the only person who finds it comfortable is Yael. I'm not going to kick you out of your bed." Then, winking, I point to the can in his hand. I shimmy my hips jokingly. "We could have fun with that . . . ," I say in a singsong.

"That's it; you're flagged," he announces. "C'mon. I'll tuck you in."

Against my will, he tugs on my hand and pulls me up, wrapping an arm around my waist and helping me down the hall.

Inside his room, I collapse onto his bed and watch him while he roots around in his drawer.

He tosses me a pair of pajama pants. "These okay?" I nod, and he adds a worn T-shirt to the pile. I giggle because it has a picture of YouDee on it.

I sit up, thinking nothing of taking my bra off beneath my tank top before I change.

I see the muscle in Miller's jaw tense. He closes his eyes. "Seriously. I need to tuck you in now. Hold off on the changing."

"You're a buzzkill," I mutter with a smile.

"Yeah, okay. You'll thank me in the morning, Alyssa."

He pulls back the covers; I grab his clothes and climb beneath them. "What does that mean?"

He does, actually, tuck me in. "Nothing." Miller kisses my forehead. "Go to sleep."

I close my eyes. But still try one more time. "Come onnnn . . . ," I say, reaching my arm out, feeling how wide his bed is. "This is a huge bed. You don't need to sleep on that thing."

He chuckles. "Yes, I do."

Miller's pillow feels like a cloud, and his mattress is so soft, and suddenly I'm too tired to argue anymore. "Fine. Good night, Miller."

"Good night, Alyssa." He turns off the light and closes the door.

I inhale deeply. This cloud smells just like Miller. I fall asleep with a smile on my face. I always was a soft mattress type of girl. And I like falling asleep here.

I OPEN MY eyes and stare blurrily at the numbers on his clock. 6:08. I sit up with a start. I'm due at the park in less than two hours. I never expected to sleep so soundly.

I creep out into the living room. Miller is still asleep, and I allow myself thirty seconds to gaze upon him, his lips parted, his face pressed against the flimsy little futon pillow. I'm tempted to wake him, direct him back to that heavenly bed of his, but he's out cold, so I decide to leave him be.

I jot him a quick note that I leave on the coffee table and turn to go. When I ease the door open, I hear his voice.

"You're still in my pajama pants, you know," he murmurs groggily. "With your heels, that's going to make for one hell of a walk of shame."

I smile and turn around. "No shame. I just didn't want to wake you." I point to my note. "I have to *work* in two hours. And I figured you didn't get a particularly good night's sleep last night."

He sits up and looks me over. A bashful smile appears on his face. His one cheek is ruddy from the pillow. "Actually I had a great night's sleep."

Miller comes over and stands before me, in sweats, chest bare. It's the first time I've seen him half-naked, and my cheeks heat at this new intimacy between us, the memories from last night.

It's not a bad feeling, not at all. It just . . . takes some getting used to. Last night surprised the hell out of me, and even the next morning, it continues to surprise the hell out of me. How natural it all seems after the fact.

He scratches his beard and studies me. "Ya know what?"

"What?"

"I'm pretty sure you tried to seduce me last night."

"I did not!"

"Yeah, you did. I barely escaped your clutches." He gives me another grin. "You practically tried to lock me in the bedroom. With a can of *whipped* cream."

"Stop." I put a hand to his chest. "You're going to embarrass me! I was exhausted and delirious and . . . out of it."

Miller looks down. "Yeah, I know."

I find his hand. "No, I mean, but . . . I remember every second." I wait for Miller to look up. I shake my head. "I don't regret any of them."

This makes a small light appear in his eyes.

I clear my throat. "And all kidding aside. Thanks for being one of the good guys."

"Of course. I'd hate for things to get weird between us."

I'm standing in his threshold, in his pajamas, holding my bra. My hair is ratty, and I can taste the horror of my morning breath. Still the same, I kiss his lips softly. "I don't feel weird. Do you?"

Miller gives me the sweetest smile. "No."

"Okay, then."

"Okay, then."

We stare at each other.

"Okay, now it feels a tiny bit weird," I say.

Miller cracks up. "Get out of here." He kisses my forehead. "I'll talk to you later, okay? Don't dodge my calls. I want those pants back. They're my favorites."

"I'm good for it," I promise.

"Bye."

"Bye." I'm all smiles as I turn around and head down the stairs.

It's not a walk of shame at all. I pretty much skip.

I skip past the gardeners, barefoot, pesky heels swinging from my hands.

I wave to them and call cheery greetings, not caring at all

that last night's makeup is all over my face and I actually look like a train wreck.

I skip past Starbucks, because I'm high on life and have no need for caffeine even after a mere four hours of sleep.

And I skip past Jake's apartment building. I skip past it and don't feel a single bit of a pull, even knowing Harper's probably inside. I draw my fingers to my lips, kiss them with a loud smack, and blow a kiss in the direction of his window before continuing on my way.

chapter 21

TURNS OUT THAT "HIGH ON LIFE" FEELING only lasts so long. An hour later, coffee is my BFF.

I grab a large on the way to the shuttle and another inside the park on the way to my dressing room. I need it to even think about keeping my eyes open, and I'm desperate for the caffeine to work its magic on the headache that seems to be the by-product of sleep deprivation and maybe of eating too much whipped cream in the middle of the night. By the time I'm supposed to be undergoing my magical transformation, my hands are shaking so badly I can barely do up the rows of tiny buttons on both sleeves.

It's going to be a rough morning.

Luckily, without my even hearing her, my personal fairy godmother slips inside the curtain and takes over for me, tackling the even longer row of buttons running down my back. "Happy Thursday, my lovely!" Chrissi trills, all sparkle and spunk in her midnight-blue fairy godmother dress and rainbow iridescent wings.

"Hi." I barely manage a grunt. It comes out sounding like "huh." It's the best I can do, trying to conserve my energy for when it really matters.

There's a waiting room off the Palace tunnel where we meet up with our park attendants before every meet-and-greet outside the Palace. Glancing at one attendant's watch, I take a deep breath. We're due out in less than two minutes.

I glance at Chrissi, then do a double take at the pensive look on her face as she taps the sparkly fingernail of her index finger against her lips.

"What is it?" I ask, feeling suddenly self-conscious. I attempt to smooth my gown with my trembling fingers.

She keeps looking me over. "Something's off. Something doesn't look right."

Inexplicably, my hand flies up to my neck, covering the hickey that may or may not be noticeable through the heavy lace.

Then Chrissi snaps her fingers. "I know what it is. You forgot your necklace."

My eyes widen as my hand slides around to my bare throat. She's right—Cinderella's trademark heart-shaped gemstone is missing from my ensemble. It's a total rookie mistake.

"Thank you!" They're going to announce us any second, and I have to dash down two flights of stairs to my wardrobe locker to retrieve it. Dashing in glass slippers, on about four hours of sleep, feeling queasy from not having time to eat much breakfast, is a decidedly less-than-princessly experience. *Oh god.*

I make it back just in time, panting and feeling like I actually might throw up. I puff my cheeks up with air and turn to meet Chrissi's worried expression. "Thank you," I whisper once more.

Then we're all business; after making a silent wish with my hand over Chrissi's wand for survival, I do manage to pull myself together to sit through two hours of hugging little girls, shaking young princes' hands, and posing for pictures with entire families. Thankfully, they're easy on me today. No one makes any weird demands; no one comments that it seems like Cinderella stayed out *waaay* past midnight last night.

Without offering an explanation for it, I let my full weight lean upon Chrissi's frame as we head back down the stairs when our shift is over. And then, when we finally make it to the bottom, when we've made it out of the glaring sun and blissfully bathed in the artificial cool of the air-conditioning unit, I groan out loud. "Craaap!" I look around. "Did I leave one of my gloves out there?" I glance at the staircase wearily. "I really don't know if I have it in me to climb those stairs one more time today."

"Don't bother going back," Chrissi says. "You know someone's snagged it as a special souvenir by now"—she giggles—"that the next Cinderella they run into will be forced to autograph."

I decide she's absolutely right and, before even thinking about getting out of my costume, collapse into the nearest sofa.

She shakes her head. "You're a mess today, lady. What's up with you?"

What's up with me. What's *up* with me.

Memories from last night flood my mind. Suddenly I'm picturing myself lying beneath Miller on his carpet, him grinning above me as he shakes the whipped cream can. I'm totally sleep deprived and overcaffeinated and a bit hysterical from all of it, and the memories are churning up giggles deep in my belly. A giddy smile starts threatening to overtake my face.

As I try to hide it with my hand, this makes Chrissi giggle. "What? What it is?"

The confession comes out on its own accord.

"I hooked up with Miller last night!"

Her eyes pop out of her head. She tosses her wand across the room as she screeches. "What?!"

"I hooked up with Miller last night."

"What?!"

"Okay, we have got to get past this." I giggle.

She flitters over to sit beside me, oversize wings bopping my temple. "Oh my god, how did this *happen*?"

We sit there, side by side on the couch, both still in costume, while I fill her in on what's been happening, the things I haven't shared with anyone—the dinner, and the boxing classes, and the impromptu hangouts, and . . . the kissing. I tell her how incredibly awesome he's been. I tell her about the confusion about his relationship with Yael and what happened instantaneously once we sorted it out.

I spare no details, because I'm realizing exactly how much I've missed dishing with girlfriends, and it's fun to talk about a boy without a lump of dread in my stomach for once.

When I start, Chrissi's eyes are sparkling in anticipation of a good tale. But her face changes over the course of the story—from excited to hesitant, then from hesitant to worried—and eventually I stop, midsentence, and ask about it.

"What is it?" I wonder, tucking a wayward wig curl behind my ear. "What's that face?"

Her smile slides back into place. "Nothing." She waves her hand in circles. "This is a good story. Go on."

"No. You had this *look* on your face. What is it?"

She refuses to answer me for a solid minute. Then, "I'm not telling you." She crosses her arms over her chest.

"Chrissi . . ."

"I wasn't thinking anything." She covers her eyes with her hand. "Come on. You were so happy a second ago and so caught up in the story . . . just . . . go on."

"I can't now." I grab her wrist, pull her hand away from her face. "Just tell me. I swear it will be okay."

Chrissi, by nature, is a bit of a worrier when it comes to other people. I'm not overly concerned about what she might have to say.

"Fine." She sighs. She nibbles on her bottom lip for a minute. "It's just . . ." She looks pleadingly over at me. "You've had a really rough summer, right? You were heartbroken, Alyssa." She pauses. "And Miller's such a nice guy. It would just . . . make me really sad if either one of you ended up hurt."

It takes me a while to process her words. Because, to be honest, even after very recently enduring quite a bit of hurt, the idea of *Miller* or me hurting each other has never crossed my mind. It seems like a silly concept when she presents it to me.

"It was just some kissing," I tell her, even though I can feel that I'm downplaying something as I say the words. "We had this fun night, and we were tipsy, and we did some kissing. There's no 'hurting' in the equation, okay?"

I don't want her worrying. I don't want her putting any kind of negative spin on this.

But she's not ready to let it go, not yet.

"And Miller? He's on the same page? It's just some kissing for him, too?"

I stare down at my glass slipper, caught off guard. "Yes," I assure her right away. "Of course."

Then I'm quiet, and she's quiet. Eventually she sighs. "See, look? I brought you down. When you were on this wonderful little . . . Miller high."

The phrase makes me smile. In part just because I like hearing his name.

"I'm just looking out. For both of you."

"I know that. But I'm okay on this one. I promise."

"Okay," she finally acknowledges. She rubs my arm. "Just please be careful. I can't take any more sadness this summer. Summer is not supposed to be sad!"

I have to agree with her on this. I'm not really up for any more sadness myself.

She stands up and helps pull me to my feet. "Are you done for today?"

"Yes. Thank the heavens! I'm about to fall over."

"I'm stuck here. Can we hang out tomorrow, though?"

"Tomorrow afternoon work?"

"Yeah, tomorrow afternoon works." Chrissi smiles slyly. "I need to talk to you about this guy I'm thinking about asking to the Character Ball."

"I can't wait to hear," I tell her. "Now . . . I need my yoga pants. This dress needs to come off."

Changing out of costume makes my body hurt, and I'm so tired post–caffeine crash, I'm practically stumbling as I drag myself toward the park exit to catch the next shuttle home. I consider treating myself to a Dragon's Kiss but ultimately decide I don't even have the energy to lift a spoon.

Twenty more yards, I tell myself. *Just twenty more yards.*

Then, as I'm nearly to the staff exit, I see something, someone, that perks me up, puts enough spring in my step to keep going forward. Miller, right inside the gates, sitting on a large boulder at the end of the row of buildings along the main street.

I smile as I approach him. "What are you doing here? I thought you weren't on till two."

He stands when he sees me, looking shy. "I ended up catching an early shuttle, so I'm chilling for a bit."

I look down. "On a rock?"

"Um, okay." Miller looks rueful. "I was kind of hoping I'd run into you. I kind of wanted to see you." He lifts his right hand, bringing his index finger and thumb close together. "Just a little bit."

My smile widens.

"How are you feeling?" he asks.

"I'm so tired, Miller." I shake my head and root around for my sunglasses, because the sun is high in the sky now and it's killing me. "I'm so, so tired."

"You gonna go home and sleep?"

"Ab-so-*lutely*!"

"Okay. Are you going to make it to class tomorrow morning, though?"

"I am hopeful I will have made a full recovery by then." I pause. "Maybe we can have breakfast after."

"Breakfast. Sure."

"I have to meet Chrissi later tomorrow. She apparently needs to dish about some guy she wants to take to the ball. But breakfast would be good."

"I'll return you in plenty of time," he says. "Provided you bring my pj's back."

I refrain from mentioning I'm planning to change into them before my nap. "They will be washed and folded," I assure him.

Miller smiles at me one last time. "See you tomorrow, then, Lys."

"See you then."

I don't move. Neither does he. We just stand there, looking at each other.

A second later, he narrows his eyes, bites his lip, and ducks his head around the corner of the building I found him in front of.

"What?" I ask.

He grabs me without responding, dragging me around the corner. I find myself with my back against the brick wall, beneath the striped awning, in its shadow. Miller's so close he's almost touching. And my heart is pounding.

He smiles at me, all sweet and goofy. "Can we pretend it's still last night? For a minute?"

"Sure." I'm confused. "Why?"

Miller comes closer still. He ducks his head, looking right and left, ensuring we're hidden from the sight of children. "I, uh . . ." His hand slowly finds my hip. He licks his lips. ". . . just sort of want to kiss you again," he whispers.

My heart pounds louder still.

"Okay," I whisper in return. "Then it's still last night."

I'm not really sure why it's last night, but if it means kissing, then I'm down with turning back the clock.

"Good." That's all he says before his lips meet mine—softly, sweetly, lingering . . . parting just slightly—before he squeezes my hand, and then with a wink and a final smile, sends me on my way. "Now go get some rest."

I have to catch my breath before making it the rest of the way to the shuttle. I climb aboard, shaking my head as I collapse into the first available seat. Chrissi asked if Miller and I were on the same page. As if it were even a question. Miller and I are always on the same page.

chapter 22

MILLER AND I END UP HAVING BREAKFAST at Dixie Daisy's. It's this small scratch kitchen and café famous locally for its sticky buns and cute box lunches. With its white wicker tables, floral cushioned benches, and pitchers of sweet tea, it resembles a grandma's kitchen in the South. I avoid Dixie Daisy's most of the time because the food is pretty much too good to resist.

Our server drops off two cups of steaming coffee without even asking. As we peruse the menu, I sip mine through a straw. I notice Miller noticing, and while he smirks just a little, he refrains from making any smart comments.

When our server returns, Miller orders the Smithfield Ham biscuit. I order the My-Oh-My omelet. With a few small revisions.

"And if they could possibly make it as a two-egg omelet rather than three. With egg whites, please. And instead of the sausage, green peppers, please. Oh, and if I could possibly have the reduced-fat cheddar instead of the Swiss." I flash an apologetic smile as I close my menu and hand it over to her. "Thank you."

This morning, before power hour at the gym, I'd stepped

back on the scale for the first time in weeks. My weight is back up; one pound over, actually, but I'm going to blame that one pound on muscle mass that I've surely put on over the course of those torturous Friday mornings. At any rate, I guess I'll be keeping my log again.

It was kind of nice to . . . not.

And this time, Miller does comment. "Why didn't you just *not* order the omelet? If there was more wrong with it than right?"

I shrug. "I like omelets."

Miller tears the edges of my empty Splenda packet. "Seems like it takes so much energy, being a pretty girl."

"It does," I answer honestly. "And I know people think a lot of it's silly." I point to my coffee straw. "But you know I care about this job. Respect Enchanted's standards."

"If that's what it's about, then whatever. People do a lot of things for their jobs—move across the country, chase tornadoes, run into burning buildings. A straw's no big deal."

Miller's so great about all of it, it makes it easy to open up to him. To tell him more.

I inhale sharply. "There's probably more to it than just the job," I admit. I feel kind of silly, and I stare out the window instead. "My family went through some pretty hard times that came out of nowhere. Felt like the rug got yanked out from under all of us. I guess . . . it made me crave stability and security in some way."

My eyes dart to Miller's before returning to the window. "I guess . . . in some ways . . . it's a control thing, too. So many things that happen in life are beyond your control. It's always been like . . . looking my best, staying in shape . . . that was something I could control."

"I don't know." Miller's regarding me seriously, pondering it.

"It seems like there's a thin line between it being something you control and something that controls you."

"You're probably right," I acknowledge. I chuckle once. "This suddenly sounds like a therapy session. I don't have an eating disorder. I really don't."

"I know." He grins. "I've seen you chow down big-time in the past few weeks."

I stick my tongue out at him.

He leans across the table and gives my hand a quick squeeze. "Ah, princess problems."

"Right?"

Two loaded plates are plopped down before us, and Miller wastes no time diving into his homemade biscuits covered with melted cheese and thick slices of ham. I start trying to scrape some of the extra butter off my whole wheat toast because I forgot to ask for it dry. But after a futile moment, I put my knife down.

Miller was right. It's indeed a thin line, and this morning I guess I'll try not to let it control *me*.

"So what's this big conversation with Chrissi about tonight?" he asks, mouth full of biscuit.

"Oh, apparently she just met this guy. She wants to give me the details, decide if it's weird to ask him to the Character Ball, such a big event, so early on."

Miller nods, still chewing, eyes on his plate.

I stare at the top of his head, eyes narrowed.

A few weeks ago, when I told the girls the Character Ball no longer held any appeal for me, I'd meant it. I hadn't really anticipated that changing. But . . .

"And I guess . . ." I take a deep breath. ". . . I should probably fill her in on the guy I'm thinking of asking to the ball."

He glances up, the look on his face undeniably crestfallen. It's so damn cute, I have to bite back my smile.

"That guy being *you*, obviously."

Crestfallen changes to surprised. He takes a moment to wipe his hands on his napkin. He finishes chewing. "You want to go to the ball with me?"

"Yes. I do. I think it would be a good time."

Miller stares out the window for a moment. Then he looks back at me. "All right, Alyssa Callahan. I accept your invitation to the ball."

I'm grinning at once. Miller's always a blast; I know he'll actually dance with me at the party.

I have a date for the ball! The reality of it sinks in, and instantly excited, I start gushing at once. "We *have* to sign up the first day, you know."

He rolls his eyes. "Figured as much."

I fork a large bite of egg whites into my mouth, feeling much better about life in general, now that I'm no longer trying to convince myself I have no interest in the *best* event in the world. "I'm just sayin', I'm way behind in the costume planning department. No time to waste!"

Miller groans as he stabs his fork into a piece of ham. "What exactly have I gotten myself into?" he wonders aloud.

I lean toward him and wink, satisfied smirk on my face. "You think you know, but you have no idea."

WHEN WE WANDER out of Dixie Daisy's half an hour later, I lean against the side of his truck, lifting my face toward the sunshine. "Where you off to now, sir?" I ask.

He glances at his watch. “I have to work later this afternoon. But I told my buddy Jay I’d swing by the outdoor courts at the gym for a pickup game.”

“So you really play basketball, huh?”

“Yup.” Miller smiles. “For a short guy, I run one hell of a point.”

I consider. He does have those amazing calves. He can probably really jump.

I tap the cab of the truck. “Feel like giving me a lift first? As soon as I stood up, I remembered that my legs are entirely useless after Friday classes.”

“Yeah, sure.” He nods. He starts to open the door for me but pauses. “Better yet . . .”

“Better yet . . .”

“Come with me.”

“And do what?”

“Watch.” He smiles. “Cheer.”

I smile back at him. “Cheer for the cheerleader?”

“I’m one hundred percent athlete today, baby.”

I giggle.

He senses his advantage and presses it. Miller grabs my hand and swings it back and forth in the space between us. “C’mmmmmon. It’s a beautiful day. Sit outside, get some vitamin D. Keep me company.”

I glance down at my attire. “I’m still in my gym clothes. I need to shower.”

“Showering is overrated.”

I raise an eyebrow dubiously. “Yeah, well, I smell. And I’m still all sweaty.”

Miller actually has the gall to pull me closer and pat my butt, just quickly, releasing me before it even registers. "D'you have any idea what your tush looks like in yoga pants?" he asks. "Please. You don't need to shower or change." He shakes his head. "There's no improving on that perfection."

I don't know what to say to that, because the fact is, I always end up grinning like such an idiot in his presence. I have no desire to go home. I want to go sit in the sunshine and watch him.

"Fine," I hear myself agreeing. "I'll come be your cheerleader."

And fifteen minutes later, there I am, camped out on the bottom bleacher, feeling very high school as I watch a group of guys goof around on the court. Well, a group of guys plus Daniella. She's good, one of the best of the bunch. Tall and muscled, girlfriend can definitely hold her own. During a time-out she says hello, tells me she plays for the women's team at Maryville.

The afternoon sun warms my skin, and the light breeze coming off the lake makes it bearable and pleasant. The remaining perspiration on my skin glistens, and I shake my head at what's become of me. At the beginning of the summer, I fastidiously applied foundation, powder, and mascara before going to the gym. These days I don't even bother to shower afterward.

I sneak a glance at Miller.

And it feels okay.

The casual game is well into its second half, I think, when my phone, sitting on the bleachers beside me, starts vibrating. I glance down and see Blake's picture beside a FaceTime request. I smile and swipe the screen.

"Hey, Blake."

"Hey, girlfraaand," she drawls. "How are you?"

"I'm good."

There's a rowdy eruption from the court in front of me, and Blake scrunches up her face on the screen. "*Where* are you?"

"Don't ask."

"Okay, I won't." She glances down, and I hear her ruffling through some papers. "I just needed to call and check in because Marianne's up my butt about room assignments. Do you want to keep your triple in the basement or move up to the third floor with the big girls this year?"

"Oh, I'm happy to stay put," I answer immediately.

"Really? Why? You're officially a junior now, Alyssa. Upperclassman. You can have a double, even a single if you really want."

"I like my triple," I say. "All of us get along, and I like the company."

Which is true. What is also true is that there is no way I can afford a more desirable room within the Zeta house.

"If you say so," Blake answers. "I don't get it, but . . ."

"I grew up with three sisters," I remind her. "I wouldn't even know what to do with a room to myself."

"Again . . . if you say so. Makes my job easier. I basically had to pull Natalie and Lauryn 'Y' off each other last night during a fight over room 302."

I giggle at the mental image.

"Anyway . . ." Blake's face grows serious. "How are you doing? Like, how are you *really* doing?"

I'd talked to Lauren "E" several times in the past few weeks. I'm not surprised word about the breakup had made its way through the sisterhood. I'm actually grateful for the gossip network for once; it prevents me from having to tell the story time and time again.

"These days, I'm fine. I'm not gonna lie, I wasn't doing so well with things for a while there, but I've pulled it together. I promise."

"I knew he was a creep. I just knew it. I want to kill that guy. Should I kill that guy?"

I put my hand up to halt her threats. "No killing necessary," I say quickly. "He's just not worth it."

"I just can't believe his nerve," she goes on. "He so never deserved you."

I shake my head. "You don't have to keep reassuring me. I know that now. And I'm in a much better place." I glance around, then start giggling at the place I'm actually at. "No, seriously . . . do you want to know where I'm at right now?"

"Yes."

"I'm watching a pickup basketball game at my complex. Well, I'm watching Miller in a pickup basketball game."

"Miller? You mean that cutie patootie from the bar?"

I tuck a piece of hair back into my ponytail. "Yup."

Blake is silent for a minute. "Because, like, you have something going on with him?"

I press my lips together to keep from smiling outright. "Yeah. Kind of."

Blake squeals a moment later. "That's *perfect*."

I tilt my head, waiting for her to elaborate. I just . . . hadn't expected her to be so enthusiastic.

"I mean, Miller is, like, the perfect type of guy to take your mind off Jake. Perfect summer fling. Easy. Uncomplicated. Probably treats you like a goddess, am I right?"

"Yeah, uhh . . ."

I mean, he is. Easy. Uncomplicated. But . . .

"So it's perfect. Then in a few weeks, when you get back, you'll have your pick of the guys from Alpha. You know they all have hard-ons for you. Hate the fact that you were always so damn loyal to Jake. They'll literally be foaming at the mouth when they hear you're up for grabs."

I force a little laugh, but I'm no longer smiling. I don't really like the picture she's painting. I turn to watch Miller again, half wishing she'd never called.

"Anyway . . ." Blake holds up a stapled packet of papers and shakes them in front of her screen. "I gotta run. Like I said, Marianne's up my butt and I need to get this list to her pronto. I'll keep you in the basement if that's what you truly want." She beams. "And I can't wait for you to get back here. You're gonna get so much quality ass!"

With a flourish she blows me a kiss, and the screen goes black.

I stare down at it for a minute, feeling a bit displaced, a bit lost.

Just when I was sort of feeling like I'd found myself again.

That's when I hear someone clear her throat behind me. And even though it seems like my stomach couldn't sink any lower, it suddenly goes crashing down another story.

I glance over my shoulder and see Yael, perched on the top row of the bleachers, presumably also cheering on her love interest. I have no idea how long she's been there. How far Blake's voice carried. How much she heard.

I hope my hand isn't shaking as I wave to her. "Oh . . . hey, Yael. How are you?"

She nods curtly, her hair nearly fluorescent in the sun. "I'm good."

She glances down toward the phone in my hand, then toward

the court. "So. You did stay over the other night, didn't you? I found Miller asleep on the futon, but he claimed he just crashed out there." Yael narrows her eyes behind her glasses. "I had another theory, but of course he wouldn't cop to confirming it."

I say nothing. I don't know what to say to her.

Yael smiles at me, and for a second I'm naively hopeful that she's going to be nice. Instead she gestures with her head toward the court. "So why on earth aren't you out there with them, then?"

I shake my head, still smiling, still hoping. "What? I don't . . ."

We watch as Daniella leaps into the air, from right below the backboard, and easily nabs the ball after someone's missed shot.

"Rebounding." She smirks. "Seems like you're even better at it than Daniella is."

The smile melts from my face.

Yael shrugs. "So ya know . . . figured you might as well get out there, too."

I stare at her evenly. "Why would you say something like that?" I ask quietly.

She doesn't answer me right away. She takes a long pull on her straw, staring into space as she considers. Then Yael turns and meets my eye. "You want to know why?"

I nod meekly.

"I just came out last year. And before that, for twenty years, I got really, really good at keeping things inside, not speaking the truth. Now, for better or worse, I'm gonna tell it like it is. Because it gets really tiring living life the other way."

She shrugs again. "So maybe you don't like my bluntness, but these days I just put everything out there for people. Just be honest, man. It is what it is. And Miller is nothing more than a rebound." Yael nods toward my phone again. "Your little friend knows it. In your heart you probably know it, too. And Miller . . . if . . . when . . . *if* he ever comes to his senses, I'm sure he'll know it, too."

That sinking feeling in my stomach turns to pure dread.

Because ultimately she's the one going home with him, and she seems pretty invested in laying out this version of the story. Even if it's one that doesn't feel at all accurate to me.

"I'm not rebounding," I protest. But my voice lacks assertion, because she's gotten under my skin.

That's what she thinks? That's what Blake thinks? Is that what . . . Chrissi thinks, too? Is that what all her worry was about? When she mentioned my hurting Miller?

"Sure." Yael shoves her straw into her mouth. "Talk to me in three weeks when summer's over and you're back at school. Getting all that . . . what was it? Quality ass from the Alpha boys." She rolls her eyes dramatically. "They sound *awesome*."

Then she returns her full attention to the game, even pumping her fist in the air and screaming, "Yeah, babe!" when Daniella makes a shot. It's clear our conversation has ended. On her terms.

The game ends ten minutes later. Miller's team wins, and he comes right over to wrap me up in a sweaty bear hug and lift me to standing. I manage a weak smile for him, but despite the sun's presence in the clear sky above, a dark cloud has drifted over the day, and I'm wishing I never came.

Because I know after he takes me home, he'll be going back to his apartment. And that if she gets a chance, Yael just might try to "put everything out there" and get under his skin the same way she just got under mine.

chapter 23

SOMEONE IS KNOCKING ON MY DOOR. I'M deep in a REM cycle, in the midst of a pretty disturbing dream that can only be described as Cinderella conceptualized by Tim Burton. In which the stepmother has maroon hair and wears glasses with thick black frames. I have to swim through the hazy sea in my mind back to reality. Pushing at my satin sleep mask, I turn toward my clock. It is 5:14 a.m. I roll over and tug the covers tight. It must have been part of the dream. No one is actually knocking on my door at 5:14 in the morning.

Yet as I come all the way back to consciousness, I still hear it. I toss aside the covers and pad toward the door in the loose Cinderella T-shirt I wear as a nightie, and only at the last minute does fear kick in, reminding me that I'm a female living by herself who should seriously consider the wisdom in opening the door at this early hour. I bend to squint through the peephole. What I see on the other side—a bearded male wearing sunglasses—in most circumstances would be considered far from reassuring.

"I hear you breathing," he hisses. "Let me in."

Shaking my head and biting back a smile, I open the door for Miller.

His eyes instantly go to my bare thighs, and I tug at the bottom of my T-shirt. "Umm, what are you *doing* here?"

"Park opens for employees in forty minutes. It's August eighth, which means that the Character Ball is exactly seven days away, and the costume request log is officially available." Miller raises an eyebrow. "I kind of assumed it would be *you* beating down my door."

"It's just entirely too early for beating on doors."

"You disappoint me, Princess. Go get dressed."

"You're ridiculous," I grumble as I wander back toward my bedroom. When I get to the door, I glance at him in a last-ditch effort to get back to sleep. "Are you sure I can't talk you into sleeping for another hour instead?"

He smirks at me. "Damn, woman, you are relentless about getting me into bed." Then he shakes his head. "Get dressed."

"I'm too tired to formulate a response to that," I tell him, shaking my head as I close the door behind me and dutifully change into something more appropriate. He's being such a pain in the ass—no *way* will I share that I'm actually pretty gleeful I have a date to the ball who's this enthusiastic about picking out our attire for the event. That his early morning drop-in is reassuring considering the state Yael left me in at the courts.

There are only three other people on the early morning shuttle, and the main gate to the park is still closed when we pull up before it. We enter through the after-hours, or before-hours in this case, staff gate and veer off the main path almost immediately to take a hidden side path that loops around to the costuming building.

Even though I had a preview when I came with Rose and Camila, I have no idea where to start. At that time, I was convinced I wasn't going to the ball. I hadn't really let myself even look. And last year I came in knowing exactly what I wanted and was in and out in five minutes flat.

"Okay, I'm officially overwhelmed," I call to Miller, plopping onto a pile of out-of-commission costumes piled in the intersection between face character costumes, fur costumes, performance costumes, and retired costumes. I gaze around. "It's like stepping into the world's best game of dress-up ever." When he doesn't respond I yell, "Where are you?"

Suddenly a convincing bellow breaks the silence, and I jump to my feet as Edwin Elephant, Aladdin's trusted form of transportation, jumps out from behind a row of costumes and grabs my shoulders.

"Oh my God!" My hand goes to my chest. "What are you doing?"

Miller pushes up the costume's trunk. "Might as well have a little fun. No one else is here yet. It's all access." He nudges me. "Come on . . . there has to be at least one performance costume or something you want to try on."

I chew on my lip, considering. "Okay, fiiiine."

And I'll admit it, I get into the game. We try on several of the performance costumes in the shadows, surprising each other with hyena howls and birdcalls as we step out for the reveal. I laugh so hard when I emerge to find Miller posed on one leg, perfectly still and composed, in flamingo garb that I'm sure I pull an oblique muscle.

When I somewhat regain my breath and my composure, I begrudgingly accept the Lizzie costume he's holding in his outstretched arm.

"What's that face?"

"I can't believe I'm stepping back into fur. Even for shits and giggles."

"You never wore Lizzie when you were doing fur training," he reminds me. "Lizzie is way too high profile for trainees. Lizzie is a privilege."

Lizzie is indeed an icon. Girlfriend to Drako the Dragon, she's the other face of the park.

That being said . . . Lizzie girl deserves an updated look. Her costume's not at *all* cute, and her facial expression is stuck in permanent swoon mode, all pouty lips and batted lashes. Drako's costume has several variations, but Lizzie always looks just a little bit dopey.

But to appease Miller, I step inside one of the dressing stalls and struggle into the shiny green costume with the long scaly tail. I'm *so* not a fan of long scaly tails. Or *claws*.

When I emerge, I find Miller standing tall and proud in the Drako costume. "Drako the Dragon. Man. Something a lowly kangaroo could never have aspired to," he quips.

I go stand next to him and giggle at our reflection in the large mirror. It's a cute couple's costume, for, like, . . . something else. Not the Character Ball. Pulling off Lizzie's head, I meet Miller's eye in the mirror, my expression one of business. "Okay, let's get serious now," I tell him.

He takes off Drako's head, surprise written all over his face. "What do you mean?"

I tilt my head. "What do you mean what do I mean? Let's find the costumes we'd *actually* wear to the ball."

"We could get Drako and Lizzie, Lys! Drako and Lizzie! They're icons! Why pass these up? They're perfect."

I stare at him, still outfitted in head-to-toe green scales. Oversize silly feet. *Claws.* I'm suddenly shedding my scales as quickly as I can. "Just . . . no. Miller, I am a fashion merchandising major, trained to worship names like Prada and Versace. I'm an Enchanted Princess! I don't do lizards!"

I leave the costume at my feet. Miller picks it up, carefully puts it back on the hanger, and then follows me toward the rows and rows of beautiful princess dresses. The closer I get, the better I feel.

But Miller merely groans. "Seriously, why are you coming over here?"

"To find our perfect costumes!" My voice is enthusiastic, and there's a big smile on my face. Surely he'll come around. He has to.

"Alyssa. It is completely counterintuitive for you to go to the ball as a princess. The whole point of the ball is to go as someone you don't normally play."

"I'm not planning to go as Cinderella," I say innocently, flipping through the dresses.

He chuckles once. "Nice try. You know what I mean. Can't you even think about branching out beyond a princess dress? Look for something you can actually *move* in?"

"I'm sorry, but"—I shrug daintily—"that idea holds absolutely no appeal to me."

I smile over my shoulder, surprised at Miller's expression. I was *kidding*, but . . . he doesn't seem to be finding me all that funny right now.

"Stay right there," I tell him. "Just . . . let me show you something."

I jog down the long row of princess dresses until I find it. I stand reverently before it for a moment, staring at the dress in all its exquisiteness. It's too cumbersome for most, and few girls are bold enough to wear it to the ball, but man . . . this dress is a showstopper.

The Swan Queen's dress.

It has a sleek, sculpted bodice and intricately layered skirt. A twenty-foot train made of feathers. A choker made of more feathers and fake diamonds that sparkle more than real stones.

This year I might be ready for the Swan Queen dress. Taking a deep breath, I remove it from its garment bag and carry it gently into a fitting stall.

I dress with my back to the mirror, not wanting to peek until I've gotten it on, which admittedly, is quite the struggle as a solo act. But I want to surprise Miller with the complete look, too. When I finally turn around, there's no holding back the huge grin that erupts on my face. The ugliest of ducklings could look stunning in this dress, and with my hair pulled back in a tight bun, even with no makeup on, I look amazing.

Ever so slowly, lifting the folds of the gown and being mindful of the long, delicate train, I walk down the aisle toward Miller. His back is to me, and I announce my presence quietly. "Ta-da."

He turns around. His face is passive as he studies me, looking me over from head to . . . well . . . tail. Miller doesn't say anything for a long minute. Then, at last, he reacts. "You look ridiculously beautiful," he says.

It's a compliment. I don't understand why he sounds so defeated.

"I know it's a lot," I acknowledge, taking a few steps closer. "But I totally think we can pull it off. And these costumes? Guarantee a grand entrance." I beam and clap my hands. "The Swan Prince costume is cool, too. It's this sleek tuxedo with a black feathered mask. It's very dignified." I stare at him pleadingly. "Can I go get it?"

Miller drops his head and sighs as he rubs the back of his neck. "Yeah, sure."

I go back to retrieve the corresponding prince costume, fueled by anticipation and excitement, and return to Miller lickety-split. Black garment bag in hand, I stare at the empty space before the mirror. Where'd he get to so quickly?

I wander through the rows until I find him in front of the office, sitting on an overturned milk crate. His shoulders are slumped and he looks dejected.

"What's wrong?" I ask brightly, hoping to displace the cloud that seems to be hovering above him. I nudge his foot with mine. "You don't look like you're having fun anymore."

What happened to the guy who knocked on my door before sunrise because he was so eager to get over here?

This guy looks up at me a minute later. "To be honest . . . I'm not."

My stomach sinks, and the garment bag falls to my side.

"We haven't actually talked about the other night, but maybe we should have." Miller meets my eye only for a quick second before gazing into the distance. He chuckles once. "It was so awesome. I didn't want to taint it in any way. I wanted to, like, preserve it. Just . . . keep living it over and over again."

He stops laughing. He looks back at me, apprehensive. "Why did you kiss me?"

I do a double take at his question. "It wasn't obvious? Because I wanted to."

He looks dubious. "You were kind of out of it."

"I would've kissed you stone sober. Which, by the way, I was more than I wasn't."

"Would you have?"

I shake my head in confusion. "Yes. What does that question even mean?"

I stare at Miller, wanting to say more. *Where is this coming from? And why?*

"Miller. What is this?"

He looks me over again. By the time he finishes, his eyes are sad. "Look at you. You're a princess. You want your grand entrance. You want your fairy-tale ending. The one you lost with Jake." He sighs again.

I try to laugh, but it doesn't quite come off. And I really wish I didn't still have this dress on. "Miller, come on."

But he doesn't come on, he just continues with it.

"It's true, at least to some extent, you have to admit," he continues. "Right now, you can't even think beyond it. For a party." He rises, coming over to stand before me. We're still the same height, as we've always been, but for the first time, we're not seeing eye to eye.

"You are a princess, and I"—Miller swallows hard—"am woefully human. I'm no prince in shining armor." He shakes his head. "You can't just insert me back into the story." He looks down at the garment bag and shakes his head. "And that costume won't even fit me," he states matter-of-factly. "The pants are too long, and we're not allowed to alter them."

I drop the garment bag like a hot potato. "Forget the damn costumes, then. This is stupid!"

He stares at me evenly. "It's not really about the costumes, Alyssa."

"I don't understand. I thought things were . . ." I struggle to come up with the right word. *Natural. Right. Perfect.* ". . . flowing." I throw my hands in the air. "You want to talk about the other night, fine. I kissed you. Again for the record, I wanted to. And I just . . ." Suddenly I feel bashful and need to look away. "I just like you." *I like you . . . so much . . . and I like me when I'm with you. I don't worry about what I eat. I don't worry about what I look like. I'm too busy being happy.* "I want to see what happens here. I was under the impression that you did, too."

Did I misread something again? What did I miss this time? With Miller, it had always seemed like we were on the exact same page. And with him sticking around now, it just seemed like those pages would keep turning on their own.

"Problem is," Miller begins, wincing toward the distance, "I know what happens."

Something occurs to me, and I fold my arms across my chest. I nod knowingly. "She got inside your head, didn't she?"

"What? Who?"

"Yael. She shared her little rebound theory with you. She's trying to convince you to walk away."

Miller looks confused for a minute, and then he shakes his head. "Yael hasn't said anything to me."

I stand there, stumped. If she wasn't responsible for this seemingly sudden change of heart, then who . . . what . . . was?

"She didn't need to," he says quietly. "The thing is . . . I've been down this road before, Alyssa." He shrugs. "I don't know exactly what vibe it is I give off, but it's like I make girls feel . . . safe. And plenty of times in the past, these girls . . ." He smiles ruefully. ". . . girls who look like you do, they find their way to me. The cheerleaders. The sorority girls. Always seems like it's when they're having a rough time. They stick around long enough to get their confidence back, I guess. They stick around long enough to make me think it's real, then when push comes to shove, it's not. Sooner or later the girl always wants the prince again, the fairy-tale ending." His voice turns quiet. "And in the story, nice guys finish last."

"That's not what's going on here!"

Miller studies me. "I don't know that. And to be honest, I don't think you know that yet. And . . . you're not just one of those other girls, Alyssa. You . . . I've always . . ." He trails off. "I don't want to go down that road with you. I like you too much for that."

"I think you're being ridiculous," I tell him.

"Maybe I am, and maybe I'm not. I haven't really let myself . . . think . . . about the other night. I've just been going with it, because I didn't want to let go of it. I didn't want to think." Miller's face is pained. "But then you came out here in that dress, so caught up in wanting to be the princess, the grand entrance, and I just feel like eventually you're going to want the fairy tale again." He shakes his head. "And once you do, chances are you won't really want me to be the one by your side."

I recoil like I've been slapped. It takes me a minute to speak. And when I do, the words that come out are not very princessly. "Um, screw you, Miller."

Miller takes a step back. It doesn't ruffle him. "I don't want to fight with you. This is precisely why . . ."

Maybe he's just protecting himself. Maybe he's been hurt,

and maybe the way those other girls treated him became something of a pattern. Maybe this isn't entirely about me.

But . . . something occurs to me, and it's something really crappy.

"You're as bad as he is."

He turns around. "What?"

"You're as bad as Jake. You're reducing me to this . . . one-dimensional person. The girl who cares more about her happily ever after than what the story even looks like. The girl who's nothing more than the princess she portrays." My eyes fill and my throat tightens as this realization comes into focus. "And that *hurts*, Miller." I shrug. "Jake, apparently he always saw me that way. I thought you actually saw something more," I whisper.

He looks conflicted. Frustrated. "I do. Just . . ."

"You're sure as hell not acting like you do." I reach around and yank the zipper on the back of the dress. I think I hear something pop, but I'm too upset to care. "You're reducing me to a stereotype. You're reducing this to nothing."

"Alyssa . . ."

"Chrissi. Blake. Yael." I tick their names off on my fingers. "They all seem to think this story only ends one way." My eyes fill with tears. "I thought you were the one other person who got how it really was. Who saw how it could be." I clutch my midsection, because suddenly I feel so entirely alone. And lonely. Lonelier than I felt when Jake walked out my door.

I shake my head fiercely. "Forget this." I turn on my heel, whipping all those stupid feathers out of my way. "Forget the ball. Forget everything." I give him one last look before I go. "You were so worried about a crappy ending. Well, there you go. You just wrote it. And now you don't have to worry about it anymore."

chapter 24

"I HATE BOYS," I MOAN. LYING WITH MY head in Chrissi's lap, staring up at my ceiling, I continue my rant. "I hate lying, cheating boys. I hate the nice boys. I just hate boys."

"Maybe you should swear off boys for a bit," she responds tentatively. "Not at all in an 'I told you so' way, but this is sort of what I was worried about when we talked last week. The last thing you need is another boy hurting you right now." She pats my cheek.

I tilt my head to look her in the eye. "You're still saying 'I told you so,' by the way. Ugh! And that's the *thing*. I wasn't looking for someone to help me get over Jake. Miller was the last person I expected to start falling for. I didn't go after this. It just happened." My lips curl downward. "He was also the last person I expected to hurt me, like this or . . . any kind of way."

"I'm sorry, lovey."

"It hurt more than when Jake said it," I acknowledge out loud. I shake my head and laugh mirthlessly. "I didn't think anything could hurt more than the night Jake broke up with me, *how* he broke up with me, but when Miller said those things to me . . ."

A moment later I push myself up on my elbows and scramble to my feet. "I *hate* boys!" I shout with renewed vigor. I dart to the kitchen and rifle through my junk drawer. I find a long, thin lighter in the back and whirl around, holding it up triumphantly.

Chrissi jumps to her feet, eyes wide, looking instantly panicked. "Um, what are you doing?"

Without bothering to give her an explanation, I stride toward my bedroom. As I dig around in the piles in my closet looking for It, I hear Chrissi on her phone. "Are you home? Get down here. I think I need backup."

By the time I find it, toss my clothes back onto the floor of my closet, and go back to the living room, the troops have amassed. Camila and Rose are standing beside Chrissi.

Rose has her hands on her hips. She surveys the scene—me, holding a lighter and a binder covered in lace and sparkles. "What in God's name are you doing?"

Staring down at the binder, I feel remarkably calm. "I'm burning my wedding binder," I announce.

"Your *what*?" Rose asks.

"My wedding binder. I've been amassing dresses, and floral arrangements, and lighting fixtures, and DIY projects, and cake designs, and boudoir pictures since I was sixteen." I shake my head. "But if seriously no one out there believes there's anything more to me than the pursuit of this binder"—I hold it up over my head for their examination—"then I'm going to prove them wrong."

Camila stares at me. A slow smile lifts her lips. "You may be my new favorite person. Do it."

Rose slaps her sister's wrist. "Don't encourage her!" She glances upward. "There's a smoke detector *right there*."

"I'll be careful." I drag the small metal trash can over from the kitchen and ceremoniously drop the binder inside. "Open the windows, Camila."

She hurries over to comply.

"This is happening, smoke detector be damned. It burns *today*." I inhale a deep breath through my nose and stick my chest out. "And I shall arise like the mighty phoenix from its ashes, cleansed and *fairy-tale free*. So there, stupid boys."

Rose comes over and plants herself between me and the can. "You have officially gone batshit crazy."

"Let me do this, Rose!"

I shift right, she follows me, and I quickly shift back to my left. I just manage to dodge her at the same time as I engage the trigger on the lighter and a small flame appears at its tip. Leaning over the rim of the can, I reach down and touch lighter to binder. There is a millisecond of "oh-my-God-what-have-I-done," which is instantly replaced by a deep sense of satisfaction as the binder catches fire.

Chrissi, Rose, and Camila gasp collectively and jump back.

"Everybody stay calm," I say. I peek into the can. "It's totally contained."

It is. For about twenty seconds. But all that glue and lace and glitter is surprisingly flammable, and all of a sudden, flames are leaping out of the trash can. A pillar of gray smoke shoots toward the ceiling.

"Where's your fire extinguisher?" Rose screams.

"I don't know!"

"You don't *know*?"

"No! I don't know!"

Our exchange is promptly drowned out by the persistent, ear-splitting beeping from the smoke detector.

"At least get some water!" Chrissi screams, hands over her ears to muffle the noise.

"Right!" I sprint toward the kitchen, trying to remember where I put the one big bowl I own.

Before I find it, I'm caught in what feels like a surprise sun shower.

My hair is damp at once, and I lift my face to the streams of water, noticing the sprinkler system in our building for the very first time.

Shocked, I glance toward my friends, who are stunned in place by the surprise soaking. "Umm . . . did anyone know our building had a sprinkler system? I never noticed," I add innocently.

At least the fire is out.

Rose snarls and grabs the can without bothering to respond. "Ow!" she screams when her hand touches hot metal. She grabs a dish towel from the counter, tries again, and hurries the can toward my small balcony.

When I see her move toward the railing, I sprint to stop her. "No! Don't dump the ashes!"

The ashes were the whole point. I need them!

Rose pauses midtoss.

"Wait! Wait!"

I run back into my bedroom, find a prettily decorated jar that once contained one Zeta gift or another, and dart back out to the balcony. I kneel before the can, reaching inside to shovel as many ashes as will fit inside the jar.

"Can I just ask . . . what you might be planning to do with them?" Chrissi asks.

She and Camila are standing exactly where they were when the sprinklers came to life; they both still seemed too stunned to move. Camila's damp hair is covering her glasses.

I twist the lid onto the jar, holding it up and examining it with satisfaction. "I plan to march over to Miller's apartment and *dump* them on his head."

No one says anything for a moment.

"Umm, that would be weird," Camila says.

I lift my chin. "Well. So maybe I won't dump them over his head. I want to show them to him, at least. Show him that I care about more than the fantasy. And he missed out on what that more was."

Rose glances at Chrissi. "Do we have any hope of stopping her?"

Chrissi studies me. She looks me in the eye; she seems to be examining the set of my jaw. "I'm not entirely sure we should," she finally replies.

I nod my appreciation and turn toward the door.

I hear Rose sigh behind me as I walk out. "Godspeed, Princess Phoenix."

Feet bare, hair wet, clutching a small jar of ashes to my chest, I storm across the Lakeside complex. It's a good ten-minute walk to Miller's building, and I amass a pretty impressive collection of stares, gasps, and comments as I make my way. But I'm a woman on a mission, and I'm immune to all of them. My gaze is laser focused, dead ahead, and when Miller's building comes into sight, I break into a jog to close the distance.

I skip every other step as I make the climb to the third floor, and when I reach his door, I forgo the doorbell entirely. A doorbell seems too meek. I pound with my fist instead.

Finally Yael opens the door. She's wearing that loathsome hipster princess tee again.

I don't bother to greet her. "Where's Miller?" I pant.

"Not here. He's working."

I take a tiny step back. "Oh."

I hadn't really thought about that. According to my master plan, of course Miller was home.

I stand in the threshold to his apartment, turning the jar of ashes around and around in my hands, limbs shaking from adrenaline.

Yael continues to stare. "Can I help you with something?" she finally asks. "Get you some shoes, or a towel, or a Valium?"

I stare past her, into the interior of their apartment. He's really not here. The frantic energy drains from my body in a sudden rush, and I lean against the door frame. "I just really needed to talk to Miller," I mumble.

I rest there for a moment, still feeling my heart pounding in my chest and waiting for it to calm. Then, with a heavy sigh, I push myself off the door frame and turn to go.

"Alyssa."

I glance over my shoulder, pushing a few damp strands out of the way.

Yael is framed in the doorway, arms folded over her chest like a member of the National Guard or something. "Do you have any clue as to why I wasn't exactly fond of you?"

My lips part in surprise.

Her right eye twitches with annoyance. "If you're even standing there thinking it's because of some stupid princess-fur divide, or because you're a blond sorority girl, then you're even more delusional than I thought."

I shake my head. "I don't . . ."

"I didn't like you because I'm protective of my friends. I watch out for them, especially when they can't seem to watch out for themselves." She looks me in the eye. "And that boy's been in love with you for, like, ever."

Shock hits my chest like a launched bomb. "What?" I whisper.

"As I expected." She quirks an eyebrow. "You had no idea, did you? You were so wrapped up in *you*, chasing after some guy who apparently treated you like crap, you probably never even noticed half of what was going on around you."

I scan my brain, desperately, trying to find anything from this summer and last that would have suggested what she is alluding to. I come up with nothing.

"He never let on!" I protest. "There was nothing to notice!"

"Yeah, well . . ." Yael glances away. "He worked really hard to hide it. He still wanted to have you for a friend."

I can practically hear her unspoken "*God knows why*."

"When all this started going down, when you two started hanging out more this summer, I told him he should probably stay away. That it would hurt more to get closer," Yael says. "He felt so bad for you, though, and cared about you so much." She shakes her head. "I said, 'How the hell are you going to put your feelings aside and just be her friend?' He said he could, but I knew he couldn't. I knew this would happen."

I squint, thinking hard about the past month and a half.

Miller never once pushed his own agenda. Even when I was at my most vulnerable, most in need of reassurance, affection, and bolstering, he never took advantage of that. Even when I out-and-out threw myself at him, he didn't take advantage of that. He never hinted at his feelings until I kissed him; he never once suggested my path back to positivity involved him. He always made it about me—getting *me* to eat again, getting *me* to feel strong, reminding *me* not to lose myself.

Miller did succeed in putting his apparent feelings aside to be my friend. He was selfless about it, actually.

"You're wrong," I inform Yael. "He did put his feelings aside. He was a really, really good friend."

I stare down at the stupid jar of ashes in my hands. I don't want to dump them on his head. I don't want to yell at him.

I just want him to look at me the way he used to. Past the princess's dress to the princess's heart.

"Turns out he did know how to look out for himself, anyway," I tell her. "He didn't need you to do it for him. You'll be happy to know he walked away." I struggle to swallow over the lump in my throat. I walk back toward the doorway. I hand the jar to Yael. "Just give these to him. They were supposed to be for him."

"Okay," she sighs. "Whatever."

I stand there for a minute, staring at her. She has always made a point of speaking her mind, but sometimes, she's wrong. And now I'm going to speak *my* mind.

"You don't really know me at all," I tell her. I lift my chin. "I'm a good friend, too. I'm a good person, blond sorority princess and all. I wouldn't have hurt him. Not the way you think."

I make my way to the stairwell, but before I begin my descent, I look back one last time. I just can't help myself.

"And for the record, those T-shirts are awful." I meet Yael's eye and shake my head in disapproval. "Have a little respect."

chapter 25

IN THE DAYS LEADING UP TO THE BALL, I don't hear from Miller.

I can't risk another run-in with Yael—to be honest, I'm kind of scared of how cutting she might treat me after my little T-shirt comment—so I avoid his apartment and skip boxing class. I could call, or text, but what I really need to do is see Miller face-to-face.

Which means the park is little help, either. That's the frustrating thing about boys who play fur characters. They're constantly disguised. I find ways to end up in the sections of the park where the kangaroo usually hangs out, but I have no way of knowing if it's Miller inside the costume when I do find the marsupial. One time, I swear the kangaroo turns his head and stares, but all I'm really looking back at are the huge plastic eyes of the costume, which reveal nothing about the person inside.

By the night of the ball, I've long given up on the hope that a random run-in is going to happen. And even the ball itself doesn't guarantee that we'll be in the same place at the same time. I have a sinking feeling that he might just skip it altogether.

I get ready with my friends, trying to push my sadness aside and get swept up in the excitement of the evening. I've always loved getting dressed up in a group, and Chrissi is blasting Enchanted music as we change into costume. It's definitely not the worst time. Harper's noticeably absent, probably over at Jake's. The realization doesn't affect me.

"You outdid yourself," I tell Rose as she literally slithers into the living room dressed as the evil, conniving Sea Snake from the *Little Mermaid* movie. Her body is wrapped in midnight blue pleather with neon green accents. Her face makeup is downright frightening, her eyes menacing, a pointed tongue poking from her mouth and coiling onto her cheek. "Where's your sister?"

"Right here." Camila comes sweeping into the living room. She's wearing the Rose Red costume, and it's kind of freaky how much she looks like Rose's carbon copy for the first time ever. She smirks. "Since Rose didn't let me be Rose once this season, tonight was the one night she couldn't have a say in it."

"Do you think you're getting my goat?" Rose asks. "You're in costume and you're going to the ball. I win."

Chrissi flitters into the living room, the yellow butterfly from Enchanted's Sleeping Beauty story. "Now, now, sisters."

"You're just not comfortable without a pair of wings on, are you?" I comment.

She giggles. "Not really. Plus, Aaron, the civilian who's coming to the ball with me?" She uses the word *civilian* to refer to the nonemployee she's taking as her date. "When he introduced himself to me at the park? He just came right over to me and said, 'Your wings are hot.'"

Camila practically spits out her drink. "That is what passes for a quality pickup line for you? 'Your wings are hot?'"

"The guy who appreciates a sexy pair of wings is the guy for me," Chrissi retorts. She waves her wand in my direction. "When the heck are you going to get dressed?"

I stand up from the couch. I already have my hair done, accessorized with feathers, and my heavy makeup applied, but the Swan Queen dress is such a monstrosity, I've been waiting till the last minute to actually put it on.

It's hanging on the back of Rose and Camila's door, and I get dressed in their room. I don't bother examining the final result in their mirror before I collect my train and go back to my friends.

Chrissi literally draws in a breath when she sees me. "You look . . . unbelievably lovely. You're glowing."

"Thanks."

The truth is, I doubt I am. At least, not in the right way.

I know the girl in the dress; I know how to be her. But tonight I feel far from comfortable in her skin. Several months ago I would have felt my best, done up to the nines, hair and makeup perfection, donning the most gorgeous dress in the collection. Tonight . . . not so much.

We gather our bags and step out into the cool night. It's eleven thirty, and the shuttles are running a special route, for employees only, for this event only.

It's a party inside the bus. People sip from smuggled bottles, and music plays loudly. It's dark, and as lots of people opt to wear masks to the ball, even when going as the princesses, there's an added element of intrigue to our trip. I'm smiling before I know it, caught up in the spirit of the Character Ball, accepting compliments on my dress, jokingly reminding passengers not to crush my feathers.

But as fun as it is, the atmosphere inside the shuttle is nothing compared to the atmosphere inside the park. The Character Ball is one of my favorite nights of the year, in a way that has nothing to do with the actual dance. Walking into the Enchanted Dominion after midnight feels just like walking into a dream. It gives me chills.

A heavy silence hangs over the park, all the familiar buildings and landmarks cloaked in darkness. It's eerie and exhilarating as we join a parade of elaborately costumed ball-goers making their way down the dimly lit main pathway to the Palace in the distance. I walk beside princesses, fairies, animals, and favorite villains. It's like all my favorite movies have come to life around me, all at once.

And in the distance . . . there is the Palace. Laser beams sweep across its exterior, reflecting brilliant streams of purple, yellow, and pink into the night sky. Tonight, the Palace is the center of the universe, beckoning to us, promising adventure and excitement. Party-goers around us start whooping and actually break into a jog in their attempts to reach the drawbridge as quickly as possible. Torches lit with real fire lead the way across.

But just as my group reaches the foot of the drawbridge, as we are about to cross over from park to party, my feet still.

If there is any chance he is here tonight . . .

Chrissi turns around and pushes her mask up over her eyes. "What are you doing? C'mon!"

I wave at her. "You guys go ahead. I just need to make a quick detour."

She starts doubling back. "Potty break? I'll wait. You're going to need help with that dress."

"No, no. Go on." I look at my watch. "Aaron's already going to be waiting for you. I'll be there in, like, two minutes."

I suspect it's going to take a bit longer than that, but she doesn't need to know that.

"You sure?" Rose asks. She glances around. "It's really dark and kind of creepy in the park. We can go with you."

I laugh. "It's the Enchanted Dominion. Crime rate of negative five. Go ahead, seriously. I'll find you inside in a minute."

After a few more minutes of convincing, Rose, Camila, and Chrissi make their way across the drawbridge and disappear into the castle tunnel. I count to five, turn on my heel, gather my feathered train, and dash back toward the park entrance.

When I reach the building, I pause with my hand on the knob. *Please don't be locked.*

By some grace of Drako the Dragon, it's not. I enter, flip on a single light, and get on with my business. Tonight, I know exactly what I'm looking for. I find it and head toward the dressing room.

Inside, for the first time tonight, I see myself in the Swan Queen dress. I look even better than when I tried it on for Miller. With the makeup, and the mask, and the bejeweled hair . . . I'm exquisite.

"You are beautiful," I tell the Swan Queen. "But tonight, you are not the princess for me."

I reach behind me, tug on the zipper, and let the dress fall in a heavy pile to my feet. I step out of it, pick it up with the utmost care, and return it to its satin hanger.

I turn toward the other hook inside the stall. And shudder.

It's hideous. Oh God, it's hideous.

The spiked tail, the bulging eyes, the scales. I step into it. And eww, it *smells*.

When I have it all the way on, when I've put the horrid mask over my head, the possibility of tears seems a bit too real.

Then, words from last summer are back in my head.

"Suck it up, buttercup."

Suddenly I'm laughing the tears away, and I hurry to put the Swan Queen costume back and get on my way.

If there is any chance he is here tonight . . . Miller will be taking advantage of the one chance to be Drako the Dragon.

And at the end of the day, I want to be his Lizzie. Claws or no claws.

When I join the crowds making their way to the Palace, no one looks at me. No one smiles, no one throws compliments. By the time I reach the Palace, I've essentially become invisible.

Tonight, because the weather has held up, the ball will take place in the open courtyard, complete with twisting stone paths, lush gardens, and tall topiaries. A bright moon shines overhead, and spotlights on the castle walls illuminate the party scene that awaits. Purple and yellow fabric banners run from wall to wall, the topiaries are wrapped in purple and yellow lights, and elaborate centerpieces grace each table. A life-size Drako the Dragon ice sculpture dominates the bar. The live band is playing dance remixes of popular songs from the Enchanted Enterprises movies.

Even though it's just after midnight, the party is already in full swing, and I realize finding the girls is going to be no easy task. Within minutes, I've already spotted three Rose Reds that aren't Camila and two yellow butterflies that aren't Chrissi. And while I'd like to find them, they're not really who I'm looking for, anyway.

If there is any chance he is here tonight . . .

. . . I have no idea how he'll feel about seeing me.

My stomach tingles with nerves, and I make a quick stop at

the bar to take a Bad Apple shot, which tastes like a horrid mix of whiskey and apple juice, for liquid courage.

Then I go about the business of finding the only Drako the Dragon in the bunch that matters.

As I push my way through the crowd, at one point I do see my friends. Chrissi has found her date, and Rose seems to be approximating a snake with her dance moves. Camila is dancing, albeit stiffly, with the Asian guy I saw that day in the cafeteria, making me wonder if the Enchanted magic and notion of romance has finally, *finally* gotten to her just a bit. Every few seconds, one of them glances around, clearly looking for me.

Inside my lizard head, I giggle. It *is* kind of fun, being in disguise.

What's not so much fun is how many damn Drakos are in attendance tonight. Because he's the central character in the park, there are an abundance of available Drako costumes for the ball, and it's always a really popular choice.

After fifteen minutes, I start to wonder if this is all futile. What if I don't find him? What if he's not here at all?

I approach three different Drakos. When I tap the first one's arm, he lifts his head to reveal a girl inside. When I approach the next one and pull back my head and smile, his girlfriend appears out of nowhere and glares at me. The third Drako I approach is a tall, thin Indian guy.

I find myself at the base of the grand stairwell leading up to the rear of the Palace. My shoulders fall, and I stare around helplessly.

Hopeless. This is hopeless. This isn't turning out anything like I thought.

Then, at the top of the stairwell, something—someone—

catches my attention. A man stands by himself at the top, gazing intently in the direction of the Palace entrance.

It's the Swan Prince.

I ascend the first three steps at once, then pause, tearing up as I assess him standing there.

His hair is gelled for the first time ever. I think he's trimmed his beard. He's even wearing that stupid mask, its long, pointed orange bill coming down over his nose.

He's so handsome standing there, too-long pants gathering in folds over his shoes.

My hand goes to my heart in response to this effort of his.

Which was entirely unnecessary.

I swallow back my tears and start waving toward him frantically to join me in the middle of the stairs.

It takes him a while to realize I'm gesturing toward him. He won't tear his eyes away from the Palace entrance.

Finally he looks at me. "Did you . . . are you waving to me? Sorry . . . I'm just waiting for somebody."

Exasperated, in a sudden motion, I flip my headpiece off, and it falls heavily over the back of my neck. "Yes! I'm waving to *you*!"

Miller tears off the swan mask. His eyes pop out of his head. He stumbles down four stairs to meet me. "What are you *doing*?"

"I . . . I . . ." I throw my hands, well, claws, up into the air. "I'm trying to prove you wrong!"

Miller stares at me another minute. Then he cracks up. "You look *ridiculous*! Your hair, those *feathers*, and your makeup, and that . . . getup."

"Yeah, well . . ." I glance at him quickly, then glance away. "You look really handsome."

He glances down ruefully. "I used an entire roll of hem tape. Damn things still won't stay up."

He's standing a step above me, and I have to look up at him. "Why?" I demand of him. "If you don't want to go down that road with me . . . then why?"

Miller swallows nervously. "I know you know I want to go down that road with you," he whispers. "So much, it felt dangerous. Those other girls I told you about"—he waves his hand dismissively—"they hurt me, yeah. But you . . ." He flashes a small, sad smile. ". . . you could flat out eviscerate me."

"Miller . . ."

He shakes his head. "It was so wrong, those things I said. They were mean. And unfair. An attempt at self-preservation, I guess." He shakes his head again. "But they sure as hell weren't true." Finally he meets my eye. "I'm sorry I said them. I'm sorry I hurt you in an attempt to protect myself. And I wanted to make it up to you."

I gaze up at him for a long minute.

"I'm not a princess, Miller." I look down at my giant clawed feet. "And I'm not a lizard, either." I join him on his step, so we're looking eye to eye again. "Somewhere in between the two, there's Alyssa. And there's Miller." I swallow hard. "And personally I think there's a lot of good stuff there.

"I know you see me," I whisper. "I know you do. Underneath the tiaras and behind the gowns." I find his hand. "And I really like the me you see. I'd like to get to know her better. But most of all I'd like to get to know *you* better. Please just give it a chance. Please don't assume this story's already written."

Miller looks at me, long and hard. So long I start fidgeting, shifting from claw to claw, feeling like I might explode.

"Miller. Say something."

He doesn't. He does one better.

The next thing I know, he's tearing the lizard headpiece all the way off, letting it fall to the ground and bounce down the stairwell. Miller grabs my face and kisses me without hesitation.

Miller lifts me off the ground with the force of his kiss, spinning me around, my heel kicking up behind me. And I get that this is real life and everything, but this kiss . . . this kiss is definitely the stuff of fairy tales.

We kiss and kiss, in the middle of the stairwell, on display for the entire party. It's not long before I realize we've gained the attention of the crowd, that hundreds of faces have turned toward us, watching, clapping, cheering.

It seems like I may have gotten a grand entrance after all. I never expected to make it dressed as a giant lizard, but I guess there's more than one way to make a grand entrance.

We pause, pull apart, and turn around to survey the crowd. I giggle in embarrassment, burying my face in Miller's chest in response. Then I wave, and he offers a low bow.

As I survey the crowd, from the corner of my eye I see Sleeping Beauty in her wedding dress and her Prince Charming, side by side, smiling and clapping with the crowd. It's Harper, and Jake, and apparently he was willing to dress up for her in a way he never was for me. And I couldn't give a hoot.

I mean, as it turns out, Jake was right, anyway. I do deserve better, better than him, better than an illusion. I deserve someone who loves me with one hundred and ten percent of his heart. The same way I have a feeling I'm going to come to love him.

It seems like everyone is rooting for us tonight. I nearly do a double take when I see Yael . . . smiling, actually smiling, as she watches the two of us on the steps. It's only a small one, and she's shaking her head all the while, but I catch her. Yael. *Smiling.*

But eventually I turn my back on the crowd, because this has never been about them, and I've had enough of what everyone else has to think about us.

Us.

I grab Miller's face and plant a final, solid kiss upon his lips. I hear the opening notes of "Cheap Thrills."

"Are we going to dance at this ball or what?" I ask him.

He looks me over, studying me from top to bottom, hesitating. "Did you want to change first?" He grins. "I think Lizzie's served her purpose here tonight. You don't need to keep that on on my behalf."

"That's okay," I tell him, pulling on his hand and leading him down the steps to the party, tail making its way down the steps behind me, in time with the music. Because the party is probably already half over, and I refuse to waste another single minute. "I think I'm good."

epilogue

THE KITCHEN CLOCK READS 4:34 A.M. WHEN we stumble into Miller's apartment, giggling and feeling punch drunk. I glance at it a second longer, because that can't possibly be right. I don't really know why I'm surprised. It was me who insisted on riding the log flume again and again and again. I just didn't really want the night to end. Miller had to drag me from the park, and the only thing that worked was the promise I could snag his pajamas again and crash at his place. In that fantabulous bed.

I perch on the counter and smile shyly at his back as he opens his refrigerator and pulls out a carton of eggs. My shy smile turns into a full-blown grin a moment later as he raises an eyebrow at me and makes a big, dramatic point of separating the whites from the yolks into two separate cups. For me.

"Hey, you don't have to work tomorrow, do you?" I ask. "Well, technically today, I guess."

"God, no." He dumps my egg whites into a frying pan. "You?"

"No. I pretty much plan to sleep all day. After breakfast, that is."

"Word. I have truly amazing blackout shades." Then Miller nods toward a side cabinet. "Can you grab me the salt and pepper?"

I nod, hopping down and heading toward the cabinet he's pointed to. I retrieve the salt and pepper but stop in my tracks to take the canisters to Miller when I notice a familiar-looking jar sitting in the corner below the cabinets. I grab it at once, fist closing around it, wondering how exactly I might make it disappear.

But of course Miller sees me . . . sees it, and calls me out, bemused smile on his face. "Care to fill me in? All Yael said to me when she handed this over was 'That girl's officially certifiable.' I've been meaning to ask . . ."

"In Yael's defense, I didn't give her much of an explanation, either." I shake my head and wrap the jar in the hem of my T-shirt, putting it out of sight. "And trust me, you probably don't want to know. Let's just keep this bad boy tucked away and pretend it never happened, okay?"

Miller looks like he's struggling to keep from laughing, but I guess he decides to oblige me. He accepts the salt and pepper without another word.

But as I stand there another minute, staring down at the jar of ashes in my hand, suddenly I have a burning desire to do one better than just tucking the ashes away. "On second thought . . ."

I walk purposely toward his sink and turn on the water. I remove the lid from the jar. Then, with a deliberate motion, I empty the jar's contents into the basin. I flip the switch, the garbage disposal coming to life with a whirring grind, obliterating my dreams and wishes instantaneously, taking them away forever.

As it turns out, I'm not bothered in the slightest.

These days, my life is more than a fairy tale, and I suppose it always was. I just didn't realize reality is sometimes even more worthy of wishing for. Miller showed me that.

We don't get to write our own happily ever afters. Life takes care of that for us. And sometimes, from the very first page, you can tell your next chapter is going to be even better than anything you imagined in your wildest dreams.

acknowledgments

FIRST AND FOREMOST, thank you thank you thank you to the fabulous Swoon leadership team, including Jean Feiwel, Lauren Scobell, and Holly West. Because of your vision and hard work, I get to do what I love. I remain forever grateful for this opportunity.

To the honest and thoughtful reading and editing team that showed me some tough love regarding my first go-round with this story, thank you. Holly West, Emily Settle, and Hayley Jozwiak, I appreciate the lessons you taught me regarding constructive feedback . . . and moving forward toward something better. Without your nudging, Miller wouldn't even exist. *(I can't . . . I just can't. . . .)*

To the talented, funny, creative, and supportive network of Swoon authors who boost me and make me smile daily, I'm so glad we're a part of the same team. Kim K., thank you for always being there, to listen, rant, and provide perspective. Beyond a fellow author, I'm lucky to call you my friend.

Thank you, members of the Macmillan family, for all the thought, energy, and time you give to my work, for all the hundreds of ways you contribute to making it as polished and pretty as possible.

Jen Raudenbush Sacks—more than twenty years ago, you used to rush off the bus, dial me up, and say, "Okay, go," as my directive to begin telling you a story. Your support and love for this endeavor, decades later, means the world. Thank you, girl.

Dad—Miller's last name isn't a coincidence; it's a tribute. I couldn't help but feel that his character embodied the genuine goodness I see in you. Thank you for this inspiration, in worlds fictional and nonfictional alike. Laine—thank you for being my number one fan, in every single undertaking of mine. Love you both.

"Jamie from Sig Nu"—thank you so much for all the ways you support and ground me. Thank you for all the things you do, all the ways you work so hard, so that I have the opportunity to pursue my passion.

Lu Bean and Christian J—I see the way your eyes light up and your attention is rapt, the way that the magic of fairy tales enchants you. Thank you, my loves, for always reminding me of the power of magic and the importance of it in our world.

And lastly, thanks to you, Walt. You cultivated a world where magic and dreams are right there for us to reach out and grab. But more important, you were a living example of never giving up on one's passion and vision. "First, think. Second, believe. Third, dream. And finally, dare." *Indeed.*

Check out more books chosen for publication by readers like you.

DID YOU KNOW...

this book was picked by readers like you?

Join our book-obsessed community and help us discover awesome new writing talent.

1 Write it.

Share your original YA manuscript.

2 Read it.

Discover bright new bookish talent.

3 Share it.

Discuss, rate, and share your faves.

4 Love it.

Help us publish the books you love.

Share your own manuscript or dive between the pages at **swoonreads.com.**